THE TREASURE OF PARAGON BOOK 6

HIGHLAND DRAGON

USA TODAY BESTSELLING AUTHOR

GENEVIEVE JACK

Highland Dragon: The Treasure of Paragon, Book 6

Published by Carpe Luna Ltd, Bloomington, IL 61704

First Edition: December 2020

eISBN: 978-1-940675-57-2

Paperback: 978-1-940675-58-9

v 2.7

AUTHOR'S NOTE

Dear Reader,

Love is the truest magic and the most fulfilling fantasy. Thank you for coming along on this journey as I share the tale of the Treasure of Paragon, nine exiled royal dragon shifters destined to find love and their way home.

There are three things you can expect from a Genevieve Jack novel: magic will play a key role, unexpected twists are the norm, and love will conquer all.

The Treasure of Paragon Reading Order

The Dragon of New Orleans, Book 1
Windy City Dragon, Book 2,
Manhattan Dragon, Book 3
The Dragon of Sedona, Book 4
The Dragon of Cecil Court, Book 5
Highland Dragon, Book 6
Hidden Dragon, Book 7
The Dragons of Paragon, Book 8
The Last Dragon, Book 9

Keep in touch to stay in the know about new releases, sales, and giveaways.

Join my VIP reader group
Sign up for my newsletter

Now, let's spread our wings (or at least our pages) and escape together!

Genevieve Jack

ABOUT THIS BOOK

Sometimes the things that keep us safe hold us captive.

She longs for a better future.
Avery Tanglewood has had enough of rearranging her life for the sake of others. After years of prioritizing her family over herself, she's ready to strike out on her own, even if she's not sure what she wants to do with her life. If only she was brave enough to face the backlash the truth will bring.

He's a prisoner of the past.
For hundreds of years, Xavier has used his dragon magic to protect his Highland clan inside a pocket of space called the *builgean*. Thanks to his unique magical abilities, generations have enjoyed peace and prosperity while cut off from the modern world. But when a fairy trickster captures him and claims his throne, his refuge becomes his prison.

Can they free each other from the chains that bind?

Avery agrees to journey into the *builgean* to persuade Xavier to help with the crisis in Paragon, but she finds a mysterious stranger in his place—a problematic complication, considering she can't leave the pocket without Xavier's assistance. Worse, although she frees the captured dragon, he refuses to comply without winning back his land and his clan first. And the longer Avery spends in Xavier's world, the harder it is to remember why she should return to her own.

PROLOGUE

Paragon

In a dark, lonely, and unmarked grave beyond the boundaries of the Obsidian Palace, Aborella waited like a seed planted in the dirt. She'd lost track of how long she'd been trapped beneath the earth. Unconsciousness had relieved her suffering periodically, but without a source of light, she had no idea how many days had passed since the empress had sentenced her to this fate. All she had left was the hope that Eleanor would change her mind and come to collect her.

Her chest ached thinking about the woman she once considered a friend. The betrayal Aborella had experienced at her hands caused her more pain than the crushing weight of being buried alive. The fairy sorceress had drained herself to the point of death trying to protect the Empress, but things had gone horribly wrong. Aborella was fatally wounded in battle, and although the empress had saved her life by feeding her a dragon's tooth, she'd taken out her anger and frustration on Aborella, abandoning her to fester in a shallow grave. Eleanor, it seemed, did not tolerate failure, even from her.

Her spirits lifted when the sound of a female voice grew near, until she realized it was a soothing timbre, not Eleanor's shrill, nasal tone.

"Sylas? Sylas!" the voice called in a loud whisper.

Aborella became more alert in her earthy tomb. Whoever this was must be in league with Sylas, Eleanor's eighthborn son and rumored leader of the rebellion.

"Oh Goddess of the Mountain! Sylas?" The female voice was closer now, just above Aborella. The sound of digging, not by shovel but by hand, met her ears. The owner of the voice must have noticed the grave and thought she was Sylas. Aborella waited, hoping, praying to the goddess the woman would succeed in reaching her. If she could enjoy a single breath of fresh air and see the stars above her, it would be the sweetest mercy.

Already the weight over her was lighter. And then dirt brushed her cheek and was lifted away. Aborella stared up at a dark shadow within a deep red hood. Gloved hands, filthy with dirt, hovered over her face, two full moons acting as dual spotlights behind the woman's head.

"Thank the goddess," the woman murmured as she determined Aborella wasn't the dragon in question. "Sylas, I'm going to kill you."

She reached toward the pile of dirt beside the grave, and Aborella's heart raced. Was she going to bury her again?

Aborella couldn't let that happen. She had to show this hooded creature she was alive. Using all the energy she had, she tried to raise her hand but only managed to twitch a finger, which the stranger didn't see as it was still buried. The woman scooped another mound of dirt. Aborella opened her mouth to scream and instead drew in a full, cleansing breath of night air.

"By the Mountain!" The stranger tossed the dirt aside. A short, high-pitched gasp came from inside the hood. "How are you alive?"

Aborella tried to answer, but all that came out was a gurgle. When had she lost her ability to speak? She knew that half her face was smashed, courtesy of Nathaniel, who had also taken three of her limbs, but when she'd first escaped to the palace, she had spoken to Eleanor. And she had just proved she was able to breathe. Which meant perhaps her lack of voice was due to fear or the fact she'd had no food or water for however long she'd been buried. Without making a sound, she forced her lips to mouth, *help me*.

Quickly, the hooded figure unburied the rest of her. It was a blessing Aborella couldn't see the stranger's expression inside the deep hood. Her injuries were extensive—one leg completely gone, the other severed above the knee, one arm torn off unevenly, facial disfigurement—and it would only depress her to see the stranger's disgust manifest at the sight. She needn't have worried; the hood hid any reaction as the woman hooked her hands under Aborella's armpits, braced her heels in the dirt, and dragged her from the grave.

"Oh, my dear goddess. You're a fairy!"

The woman must have seen her wings. Aborella held absolutely still, which wasn't difficult considering how weak she'd become. She was suddenly relieved her voice hadn't worked. If the stranger was looking for Sylas, she was undoubtedly a rebel and would kill Aborella where she lay if she recognized her. Fortunately, her regularly dark purple skin was bright white now, a symptom of her drained magic, and her face must be unrecognizable thanks to her injuries.

With any luck, the hooded one would assume she was some wayward fairy set upon by thieves and would leave her to die.

"Is it you?" A low, deep voice came from a thicket of trees to the left.

"Sylas?" The stranger turned, and Sylas stepped into view, dropping his invisibility as if it were a blanket wrapped around his being. "Stars and lightning! Thank the goddess!"

He rushed forward and swept her into his arms, kissing the face under the hood. "I'm sorry it took me so long. I had to wait for that young fuckup at the gate to fall asleep."

"I felt the tug on our bond and followed it here, but Hades if I knew exactly what it meant! How did you escape?"

"It's too long of a story to tell you here. I've been hiding in the gardens for days. We need to go." He took her hand and began to lead her away.

Aborella swallowed, fresh agony washing over her as a slight breeze irritated her wounds. She forced herself to remain silent. If Sylas recognized her, he'd cut off her head and feed her to the forest animals.

She was partially hidden behind the skirt of the stranger's cape, but as the woman turned, the light of the moon drenched her pale skin.

Sylas pulled up short, his gaze locking on Aborella. "What in Hades is that, Dianthe?"

Dianthe. That was the stranger's name. A fairy name. Interesting.

"I thought she was you!" Dianthe pointed a gloved hand toward the grave. "I thought that wicked mother of yours had tortured and buried you here as some sort of warning to us. Instead, I found her."

"Who is she?"

"Definitely a fairy. Probably raped and tortured by Obsidian Guard scum and left here to die. They didn't even make sure she was dead before they buried her. It's... sick!"

Sylas was shaking his head. "We have to leave her. There's nothing we can do."

"Why?" The hood turned toward him, the gloved hands squeezing into fists. "I can heal her, Sylas. You know I can. If she's survived this long, I can bring her through this. Fairies have unbelievable regenerative properties. If we can get her back to Everfield—"

"And how exactly do you suppose we do that?" He rubbed his eyes, his words tinged with exhaustion. "I'm lucky to be alive, woman! We're risking everything by lingering here."

Dianthe placed her gloved hands on her hips. Now Aborella wished she could speak. If she could make a sound, she'd protest going to Everfield. She'd been born there and was universally hated by its people. Even if the three of them could successfully avoid detection by the Obsidian Guard and make it to Everfield in one piece, the people there would surely execute her the second anyone recognized her.

"Fine," Sylas whispered, pacing nervously. "But this is on you. She's your responsibility."

"When have I ever shirked my responsibility to you or anyone else?" Dianthe's soft voice held a note of anger for the first time that night.

"Give me your cloak. It will make her easier to carry."

Dianthe removed the red hood and began unfastening the buttons. Aborella had never seen a fairy like her. Her skin was the color of roasted cinnamon and shone like silk in the moonlight. Most fairies were born the color of flower petals—the darker the color, the more powerful the fairy. Dianthe's deeply pigmented skin was highly unusual, and when she glanced in Aborella's direction, another difference revealed itself. Most fairies had green eyes. Dianthe's were the color of warm honey. She was beautiful but markedly strange, different from any fairy Aborella remembered from home.

The lights went out as Sylas tossed the cloak over Aborella's body and face, wrapped her up, and scooped her into his arms. Nothing more was said. Aborella had neither strength nor voice to change her fate. She closed her eyes and gave herself over to it.

CHAPTER ONE

A world away from Paragon, in a place between places, Xavier, son of Eleanor and heir to the kingdom of Paragon, also woke to perpetual darkness. The scent of stale air, moldy stone, and the metallic tang of new blood assaulted his senses. Moans of pain echoed against unyielding stone walls. Someone was being tortured. Someone was always being tortured here.

His chest grew heavy with despair as the understanding of his predicament invaded his consciousness again. To be sure, there was nothing new about his reality. Rather, Xavier's renewed anguish was caused by the intense and realistic dream he'd had moments before. He'd been flying in the sun, the sweet smell of a tribiscal vineyard filling his lungs, his wings carrying him on a soft, warm breeze. He'd dreamed of freedom, of Paragon, of flying. He'd dreamed of the mountain.

It felt like an eternity since he'd spread his wings. He almost wished he hadn't experienced the dream. The ultimate despair of his predicament only cut deeper in comparison.

Another scream reached his ears from somewhere deep inside the dungeon, and Xavier came fully into his reality. The wail of agony echoed against the stone and then pinched off as if whatever wretched soul had uttered it had run out of breath. He stretched a talon to the stone and etched a line next to the others. Hundreds of others. If he'd calculated correctly, he'd been trapped in this cage for nearly two years.

Footsteps approached—a guard with his nightly meal. The sandy-haired young man was dressed in clan colors but was oddly a stranger.

"Ye must be new," Xavier said. "I donna recognize yer face."

Without speaking or making eye contact, the guard slid the tray he was carrying along the stone floor, through the slot in the door, and into the cage. Venison, bread, greens, and water. It was a decent enough meal, although Xavier would kill for a whisky.

"Ye might be new, but it seems ye ken the rules well enough. Why does that arse ye slave after bother feeding me if he plans to leave me to rot in this hole?"

The guard didn't answer him, but then he was already halfway down the hall before Xavier asked the question. None of them ever lingered. Feed the dragon and then leave quickly, Lachlan must have told them. Wouldn't want to risk Xavier breaking the mind control Lachlan kept them all under and perhaps convincing one of them to let him go.

Anyway, Xavier knew exactly why Lachlan continued to feed him. He had to. The very existence of the *builgean* depended on Xavier's magic. If he died, their world would collapse. If he became weak, the crops might wilt and the animals would stop producing young. His magic was keeping the clan alive. His clan.

Without the *builgean* and his clan, there'd be only one place for Lachlan to go, and the evil fairy would do anything to keep from returning to his kind.

Xavier closed his eyes against the rage that burned in his blood and turned his vision red. He must get free, must save his people from the scourge that even now sat on his throne and ruled his clan.

He stared at the food. His stomach rumbled with hunger but somehow still managed to roil at the thought of his predicament. He was helpless here. Trapped. There was no way out. He'd exhausted every option. Unless one of those guards had a change of heart or his oread, Glenna, found a way to break the spell containing him. He wouldn't be holding his breath for either. In two years of trying, they'd never managed to budge the gate.

All the while he contemplated his fate, his mind kept taking him back to his dream. The sun. The mountain. The beauty of Paragon. Why was his head going back there now? It had been a long time since he'd thought of the place as home. Happy memories of his childhood were few and far between after almost three centuries. Still, he was a child of the Mountain, he supposed. You could take a dragon out of Paragon, but you'd never get Paragon out of the dragon.

A child of the Mountain. His mind flashed through images of his youth, the myths and legends of his people. Xavier had never been a religious dragon, but every citizen of Paragon understood that the mountain was the physical manifestation of the goddess. The scribes who had taught him in school always said the goddess of the mountain was his creator and his protector. Funny, in all the days he'd spent in this cell, he'd never once thought to ask her for help.

There was a first time for everything. He fell to his knees and bowed his head, his arms spreading, palms upturned, and eyes closed in the way of his people. When he spoke, he did so in his first language, one he hadn't used in hundreds of years. The words, his solemn plea for help, came to him in a rush.

Goddess, I am unworthy of your compassion, but your creation needs your help. Please, I beseech you, send a warrior to free me from this fate or else one to deliver death upon me, for in freedom I can free those you have entrusted to my protection or in death I can force my captor to do the same. I ask this by my birthright as the Treasure of Paragon. By the Mountain, let it be.

He opened his eyes to the same dark world, the same stink and despair. Nothing had changed. Still, somewhere deep inside his heart was a flicker of hope. He reached out and pulled the food toward him and began to eat. There still was no whisky, but thanks to the prayer, he had faith.

CHAPTER TWO

September 15, 2018
London, England

Avery Tanglewood sorted the magazines in the witchcraft section of Relics and Runes, separating those based on Wicca from those on Druidism and Asatru. Even though she'd lived a considerable portion of her life in New Orleans, a city known for its connection with magic and the supernatural, she'd never realized there were so many forms practiced by ordinary humans. Many ordinary people she'd met in this store applied witchcraft with varying degrees of success and talent.

Still, none compared to her sister Raven, who could absorb any spell from the page and execute it perfectly the first time or Clarissa, who could make things happen simply by singing. Even a modicum of magic was impressive to Avery, who had none herself despite being mystically tied to them both.

A long and bizarre sequence of events had brought her here. Raven had married Gabriel in June. Soon after, Avery had learned that Gabriel was actually the exiled heir to the kingdom of Paragon, a realm of a world that existed in a parallel dimension to Earth. Gabriel and Raven had managed to keep his origins secret until an evil fairy sorceress named Aborella had tried to use Avery to get to Raven and the truth could no longer be denied.

Around three hundred years ago, Gabriel and his seven living siblings—Tobias, Rowan, Alexander, Nathaniel, Xavier, Sylas, and Colin—had been evicted from their world and sent to Earth by their evil and ruthless mother, Eleanor, under the pretext that she was saving them from their malevolent uncle who'd murdered their oldest brother Marius at his would-be coronation. But in February, Raven and Gabriel had discovered everything they'd been told by their mother was a lie. She'd sent her children, the Treasure of Paragon as they were called in their world, to Earth so she could keep the throne for herself. They'd spread out across the globe, believing that diluting their magic in the human world would keep them safe from detection. Over time, the eight lost touch with each other.

Now Gabriel was working tirelessly to reunite his family. And although he did not speak about it frequently, he seemed more inclined by the day to challenge his mother for the throne.

Which was none of Avery's business really, considering she was a simple human who was connected to Raven by blood and Clarissa, Nathaniel's mate, by a magical bond. They were the three sisters, a bound trio. Unlike Avery, Raven and Clarissa were extremely powerful witches. The only special skill Avery had ever possessed was the ability to comfort Raven and Gabriel's baby... well, technically, their egg. The half dragon, half witch hadn't hatched yet. For some reason, Avery was the only one besides Raven and

Gabriel who could hold the egg without getting zapped by its defensive magic.

Which brought her to this moment. She'd decided to remain in London, living in Nathaniel's place, Mistwood Manor, at least until Raven's baby was born. She also desperately wanted to explore the magical connection she shared with Raven and Clarissa.

What would it be like to have magic? Since she'd learned of Raven and Clarissa's powers, she'd questioned whether she was somehow defective. Was she a dud? A cosmic mistake? Not only was she completely without magic, her human existence was equally dull and ordinary, a truth that came sharply into focus in Nathaniel's bookstore, which specialized in the extraordinary.

Her phone vibrated in her back pocket, and she brought it to her ear with a cheery greeting.

"Thank you again for watching the shop while we're away, Avery," Clarissa said. "We owe you one."

Clarissa was legally obligated to perform one more show for her record label, this one in Italy, and she and Nathaniel had left that morning. Normally, Nathaniel's store manager, Albert, would take over while Nathaniel was gone, but the man was ill with some sort of stomach bug. Avery had agreed to fill in during his absence.

It was the least she could do considering Nathaniel had opened his home to her these past weeks, sheltering and feeding her with no expectation that she do a single thing to repay the favor. Sure, she'd worked here for him a handful of times and made some calls for Clarissa in support of her new indie music venture, but all in all, she spent her days riding Nathaniel's horses, soaking in his heated pool, or wandering aimlessly through his orchard without contributing one shilling for her upkeep.

"Don't think twice about it, Clarissa. I'm having a blast. The people-watching in Cecil Court alone is worth the effort. It wasn't like I had anything else going on tonight." In fact, there was nothing on her calendar at all. She'd taken a leave of absence from her job working with her mother at the Three Sisters Bar & Grill and hadn't a clue what she might like to do next with her life. She understood this couldn't go on forever, but she refused to think about when it had to end.

"Well, thanks again. Nathaniel and I know the shop is in good hands. Oh, before I forget, I told Emory to stop by with some dinner for you. He's going to stay in London and run a few errands for Nathaniel until it's time to drive you back to Mistwood. He should be there with the best curry you've ever tasted within the hour."

"That's so sweet." Avery loved Nathaniel's driver, Emory, and looked forward to him stopping in. Plus curry was a favorite. "Have a great show and tell Nathaniel not to worry about a thing."

"Thanks. Love ya."

"Love you too." There was a click and the call ended. Avery smiled. The exchange of I love yous between Clarissa, Raven, and herself had come naturally over their time together. They were as close as sisters could be despite Clarissa not being related by blood. Avery called her a "sister from another mister." She couldn't remember what it was like before the woman had come into her life.

The bell over the door dinged and Avery whirled, thinking it must be Emory with dinner. Instead, a reedy man in a stained T-shirt that used to be white stood in the door.

"Welcome to Relics and Runes. Can I help you find anything?"

He didn't answer her. A muscle in his cheek jerked. His lashes fluttered.

An uneasy feeling wormed in Avery's gut. The man standing before her seemed agitated and unkempt. His red-rimmed eyes darted around the room. The stench of cheap alcohol and cigarettes met her nose. Avery's gaze caught on his inner arm where track marks and fresh punctures marred his skin.

Her smile faded.

"Can I help you?" she asked again softly. Her gaze darted out the window to the people passing by in jackets. The weather hadn't changed, and his short sleeves seemed utterly inadequate. Maybe he'd stopped in to warm up. The poor man was obviously in distress. "Are you hungry? Do you need a place to sit down for a minute?"

The twitch in the man's face grew more pronounced, and he turned around as if he might leave. He placed his hand on the knob, but instead of opening the door, he turned the lock and flipped the sign on the window to Closed.

When he turned back around, a knife had appeared in his hand. "You can help me by giving me what's in the till."

Their eyes locked. She had only compassion for the man, but what she saw in his visage was anything but kindness. Survival instinct kicked in, trumping any concern she might have had. She rushed for the back door, but before she could open it wide enough to get through, his hand slapped above her head and slammed her into it, cutting off her escape.

His rank breath hit her face. "Where do you think you're going, huh?" He spun her around and pressed the knife to her throat.

One thing she'd learned working in a bar for so many

years was how to handle threatening situations. She'd dealt with her share of drug addicts and alcoholics as well as drunk men who simply wouldn't take no for an answer. The key was to remain calm. She slowed her breathing and looked him straight in the eye, flashing her warmest, most practiced smile. "Let me move to the register. I'll give you what you want."

His eyes narrowed, and he pressed the blade harder against her skin. Warm blood dribbled along her neck, and she resisted the urge to wipe it away. His eyes flicked to her breasts. "You're a pretty thing, aren't you?"

Her skin crawled. Avery knew she was in trouble. If she somehow made it to the front door, could she unlock it and get out before he sank that knife in her back? He shifted the blade, moving it from her throat a fraction of an inch as he tried to get a better look at her chest. She didn't give him a chance. Crossing her arms in front of her hips, she circled them, thrusting his knife-holding arm up and away from her as her knee barreled into his crotch with every ounce of force she could produce. His body doubled over from the pain. She used the opportunity to catch his arm by the wrist and thrust it up the center of his back.

He screamed a string of obscenities. The knife clattered to the floor. He tried to grab her with his free hand, but with her other arm locked on his shoulder, his struggling wasn't effective. "You fucking bitch!"

"I will break your arm, asshole! I know how to do it." She rammed him into the counter, grunting at the force, and released his shoulder to reach for her phone. Big mistake. The man twisted out of her hold, his fist connecting with her jaw in a blow that sent a burst of stars exploding in her vision. She stumbled backward, crashing through the table of magazines.

Avery watched in horror as he swept the knife from the floor and raised it above his head. *Don't pass out. Don't pass out.* The room was spinning. There was no way she could get out of the way in time. He dived toward her, the blade sinking toward her heart.

"Aargh!" Faster than she'd ever thought she could move, Avery brought her knees in tight to her chest and kicked him in the gut with both feet. The knife missed its target. The man flew back. Somewhere glass shattered. Avery tried to sit up to see what had happened, but black dots swam in her vision and she flopped back on the floor. She heard a sharp crack like splintering wood. Another grunt and a thump.

"Miss? Avery?" Emory's face appeared above her, his bushy gray eyebrows bent in concern.

"Chest... hurts." A searing pain swept from above her right breast toward her throat.

He pressed a hand under her collarbone. "You've been cut. I'm calling for help." His phone was already to his ear.

Avery blinked twice, trying her best to remain conscious, but her vision had become an ever-constricting circle. In the end, she gave up and allowed herself to sink into the pressing darkness.

THIRTY-TWO STITCHES. AVERY TRACED THE NASTY slice that ran from the hollow of her throat, across her right breast, and ended under her armpit. She'd definitely have a scar, but at least she could easily hide it if she wanted to. Or show it off and make up a more entertaining story for how she got it.

It had been a full forty-eight hours since Emory had

picked her up off the floor of Relics and Runes and taken her to Accident and Emergency to get patched up. (It was the first time Avery realized the Brits didn't call it the ER as Americans did.) Since then, Nathaniel's oreads hadn't allowed her to lift a finger, which was fine with her considering how sore she was from the fight. Horrified to hear of her ordeal, Nathaniel and Clarissa returned from their trip early, Nathaniel swearing to install better magical security.

Avery inspected her wound in the bathroom mirror, poking it experimentally. The cut was red and puffy but appeared to be healing. It itched like a mother though. Wasn't that a good sign?

"I can try healing it with magic. I just need to find the right spell." Raven appeared in the door to the bathroom, lines creasing her forehead as she assessed the state of her wound.

Avery waved her hand dismissively. "It barely hurts. Don't waste the effort."

"Barely hurts? You were carved up by some psycho trying to rob Nathaniel's store... I would be shaken to my core if I were you." Raven shook her head. "How can you be so casual about this?"

Avery examined her feelings. Was she shaken up? On some level, she recognized she *should* be shaken. That was how a person was supposed to feel in this situation. But did she truly feel that way? Nope. What she *did* feel was the oddest and most unexpected sense of pride. She'd taken on her attacker... and won.

"I handled it, Raven. This shit happens." She bobbed her eyebrows at her sister. "You should see the other guy."

"Avery..." Raven gave her an exasperated look.

Her phone rang. Saved by the bell. She hated having to explain her feelings or lack of them to her sister. "It's Mom.

Weird. I just spoke with her a few days ago. I wonder why she's calling again so soon."

Raven grimaced and backed away.

"You didn't!" Avery scowled at her.

"Sorry."

Avery answered and gave her mother her perkiest greeting, then listened to her ramble about how terrified she'd been when she heard the news.

"I'm fine, Mom. It's barely a scratch. You know how dramatic Raven can be."

"Really? Put me on video."

Avery pulled the neck of her shirt up over her stitches and connected the video on her call. She pointed her screen toward the tiny nick her attacker had left on her throat. "See?"

"That's it? Raven made it sound like you almost died."

Raising the screen to her face, she gave Raven a contemptuous look. "She needs to learn to mind her own business."

"She just cares about you, as do I. I miss you. It's been weeks."

"I miss you too!" Avery smiled at her mother's image. Although she didn't miss her old life slinging beer at the Three Sisters or the responsibility for propping up her mother and father after their divorce, she did miss her mother's warm, breezy spirit.

"It's been months since I've seen you and Raven. Is Raven there? How is her pregnancy advancing? I couldn't get much out of her." Her mother's eyebrows knit with concern.

Out of the corner of her eye, she saw Raven wave her hands and shake her head. Of course her sister could blab about a little knife attack, but they couldn't tell dear old Mom the truth about the baby, could they?

"Raven is good. Like an old mother hen sitting on her egg." Avery cringed as Raven punched her hard in the shoulder. "She's probably around here somewhere. Do you want me to try to find her?"

"Actually, I have a surprise for both of you. There's something I haven't told you." Her mother's face split into a timid grin.

"What?" Avery's intuition suddenly flared like the first fireworks of summer.

Her mother moved her phone away from her face to reveal a bustling airport scene behind her. The murmur of voices Avery had assumed were from patrons of the Three Sisters were in fact other travelers buzzing in the terminal behind her. "I'm here! In London! I thought if you and Raven couldn't come visit me, I'd come visit you!"

"Is that Heathrow?" This was not good. Avery glared at Raven in panic.

"Yes. Can you pick me up?" Her mother gave a squeal through a broad, toothy smile.

Avery's throat constricted and she worked her mouth, wondering what to say. "Of course, but I don't actually own a car and Gabriel's brother lives outside the city. It'll take an hour or so for us to get to you."

"Would it be better if I took a cab? What's the address?" Her mother patted her pockets like she was searching for a pen.

"No!" Avery blurted. All they needed was a cabbie on a mission to find an invisible mansion. "You don't want to do that. I mean, his address is so hard to find. I'll come get you. Just give me a chance to round up Nathaniel and borrow a car."

Her mother flipped her honey-brown tresses behind her shoulder and grinned. "Sounds perfect. I'll just grab a coffee and wait."

"Bye, Mom. Love you. See you soon!" Avery ended the call and glared at her sister. "Why did you tell her?"

Her sister shrugged. "I thought she had a right to know."

"Well now she's in London and wants to see us, and we live with a vampire, five dragons, and a Native American healer you raised from the dead!"

"Don't forget Clarissa and Nick." Raven spread her hands and giggled.

"This isn't funny, Raven. What are we going to do?"

Gabriel entered her room, looking concerned. "Why is everyone yelling?"

Avery pointed a finger at Raven. "Thanks to your wife, Sarah Tanglewood and her never-before-used passport is, at this very moment, at Heathrow Airport having a coffee and waiting for us to pick her up."

Gabriel's black eyes widened. "No!"

"Yes." Avery raised her eyebrows. "We need to find Nathaniel. We'll have to ask to borrow Emory to go pick her up."

"Pick her up? Are you insane? She can't come *HERE!*" Now Raven seemed to get it. She stabbed a finger toward her flat abdomen. "I'm supposed to be pregnant. And what about Charlie?" Raven looked over her shoulder toward the hall and their room where little Charlie was baking cozily in the fireplace within a dragon's eggshell.

Gabriel frowned but wrapped a supportive arm around his mate. "We can have the oreads watch Charlie," he said. "But perhaps the best option is to not bring your mother to Mistwood at all. This place is... Well, it may be hard to disguise its magical qualities."

"What am I supposed to do? Leave her at the airport?" Avery asked. A knot had formed between her shoulder blades, and suddenly the cut on her chest was throbbing like a bitch.

"Has she actually seen Raven?" Gabriel's eyes darted back and forth between them. "Can you tell her we've left town?"

Avery poked her tongue into her cheek and shook her head. "If you think for a second that I'm going to entertain Mom all by myself this week and make up lie after lie for you, you are crazy. I can't do it, and it's wrong for you to ask me to. Shove a pillow under your shirt, or better yet, use your magic to look pregnant. I don't care. But you are going to face her with me."

Nathaniel strode into the doorway. "You three are about as subtle as a brick through the front window. There's no need for raised voices."

"Have you heard—?"

"Everyone in the house has heard, Avery." He picked a stray thread off his sleeve. "No one is leaving anyone at the airport. I've called Emory. He will take you and Raven to Heathrow to retrieve your mother and bring her back here. Gabriel will stay with Charlie for now. Tell your mother he stayed behind to allow more room in the car. I will ask Tobias, Sabrina, Alexander, Maiara, Nick, and Rowan to use this time to take a short holiday to simplify things. The rest of us can pass as human for a few days. We do it every day in public."

Avery winced. "Will the others be okay with making themselves scarce? I feel terrible kicking them out of their rooms."

Nathaniel gave a little nod. "I think it's best for everyone involved."

Avery locked eyes with Raven before reluctantly nodding her agreement. "I guess we're doing this. Let's go get Mom."

By the time the two sisters arrived at Heathrow and loaded their mother's luggage into the car, Raven had used her magic to create an illusion of pregnancy. Their mother raved over Raven's empty belly while Avery rolled her eyes and mimicked her from behind. By God, their mom acted as if she hadn't seen her in years rather than a few months. Avery intentionally chose the front passenger seat next to Emory and made Raven take the back with her. She'd always hated lying to her mom. This way Raven would be on the spot to answer questions.

"This Nathaniel, he's Gabriel's brother?" Mom asked from behind her.

Avery glanced over the seat at her sister.

Raven smiled. "Yes. He has a home in Oxfordshire. It's a bit of a drive. If you're tired, I understand if you want to nap until we get there. There will be plenty of time for us to talk later."

"Nap? Never. This is my first time to England!" She gave an excited sigh and stared out the window. "Why is it I hadn't heard about Gabriel's brother Nathaniel before you both came here? Was he too busy to travel to the states for the wedding?"

Raven nodded. "He owns a bookstore in London. It's hard for him to get away."

She nodded slowly and tapped her chin. "But Gabriel owns Blakemore's Antiques, and he's okay with an extended visit?"

Avery lifted an eyebrow and gave Raven a make-something-up-fast glare.

"Gabriel hadn't seen his brother in a number of years." Raven smoothed her skirt as if the subject made her slightly uncomfortable. So far she hadn't lied—precisely. Gabriel *hadn't* seen Nathaniel in centuries. "He wanted a chance to become reacquainted. Plus Nathaniel is recently engaged. We wanted to help with the arrangements, considering we were just married ourselves."

"Engaged," Sarah exclaimed, clapping her hands together. "How wonderful. Love is in the air."

Avery cleared her throat. "His fiancée is a singer recording her first indie album. She actually offered me a job as her personal assistant."

Out of the corner of her eye, Avery watched her mother's smile fade and her lips thin. "That sounds exciting, although would it be fair to take a position short term? You know, when you do come home, I'd love to give you more managerial experience at the Three Sisters. It's long past time I promoted you."

Avery tugged at her seat belt. "That would be great," she said weakly. It wouldn't be great. It would be a life sentence. If she learned to run the Three Sisters, she would definitely be expected to take the bar and grill over from her mother, just as her mother had taken it over from their grandmother. The Three Sisters had been in the Tanglewood family since before Louisiana was a state.

"Um, Mom," Raven interrupted, seeming to sense Avery's discomfort. "How are things with you?"

"Oh well..." She waved a hand dismissively. "Your father has been around a lot. He was absolutely destroyed when that *Charlotte* just up and left him like she did. I mean, the letter was so cold, and the way she just abandoned you in Sedona, Avery, it was all... just odd. He's heartbroken. I finally convinced him to box up her things and give them to charity."

"She was a nutjob," Avery said. "He dodged a bullet, believe me."

"Yes, I think we all know that." She shook her head. "But since she's been gone, he comes to see me every day. You know David... he can't be alone. To tell you the truth, I needed this trip just to get away from him." She laughed a little, and Avery's heart broke.

Aborella, posing as Charlotte, had put her father under her spell and made him believe she loved him. The fairy had tried to use the same magic on her, but it hadn't worked as well. When they vanquished the evil bitch months ago, Avery never thought of what her absence would mean for her father. She was sure it was confusing, like a part of his life was completely gone.

For a long time, they traveled in silence until Emory cleared his throat. Avery turned her head to see Raven conveniently knock her purse onto the floor.

"Oh! Mom, can you? I can't get down there like this." She rubbed the mound of her belly.

"I'll get it," her mom said hastily. She leaned over to collect the spilled items while Emory drove off the road and through the wards around Mistwood. By the time she sat back up, they were nearing the manor. "Oh! Is this it? I didn't even notice it from the road!"

Raven laughed nervously. "Everyone says that. It's the trees. They make it practically invisible."

Avery chewed her lip at the way Raven's voice rose in pitch. It was her sister's tell when she was lying. Would Mom notice? She released a relieved breath when Sarah didn't remark.

Thankfully, Emory wasted no time in parking the car in front of the entrance and popping open the back door.

Avery let herself out and sidled up to Raven. "So far, so good."

The heavy wood of the decorative front door swung open, and Nathaniel welcomed them inside. "You must be Ms. Tanglewood," he said, extending his hand.

"Please, call me Sarah."

"I'm Nathaniel. Welcome to Mistwood."

Mom shook his hand. "You have a beautiful home."

They were interrupted when Clarissa descended the stairs and hustled to Nathaniel's side, extending her own hand. "Hello, I'm Clarissa."

Avery watched all the blood drain from her mother's face. "Clariss—" For a moment, Sarah stared, openmouthed and wide-eyed. Then she swooned, toppling to the stone threshold to the sound of her daughters' screams.

CHAPTER THREE

"Mom!" Avery slapped her mother's cheek gently.

Nathaniel swept Sarah into his arms and carried her to the couch in the main parlor. Although she'd knocked her head when her body crumpled, there was no blood. She was breathing but unconscious.

"Nathaniel, can you get some ice? She's going to have a bump."

Her mother's lashes fluttered. "Avery? Oh..." She rubbed her head. "I'm so sorry."

"Why are you apologizing? It's not your fault you fainted."

Nathaniel returned with a cloth bag filled with ice, and Avery applied it to the bump.

Sarah's eyes searched the room, locking onto Clarissa. "No, what I mean is, I'm sorry I didn't tell you. She's why you haven't come home, isn't she? Because you know. She told you."

Raven moved in closer and set her hand on Avery's shoulder. "Told us what, Mom?"

Sarah's brow dipped, and her gaze flitted between the three of them. "That she's your sister, obviously."

The room exploded into gasps and murmurs.

"What does that mean?" Avery's mouth popped open. She closed it and then looked toward Raven as if her sister might have an explanation. But she seemed just as shell-shocked.

"You've got to be kidding me. Mom, are you serious?" Raven shook her head incredulously.

Clarissa was as still as a statue as she said, "I'm your... daughter?"

Their mother glanced in her direction, then squeezed her eyes shut. "You didn't know? How could you not know? You all look exactly alike for God's sake. No DNA test is needed here."

"Mom." Raven's tone was razor sharp. "Start explaining."

"It was thirty years ago. David and I weren't ready to have a child. We were too young. We could barely support ourselves."

Nathaniel appeared with a beverage tray. Avery hadn't seen him leave the room and assumed one of his oreads, Tempest or Laurel, was actually responsible. "Tea, Ms. Tanglewood?"

"Yes, please. Whatever you have there."

He poured her a cup. Mom sat up, stirred in a lump of sugar, and raised it to her lips with trembling hands.

"We weren't even married yet, you understand." She cast Clarissa a beseeching look. "We had to give you up, and the Blacks were such a good family. I knew they would give you the life you deserved."

Nathaniel's empathetic gaze fell on his mate, and he

crossed the room to stand beside her. He rubbed her shoulders supportively.

"I was told my biological parents died in an automobile accident." Clarissa's throat bobbed with her swallow.

Their mother blinked rapidly and leaned back against the sofa. "Heavens no. Why would the Blacks tell you that?"

"They didn't. The social worker told me after the Blacks died in a tragic accident when I was five."

Mom brought her hands to her mouth and gave her head two quick shakes. "But... if they died, who raised you?"

"I was fostered by... many families." Clarissa's gaze dropped to the Persian rug but not before Avery caught a flash of pain in her blue eyes. In the short time she'd known Clarissa, Avery had come to understand that her upbringing had damaged her in ways the rest of them would likely never understand.

Sarah's face paled. "What? But... by the time you were five, we were settled. We would have taken you."

Clarissa shrugged. "I don't know how it works."

"I'm so sorry, Clarissa. I never knew. I've followed your career over the years, but I couldn't contact you because..." She gestured toward her with both hands. "Well, because you're you! You're famous. I had no idea if the Blacks had even told you about us. Oh, what a mess." She buried her head in her hands.

As the initial shock began to wear off, Avery experienced a bubble of elation and rushed to Clarissa to give her a tight hug. "You're my sister. My real, blooded sister."

Raven, though, wasn't ready for hugs and acceptance. She crossed her arms and paced the room. "I can't believe you kept this from us, Mom. Why?"

Sarah brushed her bangs back from her eyes. "What

was I supposed to say? There isn't really a good time to tell your children that they have a sister out there and that she's a famous pop star."

Millions of questions tumbled through Avery's mind, and she rubbed her temples. "So Dad knows too? He was part of this?"

Their mom nodded.

Nathaniel stepped deeper into the room. "Sarah, is that why you named the bar the Three Sisters?"

For a second, Avery was confused. She'd heard Raven explain the name to him before. It was a historical name. Why was he asking a question he already knew the answer to?

"Oh no. The Three Sisters has been in the Tanglewood family for generations. It was named after a small plantation owned by three Tanglewood sisters from way back when Louisiana was a new territory. As the legend goes, someone burned the place down. One of our ancestors was accused of being a witch, can you believe it? So those three sisters opened the Inn of the Three Sisters, which eventually became the Three Sisters Bar & Grill. My bar."

"That's quite the story," Nathaniel said, suddenly acutely interested. "Three women running a plantation on their own in a colony."

Sarah shot him a lighthearted grin. "There are all these rumors in our family that they were..." She lowered her voice. "...actually witches. It pops up again and again in our family history." She giggled as if she found the whole thing ridiculous. "Although my brother and I understand that back then, the word *witch* was used to describe any woman who dared to think independently. Family legend also said they were Greek, but we all figured they were French like most of the population. Tanglewood isn't a popular surname, and we can't trace our roots back before New Orleans. We think the three women invented it because they wanted to hide their true identities. Maybe they were criminals after a new start. It would fit with the city's history." She shrugged, her narrow nose wrinkling.

"Witches," Clarissa blurted. "What a story."

Their mother took another sip of tea. "It really is. It followed my family through the years. If my girls haven't told you, it's tradition in our family for the maternal line to take the name Tanglewood. I kept it when I married David, my mother kept it, my grandmother kept it. There was a Tanglewood witch back in the 1800s—oh, I suppose she would have been my great-great-great-aunt—who people said could cure any illness. She made this elixir..." She laughed. "It was basically a snake oil cure. But people swore by it."

Nathaniel tugged at the cuff of his suit. "So more than one generation of witches."

She rolled her eyes. "A few generations didn't perpetuate the legend. Sometimes a Tanglewood woman would give birth only to boys. But for some reason, other generations kept reviving it. And now there are dozens of spooky Tanglewood stories. My brother Sam has kept some of the journals and things. He lives in Minnesota. He's more into the history than I am." She tucked her hair behind her ear again. "Anyway, don't you worry, Clarissa. Despite the weird family history, I am not a witch and cannot turn you into a frog. I can tell you from personal experience that the rumors about the Tanglewood witches are complete hooey."

Raven choked and coughed into her hand.

"No wonder we look so much alike." Avery still couldn't quite believe what she was hearing.

Their mom leaned forward and focused on Clarissa.

"No one expects anything from you. I am here for you if you want to get to know me, but I understand how difficult this must be. Whatever you're feeling, whatever you want, it's fine with me."

Clarissa took three ragged breaths and lost the fight to keep her tears at bay. "I have a family?"

Mom's eyes turned misty. "If you want one."

Clarissa left Nathaniel's side and strode across the room to their mother. Sarah stood and pulled her into her arms. Although it made a nice picture, Avery watched the two with mixed emotions. She'd grown close to Clarissa over the previous weeks. She already loved the woman like a sister. This was good news. So why the heaviness in the pit of her belly? Because she couldn't understand her physical response, she plastered a smile on her face and worked hard to display a casual demeanor. No reason to outwardly show an emotion she didn't even understand. Inside though, tension built in her shoulders and the healing cut on her chest throbbed.

The two women parted, and Nathaniel clapped his hands together. "How long will you be staying with us, Sarah? I'll tell the staff to ready a room for you."

"Only three days, I'm afraid. I wish I could stay longer but I can't. Have a business to run."

Three days. Avery closed her eyes and thanked the Lord for small favors. They could keep her busy for three days.

THAT EVENING, SINCE RAVEN WAS SUPPOSED TO BE pregnant, she and Gabriel stayed behind while Avery, her mother, Nathaniel, and Clarissa took a ride around the grounds of the estate on four of Nathaniel's prized horses. Avery's mare was a sweet-natured Appaloosa named Millie, who made no attempt to keep up with the beast Nathaniel rode, a stallion twice her size with a disposition that matched his name, Diablo. Her mother rode a Thoroughbred named Luna who was so dependable Avery thought her mom could drop the reins and have the same experience as holding them. Clarissa's horse was far more spirited, but Nathaniel's mate proved to be an accomplished rider.

Distracted as she was by the stunning grounds, Avery didn't think again about what had happened that day until they'd all shared dinner and retired to their rooms, exhausted from the day's activities. She tossed and turned, unable to sleep until finally she gave up and decided to walk down to the kitchen for a warm glass of milk.

As she stepped into the hall, a flash of light caught her eye. It was a reflection of gold in the shape of a silhouette, as if a woman in a gold lamé dress had slipped from the hall a half second before she'd turned her head and the gold flash was all that was left in her wake.

"Laurel?" she whispered. Perhaps the oread was up here cleaning. Avery followed the light past the other bedrooms and down an adjacent hallway. This was a direction she didn't normally go in the house. Mistwood was an absolutely massive manor. There were many areas she hadn't yet explored, and she felt a tingle of curiosity as she padded down the empty hall.

An open door revealed a bedroom with furniture draped in white sheets. Hmm, this wing must not be used often. A red Persian carpet runner covered the length of the hall, which was bordered in dark wood wainscoting. Framed portraits hung between brass sconces that filled the space with a warm ochre glow. Curious, she approached the first portrait.

From his lofty advantage, a middle-aged man in a powdered wig stared down at her with pursed lips from over a pair of wire-rimmed glasses. His mouth drew a cruel line, matched only by the coldness in his eyes. She had no idea who he was, but he looked like an asshole.

"Damn. Pull the bayonet out of your ass." She moved on to the next portrait. This one was of a portly woman with feathers in her hair, pink cheeks, and a fan in her hands. Her Mona Lisa smile made Avery feel like she was keeping a secret. "Ooh la la. How did you know Nathaniel?" She giggled under her breath.

She had to pass another bedroom to reach the next portrait—this one clearly of Nathaniel, although his hair was long and pulled back into a ponytail and he was dressed in a neckcloth and tailcoat. She chuckled. Clarissa needed to see this tomorrow. And if she'd already seen it, Avery wanted to be there to needle her about it. So weird. It was much easier to forget about the age difference when her mate didn't look like Paul Revere.

She sidestepped to the next picture. Everything stopped. Even her breath halted in her lungs. Cerulean eyes stared down at her from over a straight-edged nose and full lips in a perfectly symmetrical face with a strong chin. Long, auburn hair collected around his shoulders, the color somewhere between light brown and red. It contrasted sharply with the plaid that cut across the formal-looking coat he wore. Clearly he was Scottish. If the facial features weren't a dead giveaway, the kilt was. The portrait cut off at the hip, but she could make out the top of the kilt, a sword belt and sporran.

"Who are *you*?" she asked the painting in breathless

wonder. Her finger hovered over the canvas, and she tried to curb her desperate urge to touch. She could stare at that face all day. What was it about him she found so interesting? The mouth, she decided. The corner of his lips turned up impishly like he was up to no good, and the twinkle in his eye seemed to share the mouth's general disdain for authority. It was at odds, that twinkle and quirk, with the formality of the uniform. This was a man who was true to himself. This was a man who made his own rules.

She would like to meet this man.

"You found Xavier."

Avery leaped back and spun to find Nathaniel in the hall in a pair of black silk pajamas. She placed a hand on her pounding heart. "You scared me! I hope I didn't wake you."

"No. I was having trouble sleeping. Again."

"Again. Right." They'd run into each other before in the middle of the night. It seemed they both suffered from insomnia. "I've never been in this part of the house."

"I don't normally room people down here. It's such a long walk from the central part of the manor. Plus it sometimes gets cold in the winter months."

She casually pointed at the painting. "Did you say this was Xavier? Your brother?"

He nodded slowly. "I commissioned it in 1745, the last time I saw him in person."

She looked at him and then back at the painting. "I thought you all went your separate ways when you arrived here in 1698?"

"We did. But Xavier sought me out that year. He needed my help with something. Something only I could do."

"Sounds serious."

"It was. Xavier and I traveled together for almost a year

before I settled in London and he moved north to Scotland. There, he endeared himself to the chief of Clan Campbell, Archibald, first Duke of Argyll."

"He joined a Highland clan?" Avery's knowledge of Highlanders was limited to what she'd learned in romance novels. She looked at the portrait again and tried to remember anything she'd read about the Campbells.

Nathaniel nodded. "Xavier's skills with a sword were unparalleled among humans. Of course they would be, considering he was a dragon warrior who trained in the pits of Paragon from the time he was a boy. He was one of the toughest, you know?"

"Raven told me the fights were fixed so that Marius would always win."

"Oh yes, that's true. We all understood we were not allowed to beat Marius because he was the eldest heir. But if anyone could have, it would have been Xavier. I was never much of a fighter myself, but even Gabriel wouldn't take on Xavier if he didn't have to."

"Hmm." Avery stared up into the blue eyes of the portrait.

"He was initiated into the Campbell clan, and over time advanced to be war chieftain. That was a rare honor as he arrived as an outsider, an outlander as the Highlanders called us. But the thing about dragons is we can change our appearance to look any way we wish, and we have magic that allows us to understand and speak any language we hear. Over time, he grew close to Archibald and even married his second daughter, Lady Jane."

Avery felt on odd and unexpected weight on her chest to hear Xavier was married, despite the nuptials occurring centuries ago. She pushed the strange and uninvited feeling aside. Was she crushing on an oil painting?

"He didn't love Jane, of course," Nathaniel added for some strange reason. "The marriage was only to serve to cement Xavier's relationship to the Campbells. It made him truly one of them, although they never actually knew where he'd come from. Archibald, Xavier said, suspected he was a fairy."

"A fairy?" Avery chuckled.

"The Highlands are full of fae, Avery. Most humans believe the stories of the wee folk are all folklore, but as you have been inducted into the supernatural, I feel no guilt informing you that fairies are real, very dangerous, and not a bit wee at all. In fact, they look just like humans when they have their wings tucked away. Mischievous devils. Archibald would have felt quite powerful having one in the family, and certainly Xavier fit the bill. He was unnaturally strong, healed quickly from injury, and never seemed to age."

"So Archibald knew he wasn't quite human but was simply happy to have him in the clan?"

"Exactly. Archibald died in 1703 and was replaced by his son John. All was well until the Jacobite uprising of 1715 when James Francis Edward Stuart attempted to regain the thrones of England, Ireland, and Scotland for the exiled House of Stuart. He failed, but England learned he had support in the Highlands. So by 1725, the Campbells, who were loyal to the crown, were enlisted to be part of the Black Watch, six companies of trustworthy Highlanders tasked with the purpose of crushing any remaining Jacobites.

"But over the next twenty years, it was clear the Jacobite cause was again gaining traction. Those were dark and difficult times. Xavier could see the writing on the wall. Soon clan would turn against clan, and England would bring the full weight of its fist down upon the Highlands.

"One thing you should know about Xavier is he's a man of honor. He puts a high price on fairness. During all his time with the Campbells, he refused to abuse his power even when it would have benefited his chieftain. He hated war, especially the idea of a war among his own kind. John Campbell secretly shared Xavier's concerns, and after an exceptionally bloody skirmish, the two men had a meeting of the minds." Nathaniel walked toward the painting and looked fondly up at his brother.

"He's a pacifist?"

Nathaniel glance at her and laughed. "No. Xavier is a warrior, but he has to feel he's fighting a just war."

"So what did he do?"

"By that time, it was clear that Xavier wasn't aging, so John was sure he must be a fairy. He asked him to use his fairy magic to hide and protect a portion of the clan, to keep them safe from the war that was to come. That's why he came to me. Dragons, you see, have the innate ability to protect their treasure."

"I remember. Alexander has a cave in Sedona that's warded against the supernatural. And Nick told me that Rowan created an entire hidden city for her best friend, Harriet, and her people. This place, Mistwood—you can't even see it from the road. It seems to take up no space." Avery shook her head. Dragon magic was amazing.

Nathaniel nodded. "Exactly. Xavier needed something bigger."

Avery crossed her arms. "How big are we talking?"

"Together we created a pocket near Bidean nam Bian, the highest point in what used to be the county of Argyll. What you need to understand, Avery, is we were doing something no dragon had ever done before. We didn't just ward a part of the land; we copied space."

Avery shook her head. "Copied space? What does that mean?"

"We didn't take existing acreage and fold it into a pocket; we expanded what was there, duplicated it. Xavier and I, with help from the fairy kingdom, created a land that had never existed before. You won't find it on any map, but it is big enough to support thousands of Highlanders for multiple lifetimes. We created roughly six hundred square miles and protected it with the strongest wards known to our species.

"Nothing supernatural can get through those wards, and no human can find the doorway inside. The Campbells who stayed behind wiped all memory of Xavier from their history. Several hundred Highlanders followed my brother into that pocket of space, which he named the *builgean*—bubble in Gaelic—not just Campbells but others who wanted to avoid the coming battle. Xavier became the chieftain of a new branch of Clan Campbell that still exists today, locked in a world that has branched off from us since 1745."

Avery shook her head. "What are you saying? That he never came out?" She laughed. The thought seemed ludicrous. Certainly the people would eventually long to travel beyond the borders of the wards.

"Never. Xavier rules over a land of perpetual abundance, fed by his dragon energy. A land where presumably the world is the same as it was in 1745. A land completely cut off from the modern world."

"But surely you've visited him over the centuries. You helped design the wards!"

Nathaniel shook his head slowly. "Although my magic is

incorporated into the wards, his is as well, and fairy magic. As a supernatural, even I can't get through. Over the centuries, Xavier has sent a few human scouts out and they've brought me messages of his well-being. I've provided them with some simple pleasures on occasion. Books mostly. Ideas. They told me stories of their existence before I returned them to the pocket, but since the day of its creation, I've never ventured inside." He looked at her then, in the direct way of a dragon, an idea sparking amethyst in his normally gray eyes. "But you can, Avery. You're still human. I can bring you to the door. I'm the only one who knows where it is. You can go through and tell my brother what is happening in Paragon. You can tell him that we need him."

"What?" It felt like he'd knocked the wind from her lungs.

"Witches, dragons, and vampires are supernatural. They can't get through. That means, of the people who know us and understand the situation in Paragon, only you or Nick can go through the door. Nick is mated to Rowan and any length of separation will be torture for her, especially if she has no way to contact him. She'll try her hardest to keep him from going, and if he does anyway, she'll be inconsolable until his return."

"But I don't have a mate." Avery chewed her bottom lip.

"You don't have a mate."

"And I have no power."

He nodded.

"You want me to retrieve your brother from a place you haven't seen since 1745." Avery tried to process the words as she said them, but they overloaded her brain.

Nathaniel faced Xavier's portrait. "You have another advantage, Avery. You're a woman. You have a better chance of reaching him. The Highlanders will be much less threatened by a strange woman than a strange man."

Avery stared back at the portrait again.

"You don't have to decide now." Nathaniel sighed. "It's a lot to ask, especially considering what you've been through the past few days."

"Considering I haven't had my stitches out yet and I've just discovered I have a sister I never knew about, I think dropping into an experiment in time and space is more than my mind can digest at the moment."

"I understand." Nathaniel brushed his fingers over the base of the frame. "It's a good likeness," he said absently.

Avery blinked at the compelling eyes staring down at her and flushed at the warmth that pulsed through her again. She mumbled a good-night to Nathaniel, excused herself, and hurried back to her room.

CHAPTER FOUR

The next day, Avery, along with Clarissa and Raven, took their mother into London to show her some of the sights. Avery fought an overwhelming exhaustion. She'd been up most of the night thinking about what Nathaniel had asked her to do. She couldn't possibly do it, could she? Allow him to drop her into a place that was most likely frozen in time on the off chance she could persuade Xavier to return to the modern world?

She was sure it would be physically dangerous. There would be no paved roads or cars in the bubble. Most likely, it would be emotionally traumatizing as well. She had no idea what she'd meet on the other side of the wards. But her most disturbing thought as she considered the proposal was that for reasons she could not explain, she *wanted* to go. The bubble embodied everything she wanted to experience by breaking from the Three Sisters. It would be an adventure. There was no way to plan for it really. She'd have to survive on her own wits and muscle. Not only that but she was drawn to Xavier—the moment she'd seen his image, she'd been rocked with pangs of curiosity and probably infatuation.

Which, yes, was a problem. Nothing good ever came from infatuation. It was the thing that made you take the wrong bus three miles out of your way just so you could sit behind a handsome man and try to work up the courage to ask him on a date. It was why you watched the same movie again and again just to swoon over an actor that made your heart beat faster. Infatuation made people idiots.

Despite knowing that in her head, she couldn't stop thinking about the painting of Xavier or of going into the bubble. If she said no, if she refused, who would go and tell Xavier about his family and the troubles in Paragon? Not Nick. She couldn't do that to Rowan.

"Avery? Earth to Avery." Her mother waved a hand in front of her face, her long, narrow nose wrinkling with her smile.

"Oh, um, sorry. I was daydreaming."

Sarah laughed. "I see that. I asked you if you liked this dress. I think it would look perfect on you."

Avery glanced at the wrap dress in her mother's hands. "It's a little formal for my taste. It looks like something someone would wear to an office."

Mom shrugged. "It's perfect for when you come home and I promote you to manager. You'll have to dress more professionally if you want the staff to take you seriously."

Avery glanced at Raven, but help was not coming from that direction. "I don't think it's for me, Mom."

She waved a hand dismissively. "It's probably better to buy new clothes locally anyway in case they don't work out."

Avery stopped, a moment of clarity seizing her and not letting go. "No."

"I heard you. I put it back on the rack." Her mother continued to flip through the dresses in front of her.

"I mean no, I'm not going back." From the moment she'd set foot in England, she'd known the Three Sisters wasn't her future. For one pure second, everything was so clear. She couldn't go back. It would smother her.

Sarah stopped what she was doing and grimaced like she'd just stabbed her in the heart. Avery's stomach ached as she thought about the pain she was causing her mother. Could she do this to her? Maybe she was being selfish.

"What do you mean, you're not going back?" Her mother stared at her with nothing but confusion on her face.

Avery cleared her throat and folded like a cardboard house made of paper drink coasters. "I mean obviously I'm eventually coming back. But I can't go home right away. Nathaniel needs help with a special project, and he's been so generous letting me stay here. It's a great opportunity. I'm going to stay... for a while."

Raven caught Avery's eye and frowned. Her sister could always tell when she was lying.

Her mother took a step closer. "You can't intend to continue working for Nathaniel. Not after what happened. Aren't you afraid you'll be held up again working in that store?"

"This is a different opportunity, not at Relics and Runes." She waved her hands. "Um, I'll be fine, Mom, really. I just won't be home... right away."

"Well, how long will this project take?" The perturbed look on her mother's face made her feel nine years old again and like she was thirty seconds from being sent to her room.

"I think Avery wants to explore a few opportunities before she goes home," Raven said. "I think it will be good for her."

Sarah gaped, shifting her gaze between them incredulously. "Okay." She closed her eyes and nodded. "Enough said." Turning on her heel, the older woman exited the store and strode down the street without them.

Avery tossed up her hands. "She's practically signing the place over to me already!"

"You don't want to go back, do you?" Raven peered knowingly at her sister.

Clarissa, who'd been shopping near the back of the store, joined them. "Why did Sarah just hustle out of here like the place was on fire?"

Avery rolled her eyes toward the ceiling. "She's upset that I'm not going back to New Orleans."

"You're not?" Clarissa glanced at Raven for answers and got only a shrug in response.

Avery turned and her two sisters followed, threading their arms into hers at the elbow.

"It's just... It's just..." Avery couldn't find the words.

Raven shot her a serious look. "This is about more than the Three Sisters, isn't it?"

Pop. Avery felt something inside her give way, and all her blood seemed to rush to her head. Her ears grew hot, and a desperate wave of emotions barreled through her. Resentment, anger, longing. She gasped. Tears flowed from her eyes like a dam had broken.

"Oh my... Avery, what's going on?" Clarissa put an arm around her shoulders.

"I am tired of always living someone else's life!" she blurted.

Raven glanced both ways, but they were alone. She steered Avery out of the store and paused on the sidewalk. Thankfully their mother wasn't out here. She must have ducked into another store up the street.

"Tell us more," Clarissa said.

"I don't want to hurt Raven's feelings." Avery wiped her tears frantically. "Don't make me go there."

Raven gave Avery's shoulder a squeeze and glanced toward Clarissa, who seemed equally concerned and confused. "Avery, you are experiencing pain. It's running out your eyes and down your cheeks. You're shaking. Let it go. Let me be responsible for my feelings." Raven wiped a tear from her cheek.

She wanted to warn Raven to brace herself, but the words poured out without a moment's hesitation. "It's just, I spent so many years while you had cancer being a buffer between Mom and Dad, trying to be the perfect daughter to make up for the grief they were experiencing as you slowly died in that hospital bed, plus picking up the slack at the Three Sisters when Dad left and Mom was so depressed she couldn't get out of bed."

"I know. I'm so sorry—"

"And then you got better, and I thought, okay, I can go back to college and pursue my dreams. But we didn't have any money then, and honestly, even if we had, I didn't have any dreams."

"Everyone has dreams," Clarissa said breathlessly.

Avery shook her head. "No, Clarissa. Sorry, but you've never been a caregiver. I'd been playing the role for so long I forgot my own dreams. I'd let them all go. And then Raven got married and then there was the baby and oh God, the magic. The dragons. Aborella!" Avery buried her face in her hands before wiping the tears from her eyes. "It was all about you, Raven, and them. It was all about Charlie."

"Oh, Avery—" Raven's frown became more pronounced, but Avery couldn't stop now.

"And now, now after everything, it's all about you,

Clarissa." Avery tucked her hair behind her ears and stared at her brand-new sister.

Clarissa's mouth formed into a perfect O.

"I'm sorry. I love you. You are the best thing to happen to me in a long time. But yesterday when you hugged Mom, I realized that I am now part of *your* story. I'm a cog in the wheel of both of your lives." She glanced between the two of them. "Whether I'm watching Charlie or serving at the bar or working at Relics and Runes, I'm living someone else's story. When do I get to write my own?"

The tears came faster, and Raven rubbed Avery's shoulders. Clarissa seemed unsure where to put her hands and moved them from her hips to her stomach and back again.

"Okay. Okay. That's good, Avery," Clarissa said. "Let it out. But can you explain to me what it is that you want to do? Maybe I can help."

"Don't you understand? I don't know. I don't know who I am." Avery inhaled a ragged breath and shrugged.

"I know who you are," Raven said unequivocally. "You are a person who has been far too generous with your time and talents for far too long."

Clarissa swallowed. "Okay. Let me ask you this way. You just mentioned you want to write your own story, basically... find yourself. Where do you want to look first?"

Avery wiped under her eyes. She needed a break. Needed to go where the only person she could rely on was herself. She sighed and glanced from one sister to the other. "I want to go find Xavier."

Looking utterly confused, Raven asked, "Xavier? Gabriel's brother?"

Avery told her what she'd learned from Nathaniel the night before.

"Wow, Avery, that is a lot." Clarissa rubbed her palms

on the sides of her hips as if her fingers were twitching to call Nathaniel. "I can't believe he didn't tell me about this."

Raven squeezed her eyes shut and opened them again. "It sounds dangerous."

Avery nodded. "But the only other option is Nick, and I won't do that to Rowan. Besides, I think I need to go. I think this bubble is exactly the type of challenge that could bring out the best in me."

Her sisters seemed to ponder that for a moment.

"You know what's right for you," Raven finally said. "Let's get Mom on a plane, and then I will do everything in my power to help you do exactly what you want to do."

Clarissa nodded. "Me too."

The three women hugged. As tight as they squeezed each other, all Avery felt was lighter.

"Am I missing a moment?" Their mother was back with a new bag hanging from the crook of her elbow.

"We're conspiring," Clarissa said, distracting her with a wide-open grin. She took her arm opposite the bags. "Come with us. We want to introduce you to afternoon tea."

AVERY WAS RELIEVED WHEN HER MOTHER FINALLY LEFT and they hugged goodbye on the curb in front of the airport. She loved her mom, but the tension between them had grown thick enough to withstand a proton blast. Several times over her visit, Sarah had tried to force Avery to commit to a return date both directly and indirectly, and Avery had dodged her questions as if they were hurled daggers. Raven and Clarissa had run interference. She didn't want to lie to her mother, but she wasn't ready to tell her *no* or *never*. It would hurt her mother terribly, and

Avery wanted to avoid that pain until she was absolutely sure.

Her mom turned away, about to roll her black Samsonite luggage through the glass doors of Heathrow, when she stopped and smiled at Avery. "I hope you know how much I love you. All three of you."

Avery nodded.

Sarah's smile widened as she hugged Raven and Clarissa one more time and then disappeared inside.

"Do you think she suspects her three daughters are witches?" Clarissa asked.

"Two daughters," Avery said, shoving down a resurgence of disappointment at being the family dud. "I'm not a witch. And no, I don't think she has a clue."

They climbed back into the car. Raven deflated her fake pregnancy as soon as she was out of sight of the general public. Emory drove them back to Mistwood Manor.

That night at dinner Avery decided she'd waited long enough. "Nathaniel, my answer is yes. I will go to find Xavier."

The sounds of forks and knives scraping plates halted abruptly. Raven and Clarissa visibly tensed.

Gabriel glared at Nathaniel and asked, "What's this about?"

"I know where Xavier is, and as I told Avery, she is the only one who can reach him to tell him that we need him." He explained about the bubble and gave a shortened version of the history behind it. Gabriel had no problem keeping up.

"Have you lost your fucking mind?" Gabriel's eyes flashed. "Did you learn nothing from Aborella's tampering with Clarissa? If something happens to Avery, Raven and Clarissa could lose their power permanently."

That was an angle Avery hadn't considered. She'd have to be careful with herself. If she were killed somehow, Raven and Clarissa would be powerless again and the future of Paragon would all but certainly fall into Eleanor's hands. Only she refused to dwell on that possibility. After being attacked in Nathaniel's shop, it was clear to her that no place would ever be perfectly safe for her.

Nathaniel lifted his wine and swirled the red liquid in the belly of the glass. "Avery is a grown woman. She's extremely resourceful. So much so, she cared for your child on her own the entire time you were in Paragon. Not to mention she faced Aborella alone and lived to tell the tale. Unless you want to suggest to Rowan that Nick has to go? Excuse me for not wanting to be in the room for that conversation."

"She has no magic!" Gabriel protested, pointing a hand at Avery.

"Exactly why she is the only one who can enter the *builgean*." Nathaniel's finger tapped the table beside his plate.

"You can't seriously think it's a good idea to help her through the gate to the *builgean* with no idea what she'll encounter inside?" Gabriel narrowed his eyes on Nathaniel incredulously.

Clarissa leaned toward him. "We can send the shadow-mail candle with her. If she runs into trouble—"

"Actually..." Nathaniel shook his head. "I gave my candle to Sylas in Paragon."

"What?" Clarissa raised a brow.

Nathaniel glanced between Raven and Gabriel. "In the cave under the palace, while you and Rowan made sacrifices to the goddess, Sylas told me he couldn't come with us. He needed to continue his work with the rebellion. I gave him the candle so that we'd have the means to find each other when the time came."

"We'll make another," Clarissa said hopefully.

Nathaniel shook his head. "I can't… It's a complex spell, and I'd have to wait until spring to gather the right ingredients."

"Borrow Warwick's?" Clarissa shot Nathaniel a pleading look across the table.

"He's gone on a mission to collect magical herbs for the Order. He's somewhere in the Australian outback. Even if I could get a message to him, getting it back in a timely manner would be… problematic. I'm afraid if Avery goes, she does so alone," Nathaniel said.

Gabriel slashed a hand through the air between them. "That settles it. It's too dangerous. We'll have no way to help her if she gets into trouble. No way to know she's in trouble! She doesn't go."

"*She* is sitting right here." Avery's fork clattered to her plate. "And *she* has decided she wants to do this."

Gabriel growled at her. "You'd risk your sister's power?"

Raven clasped a hand over her mate's mouth. "Gabriel, Avery is right. It's her life and her choice. Plus we need her help. We need Xavier."

When Raven slid her hand away, Gabriel narrowed his eyes on her and then Clarissa. "You two knew about this, didn't you?"

"Yes."

"Raven, it's a terrible idea. It's too risky." The dark depths of Gabriel's eyes flickered with red fire.

"I think it's Avery's choice." Clarissa gave her a little nod. "It is dangerous, and I'm scared as hell for you. But I can see that this is something you want to do. Something we need you to do. And if you are brave enough to go, we should be brave enough to let you." Her eyes bore into Gabriel's head as she said the last sentence.

Avery scoffed. "Thank you, but I don't need anyone's approval. I'm an adult. Nathaniel asked me to do this, and I said yes. While I appreciate all the concern, I've decided. I'm going."

"I'll have the oreads start on your wardrobe tonight." Nathaniel pulled the napkin from his lap and folded it beside his plate as if he'd finished eating even though he'd barely touched his food.

"Wardrobe?" Avery hadn't thought she'd need anything but the clothes on her back.

"We have to assume that everyone behind the ward still dresses and acts as if it is 1745. Aside from a handful of adventurous souls who have visited me over the centuries, there have been few outside influences since we created the bubble. Most of the people there have likely never seen a pair of jeans. If you are going to successfully traverse the considerable distance from the doorway to Castle Dunchridhe, circumnavigate its defenses, and get close enough to Xavier to speak with him, you'll need to be prepared. I will help you with everything."

Considerable distance. Castle defenses. Avery's stomach clenched. Did she have any idea what she was getting herself into? She reached for her wine and took a fortifying gulp.

"I'm ready when you are."

CHAPTER FIVE

"How do I look?" Avery turned slowly, modeling the clothes the oreads had made for her. She shuffled her feet for fear of tripping over the long, heavy skirts.

"As authentic as I remember," Nathaniel said.

Gabriel, Raven and Clarissa nodded appreciatively. "It looks uncomfortable," Raven said.

"I was thinking the same thing," Clarissa added.

"Let me put your curiosity to rest. It is very uncomfortable, and it weighs a ton." Avery swayed back and forth, causing the skirts to swish over her feet. There was something called a sark, which was basically a shift, made out of white linen that she wore underneath it all. The sark she could handle. It was soft and lightweight, almost like a nightgown. But on top of it, Laurel had tied something around her waist like a donut and then layered on three full skirts. Her hips looked like they needed their own zip code.

As if that weren't enough, Laurel had tied her into a set of stays that were basically like the world's most uncomfortable bra and then a wool bodice with sleeves that tied at the shoulders. It fastened in the front and gave her breasts an attractive lift. But anything sexy about that bit of the dress was completely undone by another piece of linen that was wrapped around her neck and tucked into the bodice. At least that part of her costume served to hide her healing scar. The doctor had removed the stitches, but the slice was still an angry bright pink, darkest over her breast.

Not that it mattered. You'd have to have Superman's X-ray vision to see it under all the layers. The oreads had wrapped a subtle gray plaid blanket called an arisaid over the top of everything else and tucked it into a belt. All in all, with everything on, she looked about as attractive as a lump of wet clay.

"It does have pockets!" Avery slipped her hands into the well-hidden slots in her skirt. She had no idea if those were historically accurate, but they held a head covering and gloves the oreads said she might need.

"Small pleasures," Clarissa said.

"The shoes are wrong." Nathaniel scowled pointedly at her toes. How he could see her shoes, she had no idea. The skirts reached the floor in front of her.

"I couldn't walk in the ones they gave me," Avery said. "If I need to hike as far as you're suggesting to find Xavier, I'm going to need something practical." She lifted her skirt to reveal soft, stretchy leggings and a pair of leather hiking boots complete with thick socks. "I might as well be warm if I need to sleep outside."

Nathaniel frowned. "At least they're a dull color. Keep them covered as much as possible and try not to draw attention to your feet."

She nodded. The top half of her hair had been pulled back from her face and bound at the crown of her head with a blue ribbon. That at least matched her eyes and gave the outfit a bit of color. The rest of her jet-black hair tumbled around her shoulders in long, loose curls.

"So I guess that's it. I'm ready, right?" Avery shrugged. Her stomach was tied in knots, and she was anxious to get started on this journey. If Nathaniel dropped her into the bubble first thing in the morning, she might be able to find Xavier and have him back here in as little as a day or two. Why would it take any longer?

Nathaniel cleared his throat. "One more thing." He reached into his pocket and pulled out something small and dark. A jewelry box. He removed a round disk from inside and pressed it against her throat, just under her jaw.

"What are you doing?"

Everyone laughed.

"What's so funny?"

Clarissa laughed harder. "She can't hear it?"

Nathaniel shook his head. "It sounds the same to her."

"What sounds the same?" Avery asked.

Raven raised a hand. "You're speaking with one hell of a Scottish accent! You just said, 'Whit are ye doin'?'"

Clarissa giggled.

Raven's mimicry of the accent was comically exaggerated, and Avery scraped the mole-shaped dot from her throat and held it up to the light. "I suppose I won't get far sounding like an American. I might as well belly up to the bar and order a Corona Light. How long will this little inspiration of magic last?"

Nathaniel took the mole from her and placed it back into the small wooden box. "Long enough. It should remain effective for weeks, barring magical interference. Far longer than you will be in the bubble."

"Great, then it's all settled. I'll go get changed." She turned to leave.

"Wait," Raven said. "You know you don't have to do this, right? There's still time for you to back out."

Clarissa chimed in. "Raven's right. If it's too much—"

"I know I don't have to do this." Avery lifted her chin. "I want to. I'm going to. And the next time you see me, Xavier will be on my arm." She turned and strode toward her room wondering why she'd put it that way. On her arm. It was a strange way to word it. She shook her head at the bizarre turn of phrase and hurried to undress.

Avery hugged Raven and Clarissa goodbye outside of Mistwood and then climbed into the car that would take her to the Highlands. Traveling to Glencoe from Oxfordshire would take about nine hours. She'd asked Raven, Clarissa, and Gabriel to stay behind. She didn't want to have the stress of saying goodbye or risk that they'd talk her out of what she was about to do. Only Nathaniel could usher her along this part of the journey, and soon enough she'd have to leave him behind as well. They planned to travel to the bubble today, spend the night in a neighboring village, and then she'd pass through the wards tomorrow.

Nathaniel spent the entire car ride lecturing her on Scottish culture. He'd given her a bag of silver and gold coins that he said were Scottish pounds, the type of currency he assumed was still used where she was going. She'd need it for food and to rent a room for the night as it would be at least two days journey to the castle. Avery tried to listen, but she was far too nervous to absorb much at all of what he said. The information went into her brain and then out again moments later when Nathaniel attempted to quiz her.

She was relieved when she was finally alone in her room in a bed-and-breakfast called the Clachaig Inn, which Nathaniel said was near the gate. Avery flopped onto the bed and, for the first time in forever, slept through the night.

In the morning, after a full Scottish breakfast that included something called Lorne sausage that Avery liked so much she ate until she was almost sick, she dressed in the costume the oreads had made for her and drove with Nathaniel to a mountain called Bidean nam Bian where he said the gate resided.

"Are you afraid of heights?" he asked her.

"No." There wasn't much that Avery legitimately feared. She didn't care for alligators, but that hadn't stopped her from kayaking through an infested swamp with her sister. Heights she found manageable, even when she'd stood on the edge of the cliff in front of Alexander's cave and faced Aborella. The thing about Avery was, she didn't like to dwell on things and so she rarely had time to fear them.

"Good." Nathaniel grabbed her around the waist, spread his wings, and flew.

Avery should not have eaten that third Lorne sausage. Her stomach dropped as he rose higher and higher, to the very top of the ridge. He perched on an outcropping of stone. It was cold there, and she was suddenly thankful for the layers of wool and linen around her.

"Why are we here?" Avery had to raise her voice to speak over the wind. "I thought you were taking me to the gate?"

"This is the gate," Nathaniel said apologetically. He

didn't seem remotely cold although her teeth were starting to chatter. *Dragons.*

"This is the gate?" Avery looked around her but saw nothing.

With a wave of his hand, a scattering of amethyst dust flew from his fingers and caught on an invisible dome that cut through the thin air beyond the mountain's edge. Avery noted a large rectangle where the dust fell darker before disappearing altogether. The door.

"Is that it?" She pointed a hand toward the general area. "I don't even think I can jump that far."

"I'll fly you over and drop you in."

All her muscles tensed. "Are you—" Her head whipped back and forth as she stared over the edge. "I'll die from the fall!"

"You'll land inside the bubble. It's only about a three-foot drop. As soon as you fall through the wards, everything you see here will change."

She peered over the edge, her vision wavering and sweat blooming on her upper lip despite the cold. As she took in the distance to the earth below, she grew dizzy and nauseated and had to back away from the edge to keep from toppling over.

"Nathaniel, if you drop me and I miss the door..."

"You'll fall on this side of the pocket. But don't worry. I'll swoop down and catch you before you hit the ground."

"Why would I worry?" A nervous laugh broke her lips.

"You're not changing your mind, are you?" he asked. "You can, you know. It's a lot to ask."

It *was* a lot to ask. She'd only known Nathaniel for a short time, and she'd have to trust him with her life. Every cell in her body fought the idea of jumping over the edge or allowing herself to fall. Her logical brain understood that this was magic, but her logical mind wasn't as loud as her illogical panic center, which was, at this moment, running in circles in her brain with its hair on fire. She believed Nathaniel that the door was there and that she'd land safely on the other side, but her physical body and her instincts screamed in her head. Most of her still believed in the laws of physics despite the fact that the only reason she was standing there, on top of this mountain, was because a man who turned into a dragon on occasion had made the two of them invisible and flown her over the heads of everyday hikers.

"Avery?"

"I'm ready," she said, her voice shaking. "Quickly please. It's cold."

There was no hesitation. He swept her off the side of the cliff, flew her over what appeared to be open air, and dropped her.

CHAPTER SIX

Everfield
The Fairy Kingdom, Ouros.

Aborella woke, nestled in the roots of a zum zum tree, its leaves above her a medley of emerald, chestnut, and gold. The zum zum was used in healing because it was the only tree a fairy could draw energy from endlessly without killing the tree. Zum zums efficiently synthesized energy from fairy soil while their natural defenses guarded against overdraining.

There was only one place in the five kingdoms where zum zums grew, and only rarely were they grown inside homes. Sylas's mate must either be a healer or wealthy to afford such a convenience. As more details of the room she was in came into focus, she decided it wasn't wealth.

She was in a small cottage typical of her homeland of Everfield. A fire burned in the hearth of the main room within the warming radius of a plush sofa. Colorful tapestries hung from the walls and matched a woven rug on the floor. Everything was brightly colored and made by hand as was the custom. Artisanship had always been valued in Everfield above all else.

Sylas and the one called Dianthe must have brought her back to the fairy kingdom. She raised the fingers of her only remaining hand to her face. Pain shot through her head and made her eye twitch as her fingertips met swelling and tenderness. Had they recognized her? Considering she was still alive, she guessed not.

"Don't move too much." A face appeared before her with skin of deep luminescent mahogany and eyes the color of warm honey. Dianthe. She was dressed in a sleeveless yellow sheath dress that brought out her strange gold eyes. Aborella thought her ancestors must have drunk the sun to cause the radiance that seemed to emanate from her. A strange warm feeling bloomed deep within Aborella's chest.

"You've been out for days. You might be disoriented." Dianthe sat on the zum zum roots beside her and scooped an arm behind Aborella's shoulders. Once she'd sat her up, she brought a cup of sweet-smelling liquid to her lips. The flavor was distinct, a popular beverage in Everfield that Aborella remembered from her youth. It was a concoction of bullhorn root and apricot nectar that tasted like heaven and easily slid down her throat. She drained the cup dry.

"Thank—" Aborella attempted to say thank you, but her voice gave out.

"It's better if you don't speak. You're lucky to be alive. Your head, face, and body have been severely brutalized. I honestly don't know how you survived it. The good news is there has already been growth in your limbs. I think your right leg will fully regenerate. Your arm as well."

Aborella noticed immediately that she didn't mention the left leg. It was bad, she knew, pinched off high on the thigh. When Nathaniel had pounced on her, she'd had barely enough magic to transport the core of her body back to Paragon. Some of her had been left behind.

The loss of limb was not so disappointing as the loss of magic. Aborella's skin had been covered in magical symbols before, most of which had resided on her arms and legs. Losing the limbs meant losing the magic. She stretched the fingers of her one remaining hand in front of her face. At least some of her symbols remained, but they were barely distinguishable within her pale skin. Nothing like how they looked when her complexion was at its full dark purple splendor.

Dianthe scooted off the roots beside her and onto a stool. "I want you to know you are safe here. I can't imagine what you've endured, but it seems clear to us that the empress was behind this. Did she torture you?"

Aborella paused, then nodded her head. It wasn't a lie. Eleanor had buried her alive. If that didn't count as torture, she wasn't sure what did. As for the cause of her injuries, that was something Dianthe could never know, not unless Aborella wanted to meet the edge of Sylas's blade.

"Well, you're back in Everfield now, and this household is no friend to the crown. We will keep you here until you heal, and we can return you to your family. You do have family in Everfield?"

This was a harder one to answer. She might have distant relatives here but none who would take her in. Her immediate family had passed long ago. She shook her head no.

Dianthe sighed as if the thought made her sad. Aborella thanked the stars above that she could not speak. Coming up with a history that wouldn't give her identity away would be difficult. Everyone in Everfield knew of Aborella, and everyone hated her.

"I would love to hear your story, but all that can wait. For now just work on getting better." She stood and padded into the small kitchen area where she removed three trays of cookies from the stone oven.

The scent of cinnamon wafted through the cottage. Aborella's mouth started to water. Out of the corner of her eye, she saw Dianthe load a basket with the confections and cover it in a stitched linen towel. She slid the basket over her arm.

"I have to take these to the solarium for the convergence celebration. First night is tomorrow. If all goes well, maybe we can get you up and around the fire by the waning."

Aborella remembered the annual ceremony when Ouros's two moons aligned, both full. The celebration lasted for seven days, until the moons visibly parted and waned again. Dianthe must have made lunar cookies. Aborella was unexpectedly filled with nostalgia, and her eyes grew misty with memories. What was wrong with her? The people of Everfield had been cruel to her as a child. They'd hated her, and she'd hated it here. And if she were well enough to attend in seven days, she'd be well enough to return to the Obsidian Palace and regain the empress's favor.

Dianthe donned her red cloak but paused by Aborella's side on the way to the door. She selected one palm-sized cookie from her basket. "They'll never miss it."

Slowly, Aborella raised her hand and took the cookie, uncomfortable with the gratitude that consumed her. Dianthe didn't expect a thank-you. She pulled up her hood and drifted out the front door, leaving Aborella alone with her cookie, her pain, and a strange brew of emotions she wished would go away.

CHAPTER SEVEN

Avery's stomach lurched and her massive skirts swept over her head as she fell through the icy chill. Abruptly, her feet smacked earth, her knees gave out, and she rolled ass over noggin while flashes of mossy dirt broke through the blinding and bumpy tumble. She only stopped when her back slapped something hard and rough.

With both hands, she clawed at the fabric covering her face. She'd somersaulted into a rowan tree, its red berries bright against the lush green leaves. Rolling on her side, she scrambled to standing, smoothing her clothing and her hair. A mucky, wet *thwuck* met her ears as she lowered her left foot to the blanket of moss. *Dammit!* She'd lost a shoe in the tumble and water was now rising up around her ankle as if she'd stepped on a sponge.

Fuck! She hobbled for higher ground on her toes and shod foot, searching for her lost boot. That's when she realized the leather bag with all her money and things had come off her waist in her scuffle with the hill. Everything was in that bag: the mole to camouflage her voice, the money for a room, a box of matches to start a fire, a canteen, and food to get her through the two-day trip. She was doomed without it.

"Shit! Shit! Shit!" She limped back the way she'd rolled. Mercifully, she found the boot quickly enough, although an ominous squelch rose from her unprotected foot as she bent to pick it up. Everything was wet; her clothing was soaked from rolling along the hill, her sock was soaked, even her hair felt damp.

"Don't panic, Avery. You've been here less than five minutes." She took a deep breath and blew it out. And another. And another. She assessed her sodden clothing. "Look at it this way—at least you're not muddy."

She wrung out the sock and then placed both it and the boot on her foot again, this time double knotting the laces, a step she'd neglected that morning. The wet wool squished juicily inside the leather. Still, she was far less concerned about her soggy toes than her missing bag. Nathaniel had made it clear she'd likely have to sleep outdoors tonight and stay at an inn tomorrow as Castle Dunchridhe was more than two days' walk from the gate to the *builgean*. How would she survive without water, food, or matches?

Panic rising again, her gaze swept over the ground and between the trees, her heart beating faster with every passing minute. What if she couldn't find it? How would she survive long enough to even reach Xavier? She'd have to find water and food and shelter with no money or directions. Her breath came in pants, and she closed her eyes for a moment to regain her composure.

When she opened them again, a flash of gold caught the corner of her eye. Her brow furrowed. It reminded her of the flash that had led her to Xavier's portrait. She moved toward it. A divot in the moss marked where she must have landed and there, thrown off to the side, was the leather bag.

"Thank you!" she said toward the heavens and the guardian angel who must have intervened. The sky was exceptionally blue above her. No trace of a door or a ward. Suddenly she was glad she hadn't noticed that earlier. Had she not found her bag, she couldn't have given up even if she'd wanted to. She could not reach the door to the *buil-gean* on her own. Truly, there was no turning back now.

She slid her arms into the drawstring loops of the bag and wore it like a backpack. Nathaniel had said to head downhill and that she would eventually reach a village. She turned, decided on a promising direction, and started to walk, her wet foot squishing in her boot with every step.

Four hours later, Avery still hadn't seen a single human being or building. Not even an abandoned shack. The frothy babbling of a stream welcomed her to its bank, and she took a seat on a large stone to remove her boots. Her wet sock had never dried properly, and she peeled it from her foot and laid the wool in the sun on the rock beside her. The heel of her foot was rubbed raw, and she plunged it into the stream where the cool water soothed it. She'd been stupid to walk all this way with a wet sock in waterproof boots. She stripped off the other one for good measure and ran her toes through the grass.

Mmmmmmm. The feeling was heavenly. She'd under-estimated how heavy the boots would get on the long hike.

She took the bag from her shoulders and thunked it on the stone beside her, digging out her canteen and chugging what was left in it. Once she'd drained it dry, she dunked it under the water. When it was full again, she dug out the pills Nathaniel had given her and dropped one in. Whatever it was, he claimed it would clean any impurities from the water. After a brief fizzing, a puff of gray steam blew out of the mouth.

"Seems like a good sign."

She sniffed it, then gave it a tentative sip. Delicious. Screwing the cap back on, she returned it to her bag and pulled out one of the protein bars she'd packed. She opened the package and carefully placed the wrapper inside her bag. Nothing good would come from littering what was otherwise a pristine streambed.

Movement across the rushing water caught her eye, and she squinted at the space between the trees. There was something there. Something brown. A bear? It moved again.

It was a man! A small man with a furry brown face.

"Hello?" She waved cheerfully at him.

The man's eyes widened, but he didn't wave back. She took a bite of the protein bar. God, it was awful. Was this supposed to be peanut butter? It tasted like Play-Doh.

The furry man came closer but stopped at the edge of the stream. Now he was in full light, and Avery could see he was indeed very hairy. She wondered if he suffered from that wolf man disease she'd watched a YouTube video about once. What was it called? Hypertrichosis. Poor thing. Perhaps that's why he was living out here in the middle of nowhere.

Suddenly she wondered if he was hungry. Was that why his eyes were focused on the PowerBar?

"Would you like some?" she asked, holding up the bar. "I'll warn you, it tastes like shit, but it's better than starvation."

The man splashed through the stream and plopped down beside her on the rock. Now that he was closer, she noticed he was smaller than she was. Avery was tall for a woman, so that in itself wasn't necessarily odd. But when he'd moved across the stream, she'd noticed his limbs seemed unnaturally short. She didn't think he was a child but suspected whatever medical condition had caused his hairy face had also stunted his growth.

She handed him the last half of the protein bar and reached into her bag for the apple she'd brought. She'd prefer that anyway.

"I'm Avery."

He didn't tell her his name but bit into the bar, chewing in a way that produced cute little squeaks like a guinea pig.

"Can you speak?"

He glanced at her and kept eating.

"All right. I'm going to take that as a no." She bit into the apple. "I'm trying to find Castle Dunchridhe. Do you know if I am close?"

The little man nodded, his mouth full, and pointed downstream.

"It's that way? I just follow the stream?"

At first he nodded, but then he stopped chewing and rested a paw-like hand on her arm. He glanced downstream and shook his head, then stood and impersonated a monster with gnashing teeth and slashing claws. He shook his head again.

"There's a monster in the castle?"

He nodded.

"Thank you for letting me know." This hairy little man was her first friend here. She didn't suppose it would be a good idea for her to let on that she knew very well that the laird of Castle Dunchridhe was a dragon or that she'd been sent by other monsters to collect him.

Once she'd finished her apple, she slid her socks back on, which were thankfully dry and warmed from the sun, then donned and laced her boots. Though the furry man had finished his bar, he remained beside her, watching her intently, still looking hungry. If she didn't have to ration her food, she'd offer him another. She collected her bag and slid it onto her shoulders.

"I have to go now. It was nice to meet you. You're the first friend I've made here. I hope we run into each other again." Avery turned to follow the stream, but the little man took one of her hands and gestured with his head. He wanted her to go with him. She didn't feel like she was in any danger with him, but she was burning daylight. She wanted to travel as far as possible before nightfall.

She shook her head. "I'm sorry. I can't."

He let her go and she strode from the place, feeling the man's eyes on her back for a long while as she took his advice and followed the stream toward the valley.

CHAPTER EIGHT

Avery walked until sunset, then found a clearing and built a small fire from gathered sticks within a circle of stones. She donned the hat and gloves the oreads had left in her pockets and wrapped herself in her arisaid. Beside the crackling fire, she was warm enough, and she looked up at the stars and thought she'd never seen so many at once.

"Well, Avery, you survived day one," she whispered to herself, and after walking as far as she had, drifted to sleep with no trouble whatsoever.

In the morning, she was amazed that she'd slept through the night again. After weeks of insomnia at Mistwood, two nights of perfect rest were a blessing. She dusted herself off, ate some nuts she had in her bag, and started walking again. It was late afternoon when she saw a curl of smoke rising from a chimney above the tree line.

"Thank God." The stream had provided water, but she was down to her last two protein bars, the bottoms of her feet ached, and the sun had begun its descent, its light casting long shadows across the village streets. She needed to find a place to spend the night. Although she'd slept well enough outside last evening, she was desperate for a hot meal and a bath.

The forest opened and she had to smile. It was like walking onto a movie set. The packed dirt street was lined with two rows of stone buildings. It wasn't hard to find the village inn. Vibrant conversation and candlelight poured into the street through the windows of a large stone building with a wooden sign painted with a lion and a rabbit, THE LION AND THE HARE.

She was about to walk inside when a bell rang behind her. A man in a kilt passed her on a bicycle. She stared after him, blinking. Did they have bikes in 1745? She honestly didn't know, but then she had to remind herself that it was 2018 here just like it was on the outside, simply a 2018 that had evolved on its own, cut off from the modern world. She frowned. She couldn't wait to reach Xavier and get out of here. Thinking about this place gave her the creeps. It was almost like she'd gone to another planet.

Which reminded her... She dug in her bag and pulled out Nathaniel's box, pressing the small black mole to her throat. Now she'd speak and understand the language no matter what that might be.

Avery smoothed her hair and her skirts and entered. Inside, the stuffy air crowded around her. Smoke from the large fire along the far wall mingled with the scent of unwashed bodies and spilled ale. All of it was made worse by the faint floral scent of something that wanted to be perfume but wasn't strong enough to do anything but add cloying sweetness to the mix. She breathed through her mouth and took a seat at one of the tables, ignoring the stares of the women and men who were obviously curious about her.

"Can I help ye, lass?" A woman stood before her, her

ample bosom almost spilling out of her tight dress. *I bet she makes great tips.* Avery was too tired and hungry to think any more of it.

"I'd like something to eat and a room please."

"We dinna serve lasses here, ye ken?" The woman lowered her chin.

Avery gave her a hard look-over and then eyed the other women in the pub. They were in various stages of undress, sitting on laps, running fingers through their gentleman's hair, all while the men played cards or sipped drinks. *Oh.* This wasn't an inn; it was a brothel.

"Unless yer looking for work yerself?" That the woman said a bit softer, eyeing her hair, her throat, and her chest as if sizing up her earning potential.

"Uh, no. I don't need work... or company. I just need a room and some food. I can pay you for it." Avery began to dig in her bag. She'd much rather spend the night in a brothel than beside a tree.

The woman shook her head and placed a firm hand on her arm. "Nay, lass. I canna allow ye to stay here. I won't be part of ruining yer reputation. Take my advice and go home to your father or husband where ye belong. This is not the place for a wee thing like you."

"I'm not..." What could she say? She didn't think it would be a good idea to yell that she didn't care about her reputation or that she didn't have a man at home waiting for her. Would she even be safe in this place if the wrong person thought so?

Avery considered leaving and trying somewhere else, but she didn't know where else to go, and she was too exhausted to move. For all she knew, all inns in the *builgean* were houses of ill repute. She sighed heavily. This wouldn't do. She could not spend another night outdoors, and she needed a hot meal to quell the protests of her hungry belly. She stared at the woman, who raised an expectant eyebrow. Clearly she was a woman who did what she had to in order to survive. A woman not unlike herself.

"What's your name?"

"Evangeline. I'm the madam of the house."

"I'm Avery." She held out her hand, and Evangeline took it reluctantly. "Would you consider a wager?"

"What kind o' wager?" Evangeline gave her a shrewd stare.

She reached into her bag and pulled out one of the larger silver coins, pushing it across the table toward the woman. "I'll bet you that I can turn water into whisky and whisky into water."

Evangeline scoffed and looked at her like she belonged locked up somewhere safely away from the public. Her eyes flicked to a large Scot at the door, who placed a hand on the dirk at his hip and frowned.

"If I can't do it"—Avery spoke loudly, noticing a few men around her table had taken interest—"you keep the coin and I leave. If I can, you sell me dinner and a room, no questions asked."

The woman's eyes fell on the coin, and then she glanced around the room at the patrons who'd taken interest. Avery couldn't remember what the coin was worth, but it was clear it provided some temptation, as did the idea of Avery providing some free entertainment.

"Aye. It's a wager." The woman offered her hand, and Avery shook it.

"I'll need a shot of whisky and a shot of water," Avery said.

"A what?" The woman looked at her in confusion.

Oh shit. When the fuck was the shot glass invented?

Avery's eyes locked on a small glass in a nearby man's hand. He was sipping something that looked like wine out of it. "In a glass like that," she said. "One whisky. One water. Filled to the top. You have to be able to see the miracle take place."

Avery rubbed her hands together, trying to psyche herself up.

"This is crazy," she whispered under her breath. She turned to the men, now watching her curiously. "May I borrow one of your playing cards?"

Three men produced cards, and Avery selected one from the man who looked least likely to kill her. The woman returned with the glasses and placed them on the table before her.

"Thank you. Now, watch closely," Avery said, thrusting her arms into the air and loosening up her hands. She'd performed this bar trick a million times in the Three Sisters, but there were so many things that could go wrong in this environment. She said a silent prayer that her guardian angel was still with her and placed the card over the water. Holding it in place, she flipped the glass over and placed it on top of the glass of whisky.

The Lion and the Hare become eerily silent as both men and women circled to watch what came next. Some in the back stood on chairs so they could see. This was the hard part. The key was creating the smallest possible opening. She pinched the card lightly and gave it a gentle tug.

Like magic, the whisky rose into the upper glass and the water sank into the lower one until the two liquids had completely switched places. There was an audible gasp from her audience. With practiced hands, she nudged the card back into place, held it to the top glass, and flipped it over. Removing the card, she handed the glass to Evangeline, whose mouth gaped in wonder.

"Go ahead, taste it," Avery offered, giving her the friendliest smile she could muster.

She did and then held it up above her head. "Whisky!"

Everyone erupted in cheers. Avery took a bow.

"Are ye a witch, woman?" The man near the door asked, his hand still on his dirk.

Avery laughed but thought she'd best put that idea to rest right away considering the history of witches in this part of the world. "No. Water is heavier than whisky. It's a trick. The liquids switch places. I can teach you how to do it"—she turned back to Evangeline—"if you bring me something to eat and I can have a room. If not, I'll have to go."

Evangeline smiled warmly and swiped a hand through the air. "Sit down, lassie. I'll bring ye some stew and have one of the girls fix a room for ye."

Avery fell back into her chair and clapped her hands together. "Well then, let the water-to-whisky lessons commence!"

An hour later, her stomach was full, she was very tipsy, and she'd demonstrated the trick three more times until the man by the door whose name she learned was Aeden was able to replicate it to the cheers of onlookers. To her relief, the patrons lost interest when a bard arrived with a lute and set up in the corner of the room. At the same time, several men disappeared up the stairs with their chosen woman, no doubt to complete their transaction.

Avery decided to have another pint and watch the show. She leaned back, turning her body toward the bard. He was a slight man whose lute was only marginally smaller than his torso. His voice, however, left nothing to be desired, and

Avery found herself enjoying his song as she sipped the most delicious ale she'd ever tasted.

She'd just asked Aeden for the key to her room when the bard started singing another number. This one was called "How Lachlan Slew the Dragon." It was all about a man who killed a dragon king and took the throne for himself. Avery frowned.

"That's a strange song to be singing around here," she mumbled.

"Why ye say so?" Aeden asked. He'd brought her key and set it on the table.

"Because, you know, Xavier is the laird," Avery mumbled. "That's who I've come to see."

Aeden frowned. "Xavier? Who's Xavier?" He laughed. "I think ye best be headin' to bed, eh? Ye're in yer cups."

That was strange. He acted like he'd never heard the name. But as she swayed in her seat, it dawned on her that dragons must change their names over the years, being immortal and such. Perhaps he went by another name now. She decided then and there that when she reached the castle, she'd ask to see the laird instead of specifying Xavier. That way she'd be sure to be taken to him.

"Why are ye goin' to see the laird anyway?" Aeden asked. Before she could come up with something, he answered for her. "Ye must be vying for that kitchen position. Na wonder I've never seen ye in the village. Ye must be from the mountain?"

"Born and raised." She cleared her throat. "Yes, looking for work."

"Aye. Ye don't need to speak to the laird for that. Ask for ol' Mistress Abernathy. The woman's been runnin' the show up there for damn near thirty years." He chuckled.

"Right." Avery stood, bumping the table with her hip. "Can you show me to my room?"

"Nay. I'm not allowed upstairs. No matter—it's the third door on yer left." He raised a hand and gestured toward the stairs to the second floor.

Avery gripped her key and made her way to the room. Outside her door there was a portrait of a platinum-haired man hanging on the wall with his sword buried in a dead dragon. Engraved in brass at the bottom was LACHLAN SLAYS THE DRAGON. Weird.

She unlocked her door, peeled herself out of her clothes, and passed out a minute after using the chamber pot.

CHAPTER NINE

Avery woke with a pounding headache and thanked the stars above she'd smuggled pain relievers in her leather bag. She washed herself using a deep basin of warm water Evangeline brought her and shared a simple porridge breakfast with a few of the women before setting off for the castle. Aeden pointed her in the right direction and suggested it was only a two-kilometer walk from the village. She might have seen the top of the keep last night if not for the trees and the dark.

When she reached the gatehouse, a man in a kilt stopped her at the door. "Whit's yer business here, lass?"

"I am here to see the laird." Her mind flashed back to the handsome face in the portrait she'd seen at Nathaniel's. She was looking forward to meeting Xavier.

The guard gave her a once-over and then took her by the elbow and led her into the castle. He guided her along narrow stone corridors and up a winding flight of stairs. When they reached a room with a heavy-looking desk and a fire in the hearth, he gave her a little shove through the door.

Now inside, a few more things caught her eye. There

was a rabbit in a cage near the fire that looked too thin, as if it was starving to death. Her gaze flicked to a birdcage on the desk. The bird inside was clearly dead. And another cage hanging from a stand in the corner held the remains of what might have been a squirrel once. She swallowed down a wave of nausea.

"This lassie says she's here to see ya," the guard said from behind her.

On the other side of the desk, a high-backed chair faced the window. She hadn't even noticed anyone was in it until long legs shifted to the side of the chair, followed by a lanky body and platinum-blond hair. The man was extremely pale to the point Avery wondered if he was ill. Avery swallowed hard, her stomach twisting as she was hit with intense disorientation. The man in front of her was the one in the portrait outside her room at the brothel. The Lachlan who purportedly slew the dragon. She blinked.

The laird was not Xavier but Lachlan. So where was Xavier? Her heart pounded and panic threatened to make her knees give out.

"Who are ye?" the pale man demanded, harsh lines forming around his mouth.

"My name is Avery... Campbell," she said, thinking quickly. Wasn't the population of this bubble predominantly Campbells?

"Very weel, Avery, whit can I do for ye?" He strode around the desk to approach her. The man was eerily slender, like something out of a nightmare.

For a moment Avery couldn't speak. Her brain was so overwhelmed with terror at the turn of events that she had a strong desire to make a run for it. But running wouldn't do a lick of good in this scenario. The two men in the room could easily overpower her. She had no recourse if they hurt her.

All she had was her wits and the weapons God gave her. So she did the only thing she could do given the situation. She coughed into her hand and lied.

"I was told you might need kitchen staff." She fluttered her eyelashes and stood up taller to make full use of her figure.

Lachlan scowled. "Ya dinna need to be seein' *me* for such a thing." He stepped toward her, his gaze raking down her body. His eyes were so dark as to be almost black, and the look sent a distinct chill through her. It wasn't the male gaze she expected, so often laden with sexual energy. No, Lachlan looked at her like a pig he'd like to roast over a spit. "I suppose ye are a bonny lass. Were ye hopin' I'd take an interest?"

"I need work."

His icy stare bore into her as if he were trying to rip the truth from her gullet. Several tense moments passed.

"I donna recognize ye from around here."

"Not surprising. I never left my parents farm before now. I'm from... the mountains."

"Take my hand," he ordered. "I'll warn ye—I can tell if ye're lyin' if ye do."

Tentatively, she placed her fingers into his. What choice did she have? Almost immediately, her hand tingled where their palms touched. He was squeezing too hard, cutting off the flow of blood to her fingers. She didn't pull away though. This was a test, and she was determined to pass.

"Now why're ye really here?"

The secret to telling a lie, Avery knew, was to tell a half truth. If your brain registered your exact words as true, your body wouldn't give you away. Only, her palm was drenched with sweat and her body was growing alternately hot and cold as her mind scratched the surface of what kind of trouble she was in. She looked him straight in the eye. "My father is no longer able to provide for me. My mother is gone. I can't survive on my own. I was told to seek out the laird and throw myself on his mercy." She sagged her head and lowered her gaze. "I'm sorry I didn't do this the right way or talk to the right person. I've never been away from home before."

Another moment passed, Lachlan raking her with his dark, probing gaze. "She tells the truth," he said to the guard. His eyes narrowed as he removed his hand. He seemed as surprised as Avery was that he believed her. "Take her down to Mistress Abernathy. See if she has a place for her."

"Aye, sir." The guard bowed, then took Avery's elbow, meaning to lead her from the room.

"Wait!" Lachlan said, raising his hand again. He approached her again and took her face into his narrow, bony fingers. It was like being touched by a corpse, but Avery held her practiced smile. "You are a lovely wee thing." His eyes flicked to the guard. "Tell Mistress Abernathy it would please me if she hired this lass."

"Aye."

He released her face, and Avery didn't breathe again until they were in the hall and the guard was leading her into the bowels of the castle. The walk gave her a moment to process what she'd just learned. Xavier was no longer in control of Castle Dunchridhe. A man named Lachlan was. And if the song and the painting were any indication of what had happened to Xavier, Lachlan had killed him.

"Ye all right, lass? Yer trembling like a newborn colt," the guard said kindly.

All she could do was nod and say, "I'm all right." Although she was far from it. If Xavier was dead, she had no way to get back home and no way to get a message to Nathaniel. She owned three skirts, one top, and a leather bag with money meant to last her only a few days. What was she going to do? How was she going to survive?

She'd thought of all those things when she'd lied to Lachlan. That was why her words had registered as true. She did need a job. As of right now, she might be in the *builgean* for a very long time. And as for her parents, they were gone, or as good as in her current situation. As for coming from the mountain, she did drop into the *builgean* from one.

They reached the kitchen, and a stout woman with graying brown curls wiped her hands on a cloth of questionable cleanliness before greeting them. "What 'ave ye got there, William?"

"Mistress Abernathy, this is Avery..."

"Campbell," Avery filled in.

"Mistress Campbell is needin' work. Lachlan asked me to bring her to ye. Says he'd consider it a personal favor."

Mistress Abernathy snorted in derision. "This scrawny thing? I have work, but I'm not sure she can do it!"

Avery was nowhere near scrawny. Her figure had always been more curvy than slender, and she was tall, taller than Mistress Abernathy.

"I'm stronger than I look," Avery said. If she were honest with herself, she probably wasn't 1745 strong. These people had never known the pleasures of a cell phone or a remote control. Even though she worked out regularly and carried up cases of beer at the bar, she was exhausted, and her feet still hurt from yesterday's hike. No need to oversell her abilities. "I can cook."

That raised Mistress Abernathy's eyebrows. "It's one

thing to cook for a family, another to cook for a castle, ye ken?"

"I've cooked for large groups before."

"Ye make good bread?"

"The best. And I've served before as well."

Mistress Abernathy made a sound deep in her throat and sized her up, wiping her meaty hands on her smock. "Aye. Tell Lachlan I'll give her a try."

William bowed his head and left the kitchen.

"If ye work out, ye'll have a room in the castle and regular pay. It ain't much but enough to keep yer belly full and clothes on yer back."

Mistress Abernathy motioned for her to follow her into the kitchen and threw an apron at her. She was quick to tie it on and fall into line with a team of women. One of them pushed dough in her direction and she began to knead it on the floured surface.

Avery released a breath she hadn't realized she was holding. In the center of a storm of fear and uncertainty, she had a job, she had a bed, and she had a distraction. Now all she needed was a plan.

It had been seven days since Avery had taken the job working in Castle Dunchridhe's kitchen, and all she had to show for it were sore fingers from kneading dough, a sore back from a mattress that wasn't fit for a dog, and a collection of burns from cooking over an actual fire rather than a gas stovetop. However, she had won over the kitchen staff by introducing them to her special grilled cheese sandwiches, which she made two different ways: plain and with raspberry jam. It seemed the affections of most women, from any time or place, could be bought with the right combination of carbs and dairy. They couldn't get enough.

Avery was frying a batch for her new friends in a three-legged skillet over the fire when she felt Mistress Abernathy staring at her.

"Do ye mind me askin' where exactly ye come from?" She gave Avery a strange look. "Avery is such a strange name. I canna say I've ever heard of a Campbell named Avery before."

"I'm from the mountains." She hoped the intentionally vague explanation would be enough. She flipped the sandwich in the pan.

"Where in the mountains?"

Avery looked at her but didn't answer.

"Yer skin is quite fair for growing up in the wilds. And ye know strange things about cookin' and such. Are ye a fairy, Avery?"

"Fairy?" She laughed. "No." When Mistress Abernathy didn't seem convinced, she changed the subject. "Is it true, the stories they tell about Lachlan slaying Xavier?"

Mistress Abernathy shot her a curious sideways glance and laughed. "Who's Xavier?" The old woman walked away, shaking her head and mumbling something about young women out of their minds.

"Shhh. Stupid girl," said a voice from behind her.

She looked over her shoulder but there was no one there.

"He'll have yer head if he hears ye say that name."

Avery's eyes widened when she recognized what was speaking to her even if she didn't know the creature's name. The tone of the voice held the same tinny quality as Tempest's and Laurel's, although she sensed this voice was definitely female.

"Are you his oread?" she whispered.

"Shh. What did I just say? Do not address me directly. Look toward the fire."

Avery did as she was told. Thinking back, the bard and the painting had only called Xavier the dragon. His name was never used. Whatever had happened here, no one seemed to remember him. But her heart leaped with hope. If Xavier's oread was here, maybe he wasn't dead at all.

"Do you know where he is?" Avery whispered toward the fire.

She felt a disturbance in the air beside her.

"Dungeon," the voice whispered. "I'll come for you tonight when it's safe and take ye to him."

Avery nodded. "What's your name?" Avery whispered.

"Glenna."

The air shifted again, and she was gone.

THAT NIGHT AVERY WAS EXHAUSTED BY THE TIME SHE was dismissed to retire to her chambers. Her room was only as wide as her bed and had a sloping ceiling that limited the area where she could stand at her full height. Still, she was thankful for the bed and would have gladly made use of it if not for Glenna. When would she come? Would they have to hurry from the room?

She knew she'd fall asleep the moment her head hit the pillow, but she had to find out what happened to Xavier. He was her only chance of ever going home, or at least to what served as home these days, Nathaniel and Clarissa's. At first she tried to wait for the oread, but after falling asleep on her feet and falling into the wall, she blew out the candle next to her bed and fell asleep still dressed in her clothes.

"Wake up, girl."

Avery came awake to an invisible force shaking her by the shoulders.

"Glenna?"

"Shhh. Lower yer voice. Who are ye and how is it ye ken my laird?"

Avery lowered her voice to a level she could hardly hear. "I'm a friend of his brother's. Is he alive?"

"Aye."

Avery's heart leaped. "Take me to him."

"Ye'll be able to free him?"

Avery didn't know how to answer that without seeing where Xavier was being held. Certainly, if it was easy, Glenna would've done it herself. "I'm going to try."

She swept her bag off the floor and slung it over her back, then reached for the candlestick.

"Nay," Glenna said. "'tis too risky. Follow me."

Avery didn't have to ask her what she meant. The oread began to glow until her outline was visible in the darkness. She was dressed like the other women here but had a set of gossamer wings that fluttered at her back. She looked like a winged ghost.

Glenna silently opened the door, and Avery squeezed through before closing it softly behind her. She followed the oread to the rear of the castle, then down a stone staircase. They descended two levels and stopped at a heavy iron door in front of which slept a guard snoring like a bear. An empty cup sat on the floor near his feet and smelled strongly of whisky.

"Sleeping draught," Glenna said. "I spent all afternoon concocting it." Silently, she moved past him and tugged the door open a few inches. Its hinges squealed and Avery froze, but the sleeping man simply grumbled, wiped his nose with his hand, and fell back to sleep. Avery squeezed through the narrow opening.

The dungeon was dark and dank. The steady drip of water echoed against the stone. She covered her nose and mouth against the smell of mold, human filth, and something else. Something animal. She scanned the cells. There was a man huddled in the first one who looked more dead than alive. He didn't raise his head as she passed. The next three cells were empty. She kept going, following Glenna as she led her farther back into the bowels of the dungeon.

By the light of the oread, who glowed brighter now like her own personal star, Avery came upon a cage with polished silver bars. The construction reminded her of a modern jail, and it stood out against the dark stone walls. She squinted through the bars at a shadowy figure near the back of the cage. Glenna came closer, and her light beat back some of the darkness.

There was someone or something near the back of the cell, but the stooped figure looked more animal than a man. She strained her eyes to see. The size of a bear, he was crouched on his haunches, his skin dirty but mounded with muscle that tapered along his spine and disappeared into a pair of filthy breeches that strained at the thighs. His feet were bare. He rocked on his heels, his auburn hair hiding his face.

"Xavier?" she whispered.

His head rose, but he didn't turn to face her. Glenna frowned beside her.

"How long has he been down here?" Avery asked.

"Too long," the oread answered.

"How is it that you're the only one who remembers his name?"

"Lachlan's mind control doesn't work on me, only

humans. I've been hiding in this castle since they captured him, but I can't open the cell. It's enchanted, ye ken."

Inspecting the door to the cage, Avery was surprised to find there was no lock. There wasn't even a place for a key. She stared, bewildered. How was she supposed to pick a lock when there was no lock to pick?

She placed her hand on the bars in frustration. They felt cold, icy, and her palms tingled as if the metal was charged with electricity. Weird.

"Xavier?" she whispered again. "Nathaniel sent me."

This time Xavier did turn his head, and something deep inside her clenched. If his portrait had affected her, his presence did even more so. Everything about him was larger than life. He was Conan the Barbarian. He was a god, a titan, a warrior who could pull her apart with his bare hands. She could feel his blue gaze hot against her skin as if he were touching her.

She tugged on the bars, testing them. A shock ran up her arm.

"Ow." Her elbow twanged like she'd struck her funny bone, and then by some miracle the door gave. She swung it open wide. Strange... it wasn't locked.

"You've done it," Glenna whispered, her voice laden with awe.

Avery wasn't sure what she'd done other than pull open the door, but she understood they were on borrowed time. They had to leave now, under cover of darkness, or they had no hope of escaping. "Xavier, my name is Avery. I'm a friend of Nathaniel's. We need to go."

He rose slowly, his eyes widening as they roved over the open door. She blinked. He charged. And all the air left her lungs with an *oomph* as his shoulder hit her gut and her feet left the floor.

CHAPTER TEN

The woman on his shoulder had to be an enchantress. After all, she'd said Nathaniel had sent her, and his brother reached for magic the way Xavier reached for his sword. But how would Nathaniel know he needed help? And how had she gotten past the wards to find him?

Although he longed to ask her a dozen questions, there would be time enough once he delivered them both to safety. He bounded through the door, slamming it unmercifully into the guard behind it. Lachlan's man flew, his head cracking against the stone wall. Xavier swept the man's sword into his hand. He wasn't one to turn his nose up at an opportunity.

He took the stairs two at a time, the stone making a strange noise with every step. It was an *ugh* sound. No, it wasn't the stone; it was the girl. He shifted her on his shoulder and heard her take a wheezing breath. A pang of guilt jabbed through him. She was a lovely wee thing, and he was manhandling her like a sack of wheat.

"Sorry, lass. Almost there."

A guard appeared in the hall in front of him, sword raised. "Halt!"

Xavier slapped the sword with his own, freeing it from the man's grip with brute force, then kicked the man squarely in the chest. He heard ribs crack and the guard collapsed, wheezing. He leaped over the body, trying not to think about who it was he'd just incapacitated. It was better if he didn't know.

He tore out the back of the castle and headed straight for the stables, ripping the door off Tàirn's stall with one hand. The jet-black stallion whinnied in greeting, nudging his shoulder before lipping the woman's face.

"Och. Blah. Put me down!" she cried, wiping away the equine kiss.

He set the woman on her feet.

"Tàirn is mine, the fastest horse in here. He'll get us out."

She wheezed at him, her chest rising and falling in pants. He hoped he hadn't bruised her too badly. Hurriedly, he tossed a saddle on the stallion's back and tightened the girth, then slipped a bridle on. He was just finishing the tack when a stable boy rushed in.

"Stop there!" the boy yelled.

"Back away. Ye'll not want to be facing off with me tonight." Xavier stared at him and allowed fire to fill his eyes.

The boy's face turned ashen, and he turned on his heel and ran. Smart young man. Xavier hoisted himself into the saddle, then held his hand out to the wee lassie who was still desperately trying to catch her breath. She stared at his fingers, her face pale.

"I dinna mean to be so rough with ye, but Lachlan will have our heads if we dinna move and quick."

Her blue eyes flicked to his and held, and then her hand was in his own. He lifted her onto the saddle. She hoisted her skirts and tossed her leg over to straddle Tàirn in front of him like she'd been born to ride and had no use for the manners of a lady. He didn't know who she was, but as she settled in against him, he decided he liked her.

"Very weel. Hold tight, lassie. Tàirn, fly!"

The stallion lurched forward, breaking from the gate at a gallop. Lights ignited in windows to the sound of pounding hooves. Xavier held the woman to him to keep her in the saddle. Even an accomplished rider might struggle at this speed.

Behind him, dogs barked and the howls of angry men rang from the castle.

"I ken Lachlan's learned I'm missin'."

He banked left, the woman releasing a pronounced squeak as she pitched sideways in the saddle. At a full run, he headed toward the fairy hills. All he needed was to get far enough away from the castle to make it difficult for the sídh and they'd have a chance to survive.

As the distance flew by, the trees grew closer together, tangles of mist playing in the moonlight around the horse's legs. He didn't break until the stallion was showing signs of fatigue. Even then he didn't stop, just slowed and walked him to a nearby stream. This would have to do. He dismounted, helping the wee lass down as he did.

"We'll camp here," he said. "Whit's yer name, lass?"

The woman stared back at him for a moment, wavered, and then, bending abruptly at the waist, vomited near his feet.

Avery felt like she'd just gotten off the world's least fun roller coaster. Her ass hurt like she'd been spanked, she was sure she'd bruised her ribs, and her stomach had decided to empty what little was left in it onto the ground in front of Xavier. *Hello. Nice to meet you. I came from outside your world to throw up on your bare feet.*

"Easy, lass. Come. Drink some water."

She allowed him to help her to the stream, knelt down, and rinsed her mouth out, then took a long, deep drink from her hands. *Fuck*, she'd forgotten Nathaniel's pill to purify the water. She might pay for that later. *Pull yourself together.* She splashed water on her face and neck and rinsed her mouth again. The cold helped. Slowly, the nausea from the day's events abated. She sucked in a few deep breaths.

As she blinked away the cold droplets, she recognized a boulder near the shore. Wasn't that where she'd rested on her way into the village? She wondered if her furry friend lived nearby. Not that he'd be out now. This time of night, anyone with a bed was likely in it.

Rising from the water's edge, she saw that Xavier had already gathered wood and started a small fire.

"Ye all right, lass?" he asked her.

Avery nodded. "Yes, thank you. I'm not used to riding like that."

She balked at the odd look on his face.

"Whit happened to yer voice?"

Frantically she felt the length of her neck, searching for Nathaniel's enchanted mole. It was gone. *"Fuck. Fuck. Fuck."*

He held up his hands. "Easy. I thank ye for yer help, lass. I'm just wonderin' as ye don't sound as if yer from here."

"I'm not." She tossed up her hands. "Nathaniel sent me from the outside."

His big hands rubbed his face. "Ye don't sound like yer from there either."

She sighed. "I'm not. I'm American."

"Aye." He looked her over as if he found that confusing, but he didn't ask her again about her origins. "Sit. Tell me how ye come to be here." He gestured toward the fire he'd started, then stepped over her vomit to take a seat on a log beside the flames.

"Sorry about that." She kicked some dirt over where she'd lost her lunch. Her gaze darted to where the large black stallion rested beside the trees. "He's faster and bigger than any horse I've ever ridden. Even faster than Nathaniel's Diablo. I guess my stomach couldn't handle the excitement."

"It's the rare horse indeed that can best Tàirn. I'd worried Lachlan hadn't been exercising him since he locked me up but must have been. He's even faster than I remember."

Xavier motioned to the other side of the fire where another large log waited. "I'm afraid this is the best I have to offer ye for the night, but as ye can see, I'm a bit short of wear myself."

He gestured toward his bare chest, and Avery suddenly felt a keen awareness of every inch of his masculine presence. She swallowed and glanced away.

"I can share my arisaid if you're cold." She cleared her throat and lifted the edge of what amounted to a blanket wrapped around her shoulders.

"The cold doesna bother me."

She blinked slowly. "Of course it doesn't. You're a dragon like your brothers."

"Aye." He scratched his bearded jaw, and she felt the weight of his gaze travel over her.

"Do you think we are safe here? Will Lachlan come after us?" God, she hoped they were safe for now. She was exhausted and sore. All she wanted to do was sleep.

"He might, but I'm betting he won't. For one, he'd be hard-pressed to get any of the locals to come wi' him. These hills are home to fairies. Some of them kind. Others deadly. As a dragon, I donna fear them the way the others do. I can protect you if we are set upon, but I doubt many will rush after us here, especially not in the dark. And Lachlan, he's a coward and a crook. He'll hesitate to leave Castle Dunchridhe and the hold he has over it and will avoid facing me alone at all costs, especially here where there are those who might not be sympathetic to his cause."

Avery wasn't sure what he meant by that and struggled to get her tired brain to formulate the right questions to ask. She looked around her. Fairy hills. The only fairy she'd ever encountered was Aborella, and she'd been the deadliest and scariest supernatural being she'd had the misfortune of meeting. To think she hadn't believed dragons or witches existed a few short months ago. And now she was hiding in the fairy hills.

She thought about what he'd said, but there was something she didn't understand. "Why would Lachlan's leaving the castle affect his hold on it?"

"The castle magnifies his magic, as do the poor creatures in his office whose life force he drains when he needs power. Allows him to keep a mental hold on my clan. If he leaves or becomes too drained, his magic might fail and someone might remember."

The answer simply spawned more questions, but she

was too tired to ask them. She held her hands toward the fire.

"What is yer name, lass, and how did ye come to ken my brother?"

She smoothed her skirts and gathered her arisaid tighter around her shoulders. "My name is Avery—my sister Clarissa is mated to Nathaniel. My other sister is mated to Gabriel."

Xavier made a deep, throaty grunt. "Mated, both. Hmm. And yerself? Are ye mated to one of ma brothers as well?"

She chuckled and raised her brows. "No. I am not married or mated or anything else to anyone."

For some reason, that elicited a hint of a smile from the dragon, who covered his smirk with a hand and rubbed his mouth and beard. "What are ye that ye were able to open the cage?"

"Hmm?" She shook her head. "The cage wasn't locked."

He grunted again. "No need to hide what ye are from me, lass. I be a dragon. I will na judge ye."

She shrugged. "I'm not hiding anything. I'm a human, plain and simple, and all I did was tug on the bars. The door simply swung open." She didn't mention the shock that had gone through her arms. She was sure there was some explanation, static electricity or some other natural phenomenon.

Xavier didn't press the issue.

"How came ye here? How did Nathaniel know I was imprisoned in the castle as to send you to fetch me?"

"He didn't."

"Heh?"

"I'm here to retrieve you for an entirely different reason. Nathaniel assumed you'd still be laird of Castle Dunchridhe. I marched right up to Lachlan, believing he'd be you, then had to pretend to be a mountain-raised bumpkin in order to be hired onto the kitchen staff. I only found you when Glenna heard me say your name and led me to you." She widened her eyes, realizing she'd completely forgotten about the fate of the oread who'd helped her so much. "What happened to Glenna?"

"Traveling back to the castle. I asked her to retrieve some things for me." He gestured to his state of undress.

"Oh. Good." She was relieved the oread wasn't in danger. "How long were you in the dungeon?"

He tugged at his beard. "Two years, I reckon."

"Two years!"

"If ye did na ken I was in there, then whit reason did Nathaniel send ye for?"

Avery threaded her fingers and looked into the fire. She'd thought it would be easy to tell Xavier everything his siblings had learned about Paragon, but now she wondered where to start. The man had obviously had a hell of a time the past two years. She didn't relish adding insult to injury with the truth about his wicked mother.

"It isn't good news. Would you like me to wait to deliver it until morning?"

He frowned. "Ye come all this way. Deliver yer message whilst the devil is at his rest."

She folded her arms across her stomach and took a fortifying breath. "Your brothers and sister are together on the other side. Earlier this year Gabriel discovered that your mother, Eleanor, was responsible for Marius's death." Avery told him about what Gabriel and Raven had learned on Pyre night and then about Scoria coming to kill Tobias. She spoke about Aborella taking Raven, Gabriel, and Tobias prisoner and how Nathaniel, Alexander, and Rowan fought to bring them home. She explained about Eleanor murdering Brynhoff and naming herself empress and how a rebellion was rising in Paragon, one his siblings planned to join in the future once they had his help.

His expression remained chronically impassive as she rattled on. Finally she finished relaying everything she could think of as he sat in stony silence. A yawn stretched her mouth. "Nathaniel would like you to come back with me to the outside world and join forces with your siblings to take back Paragon."

She waited. He stared at the fire. When several minutes had passed, she began to worry there was a language barrier. "Did you get all that?"

He gave her one curt nod, his expression giving nothing away. It was as if she'd told him she'd just watched a squirrel bury a nut. When more time passed without a reaction, Avery grew impatient. "Well? Will you come back with me?"

He took three long breaths while he toyed with a ring on his finger. It looked strikingly similar to Nathaniel's, but instead of an amethyst, it contained a grand topaz gemstone. Finally, after a small eternity, he raised his blue gaze to meet hers.

"Nay, I'm sorry, Avery. I canna."

CHAPTER ELEVEN

Everfield

For three days, Aborella endured Dianthe's kindnesses in silence. Her fairy rescuer spoke softly to her and kept her company as if she were a child. She was fed delicious stews and tasty sweets and given healing teas to drink. She was rarely left alone, although Sylas never made an appearance in the small cottage.

It all made Aborella profoundly uncomfortable. Never in her life had anyone from Everfield shown compassion to her. Then again, if Dianthe knew who she really was, she'd probably be torturing her instead. Still, the woman's actions made it terribly difficult to hate her.

"Why... are you... helping me?" Aborella rasped on the fourth day, when she discovered she again had her voice.

"You can speak! Praise the goddess!" Dianthe took her hand and smiled at her warmly.

"Why?" Aborella asked again.

Dianthe stared at her in silence for a long time. Her shoulders sagged. "The answer I should give you is that any fairy would help another fairy for the sake of the goddess. I think we both know that isn't true. The population of Everfield isn't always kind or helpful." She released Aborella's hand and walked toward the fire, leaning a shoulder against the stone. Her wings folded gently.

"No." So then why was she here?

"Most people in Everfield would have left you in that grave. I don't know you. You were buried near the palace. I have no idea if you were once friend or foe to the crown. What I do know is that you haven't been a member of this community for a very long time. I'd know if you had been. I know everyone here."

"Then why help me?"

Dianthe's gold eyes locked onto her. "Sylas thought I should leave you. He doesn't trust you. He won't stay here while you are here."

Aborella hadn't once seen Sylas since she'd been there, but she'd spent so much time unconscious, she wasn't sure if she'd simply missed his coming and going. Interesting. She waited, although the silence dragged out between them.

"What is your name?" Dianthe asked.

Aborella thought for a moment, then offered her middle name, a name she hadn't been called in her lifetime. "Call me Zinnia. Zin."

"Zin, you are here because whoever you are, you know something about what is happening inside the Obsidian Palace. And the fact that they buried you alive means that even if you were once a friend of the Highborn, you no longer are. We need people like you to help with the rebellion. We need inside information."

"You admit you're part of the rebellion?"

"Defenders of the Goddess, yes. There are many of us. We grow stronger every day."

The opportunities this presented swirled inside Aborella's mind. She'd known Sylas was involved with the rebellion; she'd never thought his mate would be sharing his involvement with her so openly. If she played her cards right, could she potentially find out more about the rebellion to take to Eleanor? A list of rebels could be her ticket back into the empress's good graces.

"You are being kind to me in the hope that I will join your cause."

Dianthe shook her head. "I'm being kind to you because I believe in treating people the way I would want to be treated. No one deserves what they did to you. No one. I don't care who you are or what you've done in the past. It was wrong."

A chill traveled the length of Aborella's spine at the conviction in Dianthe's voice. In that moment, she almost believed that Dianthe truly would have helped her even if she'd recognized her for who she really was.

"As for my mate, he is compassionate but far more cautious than me. The only reason he is allowing me to keep you here is because he hopes you will join our cause when you've recovered. It should be soon. I've never seen a fairy heal as fast as you."

Aborella glanced down at her legs. One had already regenerated to its regular size and shape. She wiggled her toes. The other leg had grown back to just above the knee. Her skin was no longer as white as it had been. Now it was a pale pink with the slightest hint of purple. Her fingers explored her face and found it still healing. She had time. It would be a few more days before she'd be recognizable by anyone, and by then she'd be strong enough to use her magic to disguise herself. She was in the perfect position to gather intel on the rebellion.

"As you might have guessed, I am no friend to the crown," Aborella said softly. "Tell me more about the rebellion. What exactly is it the Defenders of the Goddess are trying to achieve?"

Dianthe smiled. "I'll make some tea. This will be a long conversation."

CHAPTER TWELVE

"What do you mean, no?" The one called Avery might have sworn she wasn't a witch, but Xavier reckoned flames might shoot out of her eyes at the anger rolling off her. He hated to disappoint the lass, but he could not return with her to the outside world. Not without first settling the score with Lachlan.

"I must liberate my clan from Lachlan's clutches, ye ken? He's an evil bastard, he is. I canna leave here without setting things right."

"I'd think you'd have a lot better chances of that if you got your brother involved. We can go back, get help." She grabbed the sides of her head in exasperation.

"If I go through the wards, there's no guarantee I can come back. The original barrier was created by the fairies, Nathaniel, and me. Lachlan is a fairy. It's possible he tampered with the wards while I was imprisoned."

Avery rolled her eyes toward the stars. "Are you telling me that I came all this way to get you and you won't leave?"

"Aye." Xavier narrowed his eyes on her. "I donna doubt

that Nathaniel has good reason to want ma help, but ma responsibility is to ma clan. Paragon is not mine anymore."

Xavier frowned as Avery slid angrily off the log and flopped beside the fire, staring up at the stars. The poor woman had come all this way to rescue him, and this was how he repaid her? What a sorry arse he was! Dark circles swelled beneath her eyes and her lids drooped heavily. Poor wee thing. He wished he could help her, but his duty was to his people first.

He still suspected she was a witch after what he'd seen her do, but it seemed rude to press the issue, all things considered. Besides, witches were not always welcome in these parts. Perhaps she was protecting herself from the burning stake by denying what she was. He couldn't say he blamed her.

"How did Lachlan become laird anyway?"

"Well, the first thing ye should ken about that is at first I thought he was human."

Her eyes fluttered. "Not surprising. He looked human enough to me."

"He's a fairy changeling." Xavier frowned when it was clear Avery had no idea what that was. "The fairies stole a healthy babe from Oliver and Gwendolyn MacKenzie, a lovely couple I knew quite well, and they replaced it with Lachlan, who played the part of their child. I knew the boy, ye ken, his whole life. I thought I did anyway."

Avery rubbed her eyes. "Are you telling me the MacKenzies never suspected their baby had been replaced? That seems doubtful."

"Aye, but ye see, a changeling isn't actually an infant. Lachlan is hundreds of years old. He only posed as the baby and then as their child, and he was careful and patient as not to raise their suspicions."

"Okay. So this fairy—I assume he was here from the beginning?"

"Aye, likely living on this very hill."

"But you said he didn't lock you in the dungeon until two years ago. Why then? Why not one hundred years ago?"

Xavier grunted his approval at her thoughtful question. She was a smart one. Exhausted, but still working things out. Curious. Nathaniel must have known as much to send her alone.

"Lachlan understood that he could not win against me fair and square. On a fairy's best day, their magic is no match for a dragon's fire. If he challenged me when I was in a position of power, he would lose."

"Then how did he get you in the cage?" Avery asked.

Another good question. He smiled in her direction although her eyes were closed and she could not see it. "Fairies, generally, have three powers in their favor. The first is control over plants and trees. Everything green. They can make things grow faster than normal, make a tree reach down and grab you with its branches. The second is illusion—they can make themselves look like anything or anyone. That's how he concealed himself as a child all those years. They can also make things appear that are not there. But the third and final power is the most dangerous. Fairies can read and control thoughts. Lachlan can read human minds, tell when they're lying, and he can whisper in their ear and make them believe what he says."

Avery yawned. "He couldn't tell I was lying."

"Hmm?"

"He held my hand and asked me why I was here. I lied right to his face and he couldn't tell."

"Well, I've no explanation for that. But I can tell ye that

Lachlan started makin' people believe that there was a beast picking off their cattle. He did it slow, over many years. A cow dead here. Another missing there. Sometimes people would claim to see a flyin' beast."

"Flying beast? What, like a dragon? Was he trying to pin the cattle deaths on you?"

"Normally the people here know what I am, and it would appear so, but as these cattle went missin' while I was in the company of others, Lachlan's goal was never to pin the thefts on me. His goal was to make the people believe a mysterious unknown beast was at large and to pressure me to do somethin' about it."

Avery tossed an arm over her eyes.

"After so many complaints, Lachlan corrupted the mind of the local blacksmith and had him approach me about building a cage fit for a dragon. Now, I didna believe the thing was a dragon, but I was beginning to wonder if there was not some type of mutant bird with a penchant for cattle involved. To appease ma clan, I agreed to build a trap for the creature. The blacksmith made the bars, and then I warded them with ma own magic. Before I ever understood what Lachlan was, he'd manipulated me into usin' ma own magic to build a cage that could hold me."

Avery grunted. "He couldn't build it himself, so he tricked you into doing it for him!"

"Exactly. Fairies may not be as strong as other supernaturals, but they are brutally clever. This blacksmith had lost half his herd to the monster, and he built the cage in record time. And I, believing I was doing the right thing, used my magic to make the cage unescapable. We placed it in the field with a cow as bait. And what do you know, we caught ourselves a dragon."

"You did?" Avery asked. "I didn't know any other dragons were here."

"That makes two of us. I'd never seen a dragon like that before. It was small like a whelp, with odd-shaped wings and teeth. It didna look like any dragon from Paragon. I wondered if Scotland had grown its own, ye ken, so I went inside the cage to see what we were dealin' with."

"Lachlan trapped you?" Avery's voice held all the despair he'd felt that day.

"Aye. Turns out the illusion of the dragon was bait for me. Lachlan's mind control doesna work on me, but his illusions don't require psychic manipulation. They're damn near impossible to detect, even by supernaturals. Once he had me trapped, he shot me with a poison arrow and moved me and the cage into the dungeon. Then he used his power to convince everyone that the dragon had killed me but that he had slain that dragon. Later, he made them forget I ever existed. That's when he became laird."

"Just like that?" Avery stared at the stars.

"Fairy mind control is a significant force to reckon with, at least for humans."

"Not dragons."

"Nay. It didna work on me, although Lachlan's cunning is almost as dangerous. He tricked me into the cage after all. Tricked me before I ken whit he was."

"What a dick." Avery yawned again, adjusting herself in her makeshift bed.

Xavier hadn't heard a man referred to as a dick before, but by her tone of voice, he surmised it was an insult. He nodded in agreement.

"So I canna return with ye because I must take back the castle and free my clan from Lachlan's hold on their minds. Most of them are na better than slaves, ye see."

When she didn't say anything for a long time, Xavier moved closer to better see her face. She released a loud, rattling snore. Smiling, he backed away from her, but he did not follow her into sleep. Instead, he slipped out of his breeches and transformed, allowing his inner beast to take control. As he spread his wings and lifted into the sky for the first time in two years, he thanked the goddess of the mountain for answering his prayer and sending him the sharp-witted beauty with fire in her eyes.

CHAPTER THIRTEEN

An annoying and persistent rustle woke Avery from a lovely dream where she was somewhere warm, sipping cocoa and reading a romance novel by candlelight. She waved a hand by her ear, trying to cling to the pleasant image in her head, but the sound kept coming. The dream slipped away, replaced by the feel of hard ground and a morning chill that made her shiver.

She gave up and opened her lids.

Two large brown eyes set in a furry face stared at her, close enough their noses almost touched. Startled, she lurched and smacked the top of her head on the log.

"Ow." She rubbed the aching spot and sat up.

The furry little man she'd met earlier in this place stared back at her, holding up one of her last two remaining protein bars.

"Oh, it's you. Are you hungry again? You seriously need to move closer to town."

He waved the bar excitedly as if asking her permission. She noticed then that the contents of her bag had been dumped next to the fire. She groaned, grabbed the leather satchel, and started tossing items back into it. Had he taken anything else? She tried to remember everything she'd packed. She was too tired for this.

"You made a mess. All you had to do was ask me."

The furry man held up the bar again in response and spread his lips into a smile that seemed to house too many teeth. She couldn't stay angry at that face. The man reminded her of a dog with his furry skin and soulful eyes.

"Oh, all right. You can have it," she said. "I have one more in here for breakfast."

He moved as if to bite into the bar, wrapper and all, and she held up her hands.

"No. Not like that. Here. Let me." She reached over and tore off the wrapper, then handed it back to him.

He bit into it immediately. She continued cleaning up the mess, then pulled the drawstring tight and put the bag on over her shoulders.

Moving to rise, she balked when her eyes caught on Xavier. On the other side of the smoldering coals of the fire, he slept, using Tàirn's saddle as a pillow. He was glorious. Now, in the light of day, he looked even bigger than the night before, all golden-bronze muscle and wavy auburn hair. No wonder she'd dreamed of romance novels. In all his bare-chested glory, he looked like he belonged on the cover of one. She swallowed so hard she could hear it.

A tug on her hand brought her back down to earth. The furry man had finished his protein bar and was trying his best to lead her away again. "Oh, I can't go with you. I need to wait for my friend." She waved a hand in Xavier's general direction.

He shook his furry head, squeezed her hand tighter, and heaved her in the direction of the stream.

"Oh geez, all right already." She sighed. "Xavier, I'm

going to see what my friend has to show me," she announced in the loudest voice she could muster so early.

Xavier grumbled and rolled onto his side.

Avery allowed the little man to lead her across a log bridge to the other side of the stream. The forest was thicker there, but he guided her along a narrow path that seemed undetectable by anyone but him. Avery was no expert, but the plant life here seemed exceptionally green and of a variety she'd never seen before. It made her feel peaceful. For the first time since coming to this strange land, her shoulder muscles loosened and the air flowed freely into her lungs.

The tranquil green forest opened abruptly to reveal a small stone cottage complete with a barn, surrounded by brightly colored flowers. She sighed at the beauty of the place.

"Is this your home?"

He gave a small, charming squeak. On stubby legs, he jogged up the three steps to the wraparound porch and opened the red wooden door. She followed and peeked inside. The place was cozy and immaculate.

"It's very nice. Do you live here alone? Do you have a family?"

He gestured for her to enter, but she shook her head.

Pointing over her shoulder with her thumb, she said, "I should go back and get my friend."

There was a thump behind her, and Xavier landed in the small yard in front of the cottage. He whistled, and Tàirn came running to him, the stallion whinnying and shaking his mane. The furry man ducked behind her legs and squealed.

"I'm here," Xavier said, his amber-colored wings stretching wide before tucking against his back.

"You're scaring him. Stay where you are."

"Ask him to invite me inside as well, Avery."

"He seems afraid of you." Avery rubbed the little man's back as if he were a child and he shivered. He must be terrified. "Maybe it would be better if you went back to the camp. I'll meet you there in just a minute."

Xavier chuckled and pointed an upturned hand in her direction. "He's a brownie, Avery. A fairy. Am I wrong to assume ye've fed him?"

"I gave him a couple of protein bars." She shrugged.

"Whit now?"

"You know, like PowerBars... Never mind. I fed him."

"Aye. Then he's offerin' this place ta ye. He'll serve ye now, long as ye feed him."

"Huh?" Avery looked down at the small furry man and for the first time saw him for what he was—not human. She took a step back and bumped into the doorjamb. "Excuse me, Mr., mmm, Brownie, could you please invite my friend in as well?"

His furry head bobbed, and he motioned for Xavier to enter. Avery backed into the cabin to make room for Xavier as his body filled the door.

"A stroke of luck," Xavier said. "Da ye have any more? It would be best if I fed him from ma own hand as well. Otherwise he may resent me stayin' here with ye."

Avery huffed. "One, but I planned to eat it for breakfast."

"Trust me. Ye'll have yer breakfast. Da ye mind?"

For a moment Avery hesitated; then she removed her bag and reluctantly handed her last bar over to Xavier. He stared at it for a beat, then tore off the wrapper, chuckling as if he found the process amusing, then handed the goods to the brownie, who ate it hastily.

"Xavier, are brownies dangerous?"

"Not to the ones who feed 'em." He winked at her and wandered deeper into the cottage.

A fireplace at the center of the room sat unused. Xavier tested the flue with his hand and then, using a few logs from a bin on the hearth, lit a fire with his breath. She'd never seen any of the other dragon siblings spit fire like that. It was strange and enchanting. She touched her fingers to her lips and wondered at the temperature of Xavier's mouth.

A soft mew came from behind her, and Avery turned to find the little man had finished his bar. He licked his furry fingers and gave Xavier a small bow.

"I hope that was enough. I'm all out." Avery rubbed her stomach, suddenly very hungry.

"We'll need breakfast and tea," Xavier ordered the brownie. "And some clothes, whatever ye can find."

To Avery's surprise, the brownie bowed low again and then disappeared into thin air. "Holy God in heaven!" Avery looked left, then right, then hooked her head out the door. "Did you see that? He just disappeared."

Xavier laughed a low, rumbling sound that made Avery feel warm inside. "I told ye he's fairy."

"Yes, but you said the fairies had mind control and could make plants grow. Not disappear into thin air!"

"Oh aye, brownies can. Very powerful buggers. But he won't stick around if we donna feed him, so we best get to it." Xavier headed for the door.

"Get to what?"

"We need to steal a cow so we have cream to feed the wee brownie each morning. We'll also need to provide him a bed, but I see the last one to live here has already done so." He pointed to a small wooden box with a mess of blankets.

"He sleeps there?"

"As long as ye feed him," Xavier said slowly, as if she was a bit dense.

"Right." Avery pressed a finger into her chin. "Where do we get a cow?"

"Come along, lass, I'll show ye."

THE WOMAN WAS COMELY. VERY COMELY. AS HE MOVED toward the door, Xavier found himself suddenly concerned about his appearance. He was filthy, after all, still dressed in the rags he'd worn in the dungeon and without access to a bath, a comb, or a blade. Where was Glenna with his things?

"Now that I think about it, ye should stay here while I filch the cow," he said. If she waited in the cottage, he could bathe in the stream before he saw her again.

"Nonsense. I'll help you. I'm a very good thief. I used to lift candy bars from the grocery store regularly as a teen. Besides, you need backup in case Lachlan is out hunting for you."

He grunted. "Nay. I plan to shift into ma dragon form and fly the bugger back here."

"Won't a dragon swooping down over a herd of cattle draw some unwanted attention?"

"I'll make maself and the cow invisible."

He walked out the door and jogged down the steps. She followed on his heels.

Avery frowned. "Where do you plan to find this poor cow?"

"The McGregors have a farm nearby, on the edge of the fairy hills. I donna particularly care for stealing, but I'll reward the man handsomely once I've reclaimed Dunchridhe."

"Invisible or not, don't you think it would be to your advantage to have a second set of eyes with you? Even if the cattle can't see you, they can hear you and smell you. If you're not careful, you'll send the entire herd stampeding, and within hours the entire village will be talking about it."

He paused and gave her a sideways glance. He seemed to be having some trouble ridding himself of her, even temporarily. "I can be very quiet when I try."

She rolled her eyes in a way that stirred his temper. "If someone sees their cow disappear, I think they might make a fuss. You don't want to lead Lachlan right to us, do you? Take me with you—I might be able to distract anyone nearby. No one knows who I am, after all."

Xavier grunted. "Ye have wee manners for a lass, ye ken. Can ye just stay behind this one time and let me handle this?"

"No," she said simply, her unblinking stare a clear indicator of her stance on the subject.

"Ye have a hard head on yer shoulders."

"Like a diamond. Save yourself some time and energy and simply take me with you."

"Aye." He mounted Tàirn and drew her up into the saddle. She winced when her bottom hit the leather and he suppressed a laugh. "Yer sure ye want ta go?"

"Yes," she said firmly, although he didn't miss the way she ground her teeth when she said it.

"Very well." He hooked an arm around her and dragged her against him. She released an audible *oomph*. "If ye're sure."

Before she could say another word, he kicked Tàirn into motion and she was too busy concentrating on her seat to pester him further. He didn't ride as hard as the night before, but they made it to the edge of the McGregors' land quick enough. He didn't miss how she rubbed her bottom gingerly when he helped her down.

"Anythin' wrong?"

"No," she said in a high-pitched and highly suspect tone. She raised her chin.

"There she is, fat with milk." He gestured toward the shaggy Highland cow grazing a few meters beyond the fence.

"Okay. What's the plan?"

He looked both ways. "No a soul around for ye to distract," he said pointedly. "The plan is ye wait here. I'll shift and retrieve her."

He moved away from her and made himself invisible, then shed his breeches, tucking them into Tàirn's saddlebag for safekeeping. He shifted into his dragon form, knowing it would be far easier to carry a cow that way, but when he turned toward his target, Avery was gone.

He cursed. The blasted woman was in the field, walking toward the heifer with a length of rope in her hands he recognized as the one he kept hooked to Tàirn's saddle! Damn obstinate female! He spread his wings, meaning to fly over her, swoop down, and retrieve the heifer before she could reach it. Only he realized he could not. Avery was too close now. If he scared the cow, it might become agitated and trample Avery, or worse, scare the rest of the herd.

He suppressed a growl. He'd have to wait for her to draw the animal near. He watched helplessly as she fed the cow a handful of grass while slowly looping the rope around the beast's neck. Then she coaxed her toward him. Slowly, cooing to her every step of the way, she moved the beast forward one step at a time until finally she was right in front of him.

He shifted back into his human form so he could speak, careful to maintain his invisibility. "All right, stand back and I'll carry her over the fence."

She blinked, turning her head toward his voice. Invisible or not, a shiver ran the length of his body as he stood before her naked. Thankfully, she obeyed, slipping the rope from the cow's neck and taking a step aside. He spread his wings and hopped over the fence.

"Are you naked right now?" she asked, a wicked smile curving her lips.

He paused. "An inappropriate question for a proper lass!"

She snickered. "Good thing there isn't one of those around here."

He did a double take, watching her over the cow. Avery was full of surprises. His lips twitched into a smile.

She raised an eyebrow. "Last night when you were carrying me out of the castle, I could see you even though others couldn't."

"Aye."

She giggled. "So... If I touched you right now, would I be able to, um, see you?"

"Aye." He gave a low chuckle and called her bluff. "Would ye care to 'ave a look, lass?"

She snorted and took a step back. "No!"

"Aye, I'll ruin ye fur all other men! Ye may go blind from the glory of it."

That made her laugh fully, straight from her belly. "Or maybe cry out of pity."

"He-he, it's a good thing we have a cow between us or

we might have to settle this—" He was about to say once and for all when a shot rang out and buzzed right by their heads.

Avery swore. "What was that?"

"It appears the McGregors have noticed ye after all." He leaped over the animal, grabbed Avery around the waist with one arm and the cow with the other, and flew both over the fence just as a band of McGregors rode up, pistols drawn.

"Whaur'd she go?" one of them yelled.

"Never mind the lass! Whaur's the cow?" another barked.

The cow chose that moment to release a deep, vibrating moo. The men rode in circles, terribly confused as the sound of their lost heifer came from the distant sky. Xavier waited until he was out of gunshot range to land and whistle for Tàirn.

"Ugh." Avery grunted as they landed hard between the trees.

"Sorry. It's difficult carryin' ye both in this form."

She smoothed her skirts and wiped sweat from her brow. "Between the gunshots and dangling from a deadly height, I think I've had enough excitement for the day. Please tell me breakfast is in my near future."

"Just beyond the stream there." Tàirn galloped to him and he removed his breeches from the saddlebag before pulling them on again. He dropped his invisibility, tied the cow to the saddle, then mounted.

Avery reached for his hand, but he pulled it away. "Weel?"

"Well what? Help me mount so we can return to the cottage and eat."

"Was it a glory or a pity?"

Her mouth gaped. "I was too busy praying I wouldn't fall to my death to notice!"

He reached his hand down to her and grinned. "A question to be answered another time then."

"In your dreams," she said with a laugh.

He hoisted her into the saddle in front of him and pulled her firmly against his chest. He didn't miss the soft sigh she released at the closeness or the way she smelled of clean linen and wisteria. Exquisite. To his surprise, his inner dragon whirled in approval within him.

He eased Tàirn into a slow walk and they led the cow back to the cottage.

CHAPTER FOURTEEN

She *had* almost gone blind from the glory of it. Avery leaned against Xavier's broad chest and tried not to squirm in the saddle. The man had spent two years in an underground dungeon and still looked like an Adonis. A filthy Adonis who smelled like wet earth and desperately needed a bath, but still a model of the masculine form.

She pictured herself with a soapy sponge in her hand and had to close her eyes against the images her mind conjured. She was more than a little relieved when they reached the cottage and she was able to slide off the horse and put some distance between them.

"Oh!" She tipped her nose toward the door. "Do you smell that? Food!"

Just then, Glenna appeared with a bundle in her arms. "Laird Xavier, I've brought yer things." She handed him the package.

"Whit took ye?" he asked kindly.

"I had to be careful. He can detect me, ye ken. Nymphs are not unfamiliar to fairies. I've had to hide all these years, carefully. He's got the entire clan lookin' for both of ye. The stable boy saw Avery. He's avoiding the fairy hills fur now, but it's only a matter of time."

Xavier nodded and sighed through his nose. "Ye'll have to go back. Spy on Lachlan. Alert us if he decides to come this way."

Avery could tell Glenna had no desire to return to Castle Dunchridhe, but she bowed her head and disappeared. Xavier frowned, clearly hating that he had to send the oread into danger.

"Breakfast?" Avery asked, thinking a meal would do them both good.

"In a moment," he said. "I must tend to something first." He blinked out of sight.

She shrugged. "Suit yourself." She ran up the steps and into the cabin, finding a banquet of food on the table. She ladled porridge into a bowl, topped it with fresh berries and cream, and dug in, nibbling on the meats and cheeses between bites. She poured herself a steaming cup of tea. She would have preferred coffee, but she hadn't seen any since she arrived. The oats were creamy and delicious and filled her up with warm comfort. By the time she washed down the last bite, she thought she might explode.

The door opened and Xavier stepped inside. She froze, slowly lowering her teacup to the table. The first thing she noticed was the kilt, a beautiful brown-and-blue tartan kept in place by a leather belt with a dirk at the hip. His shirt was a loose-fitting linen with buttons at the neck, and over it was a vest and jacket in deep blue. But it was his clean-shaven face that arrested her, as well as his hair, which he'd tied back at the base of his neck in a sort of long, masculine ponytail.

Avery was struck speechless. The man was stunning. She rested her chin on her fist to keep her mouth shut.

"Have ye left any for me?" he asked, one blue eye winking.

She leaned back and raised her chin. "Plenty. Might not be as warm as it was."

He sat down beside her and loaded a bowl. She fought the urge to stare as he began to eat.

"Whit does a woman such as yerself do in the outside world?" he asked. "Since ye said ye weren't a proper lass." The crooked smile he gave her was almost indecent, and a warm tingle uncurled in her lower belly. She took a sip of tea to loosen her thickening tongue.

"I work in a pub. I'm a bartender and a waitress."

"Ah, a serving wench. No wonder ye speak like a man."

"What? I don't speak like a man!" Heat crept up her neck to her cheeks.

"Aye, you do. There's no weakness ta ye. Ye say everything that comes inta yer mind with a fair bit of strong language as well."

"I promise you, loads of women in the outside world speak far worse than me. Out there, women are equal to men in almost every way."

"Heh?" He scowled.

"Yes. Most wear pants actually."

He looked at her strangely, and she realized that in a land where men wore kilts, that didn't hold the power she'd hoped it would.

"Many own their own businesses. My mother owns the pub where I work, and she's run it on her own for years."

He rubbed his smooth jaw. "It's different, ye say, than here?"

"More than you know." She watched him eat for a few minutes, her mind lingering on their talk of the outside world. It reminded her again that she didn't belong here.

She'd already stayed far longer than she'd planned. Raven and the others must be worried sick. She *had* to convince Xavier to return with her. "I don't suppose I can change your mind about forgetting Lachlan and going back with me?"

He shook his head.

Avery sighed. "Then what's your plan for taking back Castle Dunchridhe? None of the people remember you, Xavier. How do you plan to take Lachlan on without help?"

"Aye. The clan is under his control. Ta conquer the castle, we'll have to kill him first... free them from his hold."

"But how do you plan to do that? You could shift and attack the castle in your dragon form, but won't that be dangerous for the people inside? And if you attack in your human form, won't you be vulnerable to Lachlan's tricks and his mind control over his guards?"

"Aye. And more. Lachlan is immortal, as am I. I can try to tear him apart, but he'll be very hard to kill, and in the process, he'll use my people against me. I'm immune to his magic, ye ken. One against one, I'd not be worried. But I'll not risk ma clan."

"But then, how do you intend to kill him?"

"'Tis the problem, eh? Now that we've a place to stay and a brownie to help us, I'll be usin' all the tools at my disposal to find a way. I donna suppose ye have a book on ways to kill fairies in that sack of yers?"

She snorted. "No. You're on your own."

"Aye."

Having finished his meal, he stood. "If ye'll excuse me, I must tend to the horse and the cow."

She stood. "Right. Do you need help?"

He smiled and shook his head. "Nay. Make yerself

comfortable. Ye can have the bedroom. I'll fix myself a bed out here."

Avery had been so lost in her thoughts she hadn't given much consideration to the sleeping arrangements or that the cottage only had one bed. There was no way he would fit on the simple piece of furniture that served as a sofa in this room. Still, somehow they'd have to make do. She nodded, and he turned to leave.

"Uh, Xavier?"

"Aye?"

"Where did you bathe? I'd like to... clean up." She flipped a piece of her hair between her fingers. She was in desperate need of a bath. She hadn't even brushed her hair or teeth today.

"In the river, but I'd say it might be a wee bit cold for ye. Why not make use of the tub?"

"There's a tub?" Her eyebrows rose.

"Aye. Here, I'll help you with it." He disappeared out the door and returned with a simple wooden tub that reminded her of the bottom of a large barrel. "I saw it on the porch when I came in. Ye'll have to haul water from the pump and boil it over the fire, but I ken it'll be better for ye."

"Thank you."

"I can help ye if ye wait."

At first Avery thought he was being lecherous, offering to help her with her bath, but then she realized he was simply being courteous. It would take several buckets of water to fill the tub and no doubt he assumed that a woman would struggle to do it herself.

Avery shook her head. "I'm stronger than I look."

He tipped his head and flashed her a sideways smile, then slipped out the door.

Avery placed another log on the fire and dusted her

hands. The tub wasn't going to fill itself. She followed Xavier out the door, found a bucket and the well, and started pumping. The water that flowed was cool and sweet and came easily out of the spout as if it were already primed.

She wondered if it was this place. The brownie, who still hadn't reappeared, must have lived here for some time. Nathaniel had said that Mistwood was infused with his magic due to his long-term residence there. Might this property be infused with the brownie's magic?

She carried the bucket back to the cabin and poured it into the cauldron near the fire and swung it over the flames. Then she collected another and another, alternating one in the tub and one over the fire, until the water started to boil. She used a wadded towel to carefully tip the boiling water into the cool liquid already in the tub, then tested it for temperature.

"Perfect." The tub wasn't large enough for her to fully stretch out, but it would do. She began the arduous process of unfastening each piece of her clothing, cursing the rigors of eighteenth-century fashion, until finally she pulled her chemise over her head and stepped into the water.

The tub was deep enough to almost cover her with her knees bent. She leaned her shoulders against the edge and closed her eyes, allowing the heat of the water to soak into her. After a few heavenly moments, she reached for her bag and the small bottles of bathroom sundries she'd stashed away. She'd never used them at the castle, only the homemade soap they'd given her. No better time than the present. She started to scrub and immediately felt better. The welcome scent of modern shampoo wrapped around her, and she bent her knees closer to her chest to sink beneath the water and rinse her hair.

She broke the surface, wiped the water from her eyes, and came face-to-face with fur and brown eyes. *"Ahhhh!"* The scream broke her lips before she could stop it.

The brownie jumped, emitted a high-pitched squeak, and scurried into the bedroom, slamming the door behind him. Avery reached for a towel, her skin dripping on the woven rug, and realized she didn't have one. She tried to reach for her clothes instead. The door opened. She froze.

Xavier's blue eyes locked on her, grew wide, and then he blinked out of sight.

"It doesn't help if *you're* invisible!" she yelled, her fingers finally finding purchase on her arisaid and pulling it to drape over the top of the tub.

"I thought it would make ye more comfortable," Xavier said, blinking back into her field of vision with a roguish smile on his face and a laugh in his voice.

"Why would it make me more comfortable if you can see me but I can't see you?" She tugged the cloth higher on her neck.

He smiled wider. "Well, at least ye can pretend I didna see you as God created ye."

Avery stood up, wrapped the tartan around her and stormed toward the bedroom. When she opened the door, the brownie raced past her and hid behind Xavier's legs.

"Oh, for the love of all that is holy!" Avery cursed and slammed the door behind her.

CHAPTER FIFTEEN

The woman reminded Xavier of the Mountain—the goddess of the mountain. She reminded him of home. Avery must have fire in her blood the way her blue eyes burned when she countered him with her wit. She wasn't spoiled, that was certain. Her skin might be as smooth as a Highborn lady's, but she carried water like a Highland farm girl. She was an enigma.

Xavier looked down at the brownie hiding behind his legs. "I donna ken whit she's so up in arms about. Nothin' ta be ashamed of on that one."

The furry man nodded. Xavier carried the tub outside to drain it and then returned it to where he'd found it. Upon reentering the cottage, he heard the bedroom door open. Avery emerged dressed in a blue skirt and a jacket lined in fur with gold stitching. Xavier had spent enough time in the care of oreads to know when a garment was made by the supernatural.

"Lovely," he murmured.

She smiled, running her fingers through her wet hair.

"Our furry friend outdid himself. This isn't just beautiful, it's functional. Light and soft."

"'Tis fairy made," Xavier said. "I suspect this brownie fancies ye to give ye that."

In fact, the brownie was staring at her with such reverence, Xavier wondered if the poor beast didn't adore the woman something fierce, and didn't that raise on odd and unexpected ache in his chest? He watched Avery dig in her bag for a hairbrush and draw her long hair over her shoulder to brush out the ends.

He approached her and reached for the brush. "Allow me."

"You're going to brush my hair?"

"Aye." When she made a strange face, he added, "I've seen women do this for each other, and since there are na women here, it's ma duty to fill in."

She met his eyes and gave him a little nod, then followed his suggestion to sit on the bench near the fire. The heat would help dry her black locks. He stood behind her and began to run the strange brush through her hair.

"Whit is this tool constructed of?" he asked. The material was smooth as stone but lighter than wood.

"Plastic."

"Whit's plastic?"

She giggled. "It's a man-made material from the modern world."

"Much has changed since I laid the wards."

"More than I can explain."

The room grew quiet aside from the crackle of the fire and the sound of their breathing.

"Can I ask ye something, Avery?" He slowed his brushing.

"Sure."

"You've a scar across yer chest."

She glanced over her shoulder at him. "You saw more than I thought you did."

He grunted. "It was above the surface."

She smiled softly. "I was robbed at knifepoint. The man cut me when I fought him off."

"You fought a man with a dirk? And withoot one yerself? Yer lucky to be alive."

She snorted. "Actually, I injured him far worse. Kicked him through a glass countertop. He had to be hospitalized."

Xavier couldn't help but smile at the thought of Avery making a joke of her assailant. *"Curaidh."*

"What does that mean?"

"It's a Gaelic word for warrior. Ye've a warrior's blood in ye."

"You think I'm a warrior?"

"Aye. Normal women donna rescue dragons by their lonesome."

She smiled and looked down at her hands. "I've been thinking," she said. "I understand that you don't want to come back with me, but Nathaniel would be far more help than I would to take back the castle. Why don't you fly me out of the ward, and I'll tell him you need his help? If you made the ward, you should be able to allow him through, right?"

He brushed her hair from crown to end, marveling at the black shine in the firelight and the scent of wisteria that filled his nose with each swipe. His inner dragon twisted and chuffed. He didn't want her to go.

"I can't."

She frowned. "Why not?"

"The ward was constructed with the strongest magic

known to fairy, dragon, and witch. A ward of its size has never been constructed before."

"Nathaniel told me. He said he helped you."

"Aye. He helped me and yet he can't pass through it." Her hair felt like silk and he caught himself running his fingers over it unnecessarily. "Ye will recall the door is straight up. If I fly you out of it, I'll also have to fly ye to safety, and the risk is, if Lachlan has tampered with the ward, I may na be able to return."

"I remember you saying something about that before."

"And while I could toss ye through the door, unless there be someone on the other side to catch ye, I'm afraid ye'd fall to your death."

She released a deep breath and turned back toward the fire. "I'd rather not be thrown into the void. Yes, I can see now where it's not a viable plan."

He hated the look on her face. Avery was practically a stranger to him, but already she'd proven talented enough to win employment in the castle, cunning enough to fool Lachlan, brave enough to find him in the dungeon, and mysterious enough to somehow free him from his cage. He shouldn't forget beautiful. She was achingly beautiful and as stubborn as a mule when she wanted to be.

He drew the brush down the length of her hair once more. "What if we make a pact, ye and I? I need yer help, Avery. You're the only one I can trust at the moment to help me right this wrong. If ye'll stay and help me, I promise to take you home just as soon ma sword sets Lachlan's head to roll."

"And if we fail?"

"Well then, I reckon ye'll be able to walk out on yer own. If I die, and make no mistake, he'll have to kill me this time, the wards will fail. You can take Tàirn and ride west.

Maybe twenty miles as the crow flies and you'll pass right through into yer world."

She rubbed her thumb against her palm. "I suppose I made my choice when I dropped from Nathaniel's arms."

Guilt tugged at Xavier's heart. He frowned and set the brush on the bench beside her. "Nay, lass, there is one other way. I can take ye back to the door and use my ring ta try ta open a passage through fur ye. It might work in the spot directly under the gate. Ye see, there is only one door into the *builgean* because from the outside, that is the only point reachable. But it is a different matter from the inside. If we go ta the ward, I might be able to pass ye through." He wasn't sure it would work. If Lachlan had altered the wards, it wouldn't.

"But you couldn't come with me."

"No."

"And you'd have to face Lachlan alone."

"Aye."

She turned again to face him. "Are you willing to do that for me?"

He stared at her long and hard, and the oddest thought popped into his head. Her eyes were blue like his. If they ever had children, the bairns would be blue-eyed and perhaps dark-haired. What an odd thought. He barely knew the woman. Besides, he wasn't sure dragons and humans could produce young.

"Aye, for ye I would."

Avery had promised herself she'd stop living her life for others. She'd carried other people's burdens for too long, first for her sister, then for her mother, and finally for her father. That last one had almost gotten her killed when Aborella, a deadly fairy from Paragon, had used him for her wicked ends. Now Xavier was asking her to help him kill another fairy, one that might be even more dangerous than Aborella.

Avery had come here to learn who she really was, to do her own thing, have her own adventures. If she stayed and helped Xavier, was she being true to herself? More importantly, after everything that had happened with Aborella, was she willing to face off against a powerful fairy again?

Only, the more she thought about it, the more her instincts told her to stay. This place and this man challenged her in ways she'd never been challenged before. The way he looked at her now, almost pleading for her help, was dripping with respect and pure unadulterated hope. He needed her. It didn't hurt that the sight of him made her ovaries quiver either. The man was a piece of art.

But she couldn't and wouldn't stay for him alone. That wasn't a good enough reason. Her thoughts trailed to the scar still pink along her chest. She wasn't helpless. When she'd faced Aborella, she hadn't even known fairies existed, and now, even though she was not blessed with the powers of her sisters, she was here. She had freed Xavier. It made her feel proud, like she'd earned his label for her—warrior. Was she the only one willing and able to help him face Lachlan? If so, she wanted to rise to this challenge. This was who she was, and she would not back down from it.

"I'll stay," she said firmly. "I'll help you." The crooked smile he rewarded her with seemed to wrap around her like a blanket, and the heat it produced made everything inside her melt like warm butter on toast. She caught herself staring and looked away. "So where do we start?"

Xavier cleared his throat. "Well, I hadna quite got that far yet."

She gave him a withering look. "You must know that fairies are vulnerable to iron." She remembered the way Maiara had injured Aborella with a fireplace poker. It hadn't killed her, but it had weakened her.

"Aye. But how is it that ye know it?"

She bobbed her eyebrows. "I've been around this Tinker Bell hill before." She told him about Aborella and Sedona.

"I ne'er liked that fairy," he said. "Aborella played an increasin' role in the palace when I was a bairn. None of us liked her."

She nodded in agreement. "So where do we get an iron weapon? What is your sword made of?"

"Steel. All our weapons are steel. Have been for a century."

She sighed. "So we need an antique iron weapon that's still strong enough to slice off a fairy's head."

"The head. Aye. Even immortals need a head."

They both nodded knowingly.

"Where do you keep ancient weapons? Do you have a museum or something?"

He narrowed his eyes. "Mostly folks keep their ancestors' wares."

"Should be easy enough. All the people here have been around for generations, right?"

Xavier rubbed his chin. "In theory, but goin' door to door askin' for iron weapons might not serve our cause. Lachlan will have poisoned the clan's mind about me by now, and Glenna says they're after ye as well."

"Right." Avery spread her hands. "There must be another way. This shouldn't be hard. We are literally living in a cottage with a brownie. Shouldn't one fairy know how to capture another?"

Xavier raised an eyebrow and muttered something in Gaelic. The brownie appeared by his side. After an exchange of words and squeaks, the furry man led them both to a trunk at the back of the cottage. Avery had noticed the chest before, but it was covered in a musty quilt and a layer of dust. She removed the quilt and a puff of dust rose into the air. She coughed and covered her mouth and nose with her hands.

Xavier reached down to lift the lid and magic swirled in the air. Avery only recognized it from the time she'd raised the circle with her sister Clarissa. The air grew thick and her skin tingled. The chest vibrated as if there was something alive inside it.

Xavier lifted the lid.

"Books!" she said.

Xavier glanced back at the brownie, and the furry man bowed and then disappeared. "This was not whit I was expectin'."

"What were you expecting?"

"I didna want to scare the fella by askin' how to murder his kind, ye ken?"

She nodded.

"So I asked to learn more about fairies. I wasna expectin' a library."

She selected one of the tomes and opened it. "This is filled with sketches of fairies. All the labels are in Gaelic."

He grunted and selected another book, flipping through the pages. "Must be somethin' here. And it looks like most of them are in English."

Avery groaned and tilted her head back. "When I said I

would help you, I didn't know there would be research involved."

"Ye donna like books?"

"Oh, I love to read... fiction. I'm just not much of an academic. School was never really my thing. I mean, certain subjects clicked. Others..."

"Aye. Ma talents as a young dragon lay more in the fighting pits than the classroom as well."

Darkness passed behind his normally bright eyes, and she couldn't help but wonder at what haunting memories must have caused such an expression. "Did you like fighting?" she asked, closing the book in her hands. The man in front of her was far more interesting than anything within its pages. "Nathaniel said you were the best of any of his siblings."

Xavier gave a deep grunt that she interpreted as agreement. "In Paragon, every dragon male is taken to the pits when they're old enough to hold a weapon. We were no exception. The Highborns entertain themselves by watching their whelps fight."

"Highborns—that was the aristocracy, right?"

He nodded. "Our father, Killian, coached us, but he took special interest in me. Because we were heirs to the throne, our lessons were longer and harder than the others'. Not that it mattered. The other Highborn children were taught never to win against us, just as we were taught never to defeat our eldest brother Marius."

"Some of the matches were fixed?"

"Aye. They were, although it was an unspoken rule. A confusing one at that for a bairn who didn't know the why of it. I remember one match when I rebelled and let a male from a lower caste win. He broke my arm and my wing. I crawled to Killian, injured and in the worst pain I'd ever felt, and he picked me up and sent me back into the pit."

Avery's stomach turned. "He made you fight injured?"

"Aye. 'Donna come out until ye've won,' he said. And I dinna. I pummeled my opponent bloody. Couldn't move for a week afterward."

The idea of a young Xavier fighting for his life in the pit gave Avery a chill. She opened her mouth to say something and couldn't find the words. In the end, she gave up on trying and looked down at the books in her hand.

Xavier reached in and picked up another tome. "So..."

She sighed. "All right. Well, I guess we should get started... reading... these old books." She rocked back on her heels.

"Would ye like a whisky to dull the pain?" He gave her that charming, crooked smile.

"That'll work."

She settled into a chair at the table while he fetched a bottle and two glasses from the stash of supplies the brownie had provided. He poured them both a healthy dose and sat down across from her. She opened the book and began reading a painstakingly detailed account of the first fairy sightings in Scotland. She sipped her whisky.

"Are we ever going to talk about the fact you saw me naked, or are we going to pretend it didn't happen?" she asked, not looking up from the text.

"Which da ye prefer?"

"How much did you see?" When he didn't answer right away, her eyes flicked up to his.

He sipped his whisky and flashed that crooked smile again. "Enough I'm lucky not to 'ave gone blind from the glory of it."

CHAPTER SIXTEEN

Everfield

It had been six days since Aborella had been rescued from a hole in the ground, and she was feeling more herself than she had in months. Her skin had regained its deep purple hue, and her limbs had grown back enough that she could walk around the cottage, albeit with a limp. Both her wings were healed as well, and they fluttered often as she inspected every corner of the cottage at every opportunity.

She'd been careful to use her regained magic to hide her identity. To others, her skin appeared a deep rose color and her normally silver eyes sparkled green as new spring leaves. Perhaps the only thing that remained truly hers was her platinum hair. That at least occurred frequently enough in the regular fairy population to not give away her identity.

"Will you take part in the waning ceremony?" Dianthe mixed another batch of cookies in a giant bowl on the counter. The woman's oven was always on as far as Aborella could tell. She was a baking machine, a goddess of home and hearth. "You seem well."

"I think so." Aborella hadn't left the cottage since arriving here and was looking forward to a change of scenery. Plus she hoped the opportunity would arise for Dianthe to introduce her to additional Defenders of the Goddess.

"We haven't talked much about what happens next, but I'm assuming you'll want to make a fresh start. I've talked with Briar Blackcliff at the mill, and he said he has a job for you if you're not opposed to working on the line. It's not hard work collecting pollen, but it is repetitive. If you go tonight, I can introduce you."

Although her initial reaction was to sneer at the idea—the High Sorceress of Paragon reduced to collecting pollen for fairy food production?—an unexpected longing filled her. The idea that she might start anew, leading a simple life like this one, a life where she might grow to have relationships based on basic kindnesses, gave her an unwelcome warm feeling behind her ribs. She cast it aside and focused on the task at hand.

"Will other members of the Defenders of the Goddess be there? Everything you've told me about the DOGs has convinced me it's where I need to be. I'd love to become more involved."

"Now that Sylas is back, he's reconnecting with the leaders from the other five kingdoms. We need to be careful right now. He's a fugitive. One wrong move could land him back in the dungeons of Paragon. It will be some time before we meet with other DOGs again." Dianthe rested her spoon against the side of the bowl and lowered her eyes as if she were reciting a silent prayer.

They'd been here before. Dianthe had spent hours

explaining the rebellion to Aborella, but without any real details the fairy sorceress could act upon. In short, each of the five kingdoms had a network of DOG sympathizers, but members never used their real identities. Instead, they each went by a code that was constantly changing and had to do with their rank in the organization rather than their specific person. Sylas was currently Everfield, red zone, number one. ERO for short. For the two years he was imprisoned, someone else had served as the ERO.

This was why the kingdom of Paragon could not squash the rebellion. It was like a hydra—cut one head off and another would take its place. And the more Aborella learned about the movement, the more she was convinced that the five kingdoms were crawling with rebels.

The saddest part was she had to acknowledge the DOGs had a point. She'd learned from Dianthe that more than half of what Everfield produced was collected by Paragon as a tax. The remaining half had to feed, clothe, and shelter the population. Many shop owners attempted to hide a portion of their production to help needy families, but the Obsidian Guard had cracked down recently. Random raids now occurred with common frequency, and if the Guard found any undeclared property, the punishment was immediate beheading.

Sometimes illegal activity wasn't even necessary to draw the Guard's attention. She'd learned of several fairies who had been tormented by the Guard for sport. Had Dianthe not been the one to tell her that, Aborella might have thought it was a lie. But the fairy had been brutally honest from the beginning and shared specifics that made Aborella's blood run cold.

At first Aborella wondered if Eleanor was aware of what was going on or if the Highborn class had orchestrated the tactics without her knowledge. But the more she thought of it, the more she was sure Eleanor was behind the crackdown and likely condoning the raids. Her entire purpose was always to unite the kingdoms under herself by any means. What better way than to create such mass poverty as to break the individual governments and force them to accept her offer to join Paragon, the only remaining truly prosperous kingdom?

A tug deep in her torso stole her breath, and she rubbed her chest. She was struck by a sudden and overwhelming urge to return to the Obsidian Palace. Was it her second sight warning her of danger in Everfield? No. As she examined the strange sensation, she chalked it up to apprehension. Despite what Eleanor had done to her, the empress would be unhappy if she discovered where Aborella had been this past week. The feeling in her gut was undoubtedly her body warning her that the longer she stayed in Everfield, the greater the risk that Eleanor would discover she was missing and punish her for it. She was relieved when the feeling faded.

"I'll take the job. I'd love to go tonight and to meet Briar," Aborella said. After all, she couldn't go back to Paragon without something, anything, to buy her way back into Eleanor's good graces. She needed more information, and speaking with this mill operator might buy her that.

"Excellent." Dianthe's grin was warm and genuine. She handed the bowl to Aborella. "Now help me shape these into moons for tonight."

CHAPTER SEVENTEEN

Xavier was having trouble keeping his mind on his book. It was Avery—her scent, her spitfire spirit, the way she bit her thumbnail gently as she read. It wasn't a simple attraction. His dragon had taken an unparalleled interest in her, prompting him to watch her when he should have his eyes on the words in front of him. Everything about her was intriguing, including the mystery of her relationship with his family. She knew more about them than he did at the moment.

"I think I found something!" Avery's eyes flicked up, and he pretended to be reading instead of watching her as he had been.

"Oh?"

"Listen to this. There was this blacksmith named Alasdair MacEachern who had a son named Neil. His wife was dead, so he was raising Neil on his own. This guy lived near a fairy knoll, and so he always hung a rowan branch over his cottage door to keep the fairies from stealing Neil because he was such an adorable young *bairn*—I guess that means child, right?"

Xavier nodded.

"Anyway, one day when Neil was around thirteen, Alasdair, who was a blacksmith, had to travel a distance to deliver his wares to a customer. He told Neil to replace the rowan branch above the door before bed. But Neil got distracted and didn't. And guess what? The fairies took him."

"Hmm." Xavier rubbed his chin. "And I suppose they replaced him with a changeling like Lachlan. There are many stories like that."

"But that's not the end of this story. Alasdair, suspecting his son had been replaced with a changeling, visited a wise woman in the hills who was suspected of being a witch. She confirmed his fears and helped him get his son back."

"How'd he do it?"

"First he had to burn the changeling in a massive fire with some magic words, which is clearly disturbing considering the thing looked like his son. But he did it and the creature went up in smoke."

Xavier scoffed. "I think it will take more than fire and a few magic words to rid this world of Lachlan."

"I'm not suggesting you burn him. There is more to this story, Xavier. The witch told Alasdair to take a bible, a sword, and a crowing cock by the light of the full moon to the fairy knoll, where Alasdair used those three items to trick the fairies and rescue his son."

Xavier narrowed his eyes. "A bible—"

"—never mind. I have no idea. The cock completely threw me off. Anyway, he got the boy back, his real son!"

"Oh?"

"Only, the kid had completely lost his ability speak." Her eyes widened.

Xavier sipped his whisky.

"Later, that boy Neil, who'd apprenticed under his father as a blacksmith, forged an iron sword for the chief of his clan, a one of a kind fairy-killing blade. Here's the important part... Neil had remembered how to do it from his time among the fairies."

"Are ye suggesting the blade was forged with fairy magic?"

"Yes. Forging that fairy blade broke the curse over his tongue, and Neil began to speak again. As soon as he said his first words, all memories of the fairylands left him, but he still had that one blade. It says here that Neil was never able to forge another weapon of its kind but that the chief of his clan never lost a battle so long as he used that sword. It was nicknamed *murtair sídh.*"

"Fairy killer," Xavier translated.

"If this is real, this blade could kill Lachlan." Avery slapped her hand down on the page. "Is there any chance the sword is here? In the *builgean?*"

Xavier stood and paced. "Clan MacEachern originally hails from the Isle of Islay, but over the generations they've mixed with the Campbells. A few of their descendants live here, near the loch. They have a preference for water, ye ken. It's possible they'd have the sword. It would have been something their clan would wish to secure from the British, and there'd be nowhere safer to hide it than here."

"Excellent. Where do they live? Let's go ask them."

He chuckled. "We canna simply rush up to their door and ask if they have a magic sword. For one, Lachlan probably has them brainwashed against me. If they see me, they may attack or report back to Lachlan."

"So I'll go. I'll..." She drummed her fingers on the table. "I'll pretend to be a mother who has lost her baby daughter to the fairies and has it on good authority that they have a weapon that can help get her back."

He narrowed his eyes on the woman. "It's frightening how fast ye came up with that, lass. I damn near believe ye, and I ken it's not true."

She gave him a toothy grin.

"But remember, Glenna said Lachlan has put out the word to look for ye as well."

"Even if Lachlan produces a sketch of me to pass around, what are the chances it would have made it to the MacEacherns' already? It can't be very good. We were in the same room only a handful of times. I have new clothes. I'll cover my hair. I doubt anyone will recognize me. And if they do, I'll scream and you can come and rescue me."

"It's a good plan, lass, but I have a better one. I'll disguise maself, and we'll go together. It will be more believable for a couple to be seekin' their bairn."

"How far is it?"

"About a half day's ride."

Avery nodded. "We'll leave first thing tomorrow then."

THAT NIGHT, AFTER A MORNING OF CATTLE RUSTLING, hauling a dozen buckets of water for her bath, hours of studying old books, and more than her share of whisky, Avery should have been bone tired. But she tossed and turned in the bed, unable to think of anything other than Xavier, asleep on the floor in the main room. Was he comfortable? It was a cold night, but her thick blanket kept her warm and cozy. Dragons didn't get cold of course, but she couldn't help fantasizing about what it might feel like to snuggle in beside him and share the mattress.

She pushed that last thought out of her head. She'd only known the dragon for two days, and she was not the type of woman to rush into a physical relationship. But damn if she didn't understand now what her sister had experienced with Gabriel. The crush Avery had on Xavier was positively distracting. Only the memory of him brushing her hair eventually lulled her to sleep.

In the morning, she woke to the sound of footsteps on the weathered boards of the cottage's porch and the glow of diffuse light shining through the window sheers. She peeked out and saw Xavier serving the brownie a bowl of milk that the little man lapped up ferociously until there was cream soaking his whiskers all the way to his ears. The brownie served the one who fed him. If they wanted the fairy's allegiance, it was paramount that they take care of him.

The cool morning air gave her a chill, and she dressed quickly, brushing her waves into a bun high on her head. She would never again take central heating for granted. She wrapped her arisaid around her before leaving the room. A wave of guilt hit her when she saw Xavier's plaid and a pillow in front of the fire. Even the brownie's simple bed was better appointed. She decided at once that she'd offer to switch places with him that night. Every other night in the bed was more than fair.

"Good, ye're up. Have a wee bit of breakfast and we'll be on our way. The brownie found ye some of that coffee ye mentioned before, although I tried a bit and I don't understand all the fuss."

"You got me coffee?" Avery ran to the brownie and kissed him roughly on the head.

He gave a little squeak and disappeared. Xavier cocked an eyebrow as she poured herself a mug of the hot brown beverage and added some of the fresh cream Xavier hadn't fed the brownie, along with a spoonful of honey since sugar wasn't on the breakfast table. She closed her eyes and took a fortifying gulp.

"I ne'er thought I'd be jealous of a mug," he said, giving her a wink. "You look like ye've found ecstasy."

Her cheeks warmed. "Would you like to try it? I think it's better like this, with milk and something sweet."

He approached and took the mug from her, then proceeded to take a sip from the precise spot where her lips had been. For the entire time he drank, he never took his eyes off her. It was absolutely the hottest thing she'd ever experienced, and she squirmed in her chair. She cleared the thickness that had formed in her throat.

"Do you like it?" she squeaked.

He made a deep masculine sound. "Vera much. Yer right, it is sweeter that way." He handed her back the mug, his crooked grin doing delicious things to her insides. She released a breath when he looked away and said, "Enjoy it. I'm not sure where our friend obtained it exactly, but it isna a popular beverage here."

She looked at him quizzically. "How is it here at all? It can't have been a popular beverage here when the ward went up, and anyway, it tastes fresh."

"It is fresh. Before Lachlan, I used to send a brave man or two outside the *builgean* every few years ta bring back news of the world and a few things we didna produce. When coffee became popular on the outside, we established a few of the plants on the hills behind the castle, right beside the valley of tea."

Avery laughed awkwardly. "Coffee and tea can't grow here. It's too cold."

He gave her a heart-melting, crooked grin and popped a

corner of toast in his mouth. "It only takes a bit of magic. 'Tis another reason Lachlan canna kill me. Even if he could somehow replace ma magic in the wards and keep them up, 'tis my power in the ground and in the water that keeps the sheep fat and the cows heavy with milk. The *builgean* wouldna be sustainable after ma death."

Avery remembered Nathaniel's orange tree. Clarissa had bought him the plant for his birthday many years ago, and the tree still thrived despite its incompatibility with the environment. Dragon magic was a powerful thing.

"These days, there's only one man who produces coffee from the beans for the few who drink it."

"Mmm. I'll savor every sip." She took another gulp, then ate quickly and finished every drop of the coffee before grabbing her bag and joining Xavier outdoors.

He helped her onto Tàirn, where she pretended not to notice how good it felt to tuck herself into his chest. They set off toward the loch.

"Avery..." When he said her name, drawing it out and rolling the *R*, it sent electric butterflies fluttering free inside her. "I'd like to know more about ye. Why is it that Nathaniel sent ye specifically?" His soft voice was filled with sharp curiosity. "Why not a member of the Order of the Dragon?"

"That's a good question," Avery said. "For one, the witches and wizards of the order don't know everything that happened like I do. Nathaniel has many secrets from them even if they do know he's a dragon. Besides, although they're human, they've been imbued with this magic. It's questionable whether they could cross through the gate. Two, the only other human who would be capable of answering all your questions is Nick, and he's mated to Rowan."

"My sister is mated as well?"

"Yes. And Nathaniel didn't think she'd do well with the separation."

"Aye. A mated dragon has an innate need to keep their mate safe. She wouldna know if he was safe here. It would drive her mad."

"Yes. That's what he said. But in the end, I think his asking me had more to do with the cards."

"The cards?"

"The tarot cards. I was staying with Nathaniel. This is a long story actually." She combed her fingers through the base of the horse's mane and wondered how much she should tell him about herself.

"We have plenty of time."

"For you to understand, I have to start at the beginning."

When he was silent, she continued. "I was born in Michigan." She realized he probably wouldn't know where that was and added, "That's a state in what is now America."

"I know the Americas," he said. "Although most I know who tried to go there did not come to a pretty end."

She narrowed her eyes, trying to remember her history. "It's better now than when you raised the wards. Established."

"Aye."

"My sister Raven and I had an ideal childhood there until I turned ten and our grandparents passed away within a month of one another. Grandpa went first. Caught some kind of virus and pneumonia. Once he was gone, Grandma didn't want to live anymore, and she simply followed him home. My mother said she died in her sleep."

"I am sorry."

"Oh, uh, the death itself wasn't hard for me. We weren't

close to my grandparents. They lived in New Orleans, quite a distance from where we lived, and we rarely visited. But the strange thing was that their pub, the Three Sisters, was left to my mother."

"Why is that strange?"

"Because I have an uncle—my mother's older brother—and he, for all intents and purposes, was closer to my grandparents, but there's this very strange matriarchal family tradition in my family. All the women keep the family name, and the pub specifically has always been owned only by the daughters Tanglewood."

"Tanglewood?"

"That's my last name. My, er, surname, Tanglewood. Tanglewood was my mother's last name, and her mother's last name, and her mother's mother's last name."

"Aye. Like for the males here."

"Yes. So, when I was ten and Raven was nine, my mother took over the Three Sisters. Our parents moved us to New Orleans in the dead of summer. It was hard on all of us. But for me, the move was devastating. I was already this terribly awkward sixth grader who had to leave all her friends behind. At a time when I was self-conscious about my appearance, the humidity made my hair frizz and all my favorite school clothes were wrong for the weather. I was dreadfully unhappy, but I couldn't complain about it because my parents were completely overwhelmed with learning the new business."

"You didn't want to be a burden?"

"Right. I endured. I made new friends. And, of course, I had Raven. She was the only friend I brought with me from my childhood, and we became as close as two sisters could be. And then, in high school, she got cancer."

"Whit is cancer?"

"It's this disease where these tumors grow inside your body. Sometimes the doctors can stop it and sometimes they can't. At first Raven went into remission—that's what they call it when the medicine works. She graduated and attended university on a scholarship."

"Were ye also at university, bein' that ye were the older sibling?"

"No. I never got to go." Avery concentrated on keeping her voice from betraying her disappointment. Whenever she spoke about not going to college, her insecurity reared its ugly head, and yet again she wondered if she'd missed out on an important rite of passage. "The year I graduated from high school, my parents asked me to take a gap year. Raven was sick, and they wanted me close to home. To be honest, I wouldn't have left anyway. And then when she got better, we knew her remission was probably temporary and my parents needed help at the Three Sisters. I pretended I didn't want to go to college and stayed at home to help in the pub so that my sister could have the experience while she could."

"Ye sacrificed yerself for her happiness."

Avery winced but was quick to clarify. "I wouldn't call it a sacrifice. At the time, I thought I'd have my chance. And to be honest, I wasn't sure what I wanted to do or be. But then Raven's cancer returned. My father couldn't tolerate the stress that brought on our family, and he divorced my mother. After that happened, any thought of moving on dissolved in the destitution of huge medical bills and my mother's desperation to keep the pub, which had been in her family since the 1700s, solvent."

"Do you resent it, that ye didn't get the experiences yer sister did?"

"I didn't at first. To be honest, I never loved school, and

the traditional college experience maybe wasn't for me. But I do resent that I never even stopped to think about what I wanted. That's not on anyone else, just me. One year led into the next and I simply kept going, never really thinking about what I was doing at all, only that I was doing it for my family.

"And then, like a miracle, Raven got better. Gabriel fed her his tooth and healed her." Avery shook her head, still awed by how everything had happened for her sister. "Afterward, you'd think something would've changed, but it didn't. I was still doing the same things, only now there wasn't a purpose in it. Gabriel paid off her medical bills. My mother's business recovered. My father moved on with his life. And I still worked at the Three Sisters. I still hadn't stopped to think what I wanted to do, so I kept doing what I'd always done."

She looked down at her fingers as they threaded into the horse's mane. "I just woke up one day and realized I wanted to live for me."

"Aye." His chin brushed the side of her head as he nodded. "I remember feeling a similar way in Paragon about our royal duties. I would ne'er be king, yet every wakin' moment I was forced ta train for the crown. Train in the pits I told ye about. It was tradition there, one of the many royal duties expected of us despite all the honor going ta Marius as the firstborn. I suppose I shouldna have minded. In the end, he lost his head for it."

"I heard. But then you ended up here, ruling your clan. I guess it turned out okay for you, aside from being captured and imprisoned by an evil fairy." She chuckled darkly.

"That one thing, yes, hasna gone my way." They both laughed together. "I suppose it's been lonely a time or two as well. Aside from ma Glenna, I've had ta watch friends come and go. Human lives are short."

As a human herself, Avery frowned at that. Her life *was* short. She wished she knew what to do with it.

"Nathaniel told me you were married once. Do you miss her?"

For a long time, Xavier didn't speak. Avery wondered if she'd dredged up bad memories. She considered apologizing and suggesting he didn't have to give her any details. But he sighed and answered in a soft, even voice.

"No. I never loved her properly. Truth is, Jane was mentally unfit, which is why her father put her in ma care. I tried, ye ken. I protected her up until the day she... fell from her window. I never loved her though, and our marriage was in name only."

"Oh." Avery silently chastised her heart for giving a little leap. What kind of sicko was happy about a man living out a loveless marriage that ended in his wife's probable suicide? Her, that's who. Some part of her wanted Xavier, and the idea he'd loved someone else enough to marry them had been a pinprick deep inside her heart. No matter how much her brain told her it was a nonsense thing to think, she secretly wanted to be Xavier's first and only love.

Avery shut her mouth to keep from blurting out her inappropriate feelings. Silence descended as Tàirn's hooves thunked against the trail.

Finally Xavier cleared his throat and spoke again. "How did you end up here? You said it was because of Nathaniel's tarot cards?"

"Ah, yes." She swallowed. "Nathaniel read my cards and told me that I was a caterpillar who had already made itself a cocoon and if I returned to New Orleans, I wouldn't do so as a caterpillar but as a butterfly who had cut off its own wings."

"Oh. If that ain't a punch in the gut."

She laughed. "I know, right? At first I was really shaken by it. But then I realized the cards were showing me the truth. I wasn't sure what I wanted to do with my life, and everyone around me was pushing me this way and that. Nathaniel wanted me to work in his bookstore. His mate, Clarissa, wanted me to be her personal assistant. My mother offered me a huge promotion to return to the Three Sisters. And the truth was, I didn't want any of it. But if I chose one of those things, I knew it would keep me from what I was meant to do."

"This was an escape for ye?"

"Yes, in a way." Avery's heart beat faster. Was she really doing this? Was she going to tell him the truth? Maybe it was the rhythm of the trail or the warm press of him against her back, but the words flowed out of her like tugged ribbon. "I saw your portrait hanging in Nathaniel's house, and I... well, I wanted to meet you. I know that sounds insane. There was just something about it. I wanted to be the one to find you, so I volunteered."

CHAPTER EIGHTEEN

A buzz traveled through Xavier's blood as if he'd swallowed strong whisky. Had he heard her correctly? She'd volunteered to come for him, curious after seeing his portrait? That would indicate an attraction. Could it be that the lass experienced the same heat in her blood when she looked at him as when he looked at her? His dragon stirred at the thought, and he inhaled deeply of her wisteria-and-linen scent.

With his nose close to her ear, he asked, "Da ye regret comin' now that the task before ye is more than ye expected?"

"No," she squeaked, turning her head so that her mouth was close to his.

He was suddenly and completely aware of her presence between his thighs. He shifted in the saddle, uncomfortable as his body responded to her nearness.

"I don't regret coming. This is the most alive I've felt in some time."

"Aye." He tightened his hold on her waist, and she leaned into him as they rode.

It was late afternoon by the time they arrived at the MacEacherns', and he helped her down from Tàirn. He'd changed his appearance as they'd approached the cottage, and now Xavier watched the corner of Avery's mouth twitch as she took in his balding head, bulbous nose, and soft belly. He'd taken three inches off his height as well, adjusting his clothing with the illusion to appear as a common farmer.

He helped Avery cover her hair and smudged her cheeks with a bit of dirt but found it hard to believe the disguise would fool anyone. The woman would look like a queen in a grain sack.

"What's wrong?" she whispered.

"Hmm? Nothin' but that it takes effort to make ye look common." He smudged more dirt on her other cheek. He caught her trying to hide a smile. "Try not to draw attention to yerself."

She nodded, then shifted her gaze toward the water. Avery blinked at the overcast loch edged in fog. "What do you call this place?"

"This is Loch Seinn. Ned MacEachern is one of the few souls brave enough to live this close to the fairy hills. As I recall, he's a wee bit odd. Makes his livin' as a fisherman."

"I can handle odd."

A wide dirt path led up to the stone house with its thatched roof. Three goats met them at the door, noses sniffing curiously, and then bleated and pranced off to more important adventures. Behind the house, the water lapped against a rocky shore.

Xavier rapped on the front door and waited.

A few words of Gaelic filtered through the wood, and then a woman with pale skin and large brown eyes opened the door. "Can I help ye?"

"I hope so," Xavier said in a voice that was not his own. "My wife and I heard the great-great-great-grandson of Neil MacEachern lived here. We have an important question for him, if he's willing to speak with us, and some whisky for the both of you as a way of sayin' thanks." He extended the brown bottle he'd brought from the brownie's cottage toward her.

"Aye, well, ye better be comin' in then. He's tending the horse in the stable. Fergus, go and fetch your father." She slapped the shoulder of a dark-haired boy who was whittling something near the fire, and he dropped what he was doing and ran out the door.

The air inside the cottage was close and warm, and Xavier folded his hands politely.

"Would ye like some tea? Have you come a long way?"

"Aye, vera kind of ye," Xavier said.

Moments later, cups in hand and gathered around the table, they were joined by a stoic gray-haired man who greeted them politely but only sat reluctantly at his wife's pleading.

"Are you Ned MacEachern?" Xavier asked. They'd agreed in advance that he'd do the talking, considering Avery had lost Nathaniel's magic and her accent might cause suspicion.

"Aye. Who's asking?"

"I'm Oliver and this is Elsbeth from Clan MacTavish," he said. "We need yer help."

Ned narrowed his eyes. "MacTavish, you say? I thought I knew every MacTavish from our kirk?"

"We're not from Cnocmeall but Gleansrath Kirk."

"Gleansrath. You *have* come a long way. Whatever can we do for ye?"

"My wife, Elsbeth, and I have recently lost a child."

"Oh, I am terribly sorry ta hear that. Sometimes the Lord's will is hard ta understand."

Xavier shook his head. "'Twas not the Lord's will. The fairies stole her. Stole her right from our home and took her to the land of light."

Upon hearing that, Mrs. MacEachern went perfectly still while Ned gasped and crossed himself. "May the Lord protect us all from such a fate. Ye 'ave my sympathy."

"Yer sympathy is kind, but what we need is yer help."

The man studied Xavier, then laughed long and hard. "What power do ye think I might have over fairy folk? I canna help ye with that. No one can help ye."

Mrs. MacEachern reached for her tea and took a long sip, her shifting eyes betraying her. She had a secret. Xavier kept his eyes on her as he asked, "Is it true ye are the great-great-great-grandson of Neil MacEachern?"

"Aye."

"We have it on good authority that Alasdair once saved his son Neil from the fairies and that son produced a sword that could be used against the wee folk. Please, we need that sword ta get our wee bairn back."

Ned scoffed and shook his head. "Ye've been told wrong. That myth was the raving story of a madman. Even the family dinna believe it."

"But you have the sword?" Xavier leaned across the table toward the man, willing him to turn the weapon over.

"Your reliable source shoulda told ye that Alasdair was a blacksmith. He made many swords, and aye, some of them are still around. Some may even be in ma possession. But I'm not of the mind to be handin' them out to any stranger that comes ta ma door."

"I will pay ye handsomely for it."

"I dinna have it, I said, and even if I did, I would not give it to ye."

Xavier's fists clenched. Perhaps the man needed more incentive to cooperate. He reached for his dirk.

"Mrs. MacEachern," Avery said in a voice as sweet as honeycomb and sounding almost as local as he did. "I can see ye are well familiar with whit it's like to love a bairn." Avery's voice cracked, and a tear carved its way down her face. She reached out and held the woman's hand. "I ken it seems that an old sword will be useless against the evil that ravaged our small family. Gwendolyn was our only bairn after so many years of tryin'."

Avery's tone was so bereft a lump formed in Xavier's throat despite his knowing she was making the entire thing up. Even with his abilities to cloak himself in illusion, he wondered if Avery's talent at deception might be superior.

Mrs. MacEachern tilted her head in sympathy. "Loss is somethin' I ken well."

For some reason, that made Ned irate. He stood from his chair and slapped his wife in a way that shocked Xavier to the core. He rose and placed himself between Ned and his wife, fists raised. The look he gave the man made it clear he did not approve. But before the two could come to blows, Avery's hand landed on his arm, and all the anger seemed to drain out of him.

"Please, we dinna come here to fight," she said.

Ned eyed them both with disgust. "I gave ye yer answer. Finish yer tea and get outta ma house." He gave one last look of warning to his poor wife before leaving the cottage in a huff.

"What was that about?" Avery asked breathlessly.

His wife spoke in a voice as soft as a whisper. "I can get ye the sword."

Avery leaned toward her. "I promise ye, we will return it once we've tried... tried everything there is to try to get my Gwendolyn back." Her hand squeezed the woman's. "Please, I beg of ye, just one week. If ye lend me the sword for one week, whatever happens, I will accept it as God's will and return it to ye here right after. Please. What mother could forgive herself for not tryin' everythin'?"

The woman lowered her chin and stared at Xavier as if she could see straight into his dragon heart. "I will give ye the sword and ye can keep it for all I care, but ye must do something for me first."

Xavier frowned. There was something strange about this woman, not the least of which was how little she'd reacted when her husband had slapped her. "Whit is it ye want?"

She pointed a finger toward a ladder near the back of the cottage. "There's a box upstairs. Bring me what's inside it, and I will tell ye where the sword is."

Tentatively, Xavier rose and moved across the room, his eyes darting back to the woman and to Avery, who rose and followed him. He climbed the ladder and peered into a short loft above the main part of the house. He had to crawl into the space, which was just big enough for a child. A mattress on the floor with a mass of blankets seemed to indicate this was in fact where their child slept.

Avery climbed the ladder behind him. "Do you see a box?" she whispered.

"Aye." He'd found it in plain sight at the back of the room.

"Well?" Avery whispered.

"It's made of iron." A tingle ran along his spine.

"So?"

"So why can't the woman retrieve it herself?" He looked

back at Avery. There was only one reason someone would hide something inside an iron box.

Avery shook her head. "Who cares? Give her what she wants so we can get the sword and get out of here before her husband comes back and takes away our only chance."

Fairies couldn't touch iron without being burned, and they were close to the fairy hills. Was it possible Ned's wife was one of the wee folk? He shook his head. She looked human, and they had a child. Perhaps the box was simply locked and the woman needed him to open it. He lifted the lid. Not locked, and what he saw inside made him revisit his earlier hypothesis.

Avery appeared beside him. She must have given up on waiting at the top of the ladder. "What is that? It looks like a fur coat."

"'Tis a fur coat. She's a selkie." Xavier scowled. This was a dilemma. "MacEachern has this in an iron box so she can't touch it."

A distinct line appeared between Avery's eyes. "Selkie... Those are the seal people who shed their skin." She gasped. "Are you telling me that the woman downstairs is being held here against her will because that asshole who beats her and wouldn't even consider helping us has her skin in an iron box?"

Xavier raised his eyebrows. "She's his wife. We can't give it to her. She'll leave him and return to the sea!"

"The hell we can't." Avery grabbed the skin out of the box and crawled toward the ladder, her skirts bunched around her waist.

"Wait! Ye donna ken the way things are!" Xavier whispered loudly. He tried to catch her, but even disguised as a smaller man, his larger size slowed him in the cramped space.

Avery lowered herself onto the ladder with surprising grace. "All I need to know is that a shifter, just like you, is enslaved here against her will with a domestic abuser. Even if she wasn't going to give us the location of the sword, I'd give this back to her." She shook the skin righteously and descended into the room below.

"Damn pigheaded woman," Xavier murmured and hurried after her.

AVERY CHARGED INTO THE MAIN ROOM OF THE COTTAGE and watched the woman's dark brown eyes grow to a size befitting her seal form. She lunged for the skin.

Avery dodged to the side and held the pelt over the fire. "First the sword."

Xavier entered the room with his hands outstretched toward the selkie.

"Keep your promise and I'll keep mine."

"Aye, I will. But be warned, Ned is no ordinary fisherman. He's an expert swordsman from a long line of weaponsmiths. He practices two hours a day, every day. If ye take that blade, ye better run before he gets wind of whit ye done."

"I understand." Xavier nodded.

"Move those stones aside." The selkie gestured toward the wall that surrounded the fireplace.

Xavier followed the woman's gaze to a spot above the mantel and jiggled the stones. One large piece of masonry came away from the wall with a tooth-vibrating scrape. Avery turned her head for half a second to see what was there, and the pelt was torn from her hands. She turned back to see the woman running for the door with it.

"Fuck!"

"I'm afraid ye not only cost Ned a wife but poor Fergus a mother," Xavier said sadly.

"How can you say that after the way he slapped her?" Avery stared at him, absolutely appalled.

He grunted. "There's what's right and then what is. The selkie will not come back, not even for her son. Ye've saved the selkie but orphaned the boy."

She frowned and pointed her chin toward the mantel. "Please tell me there is actually a sword behind that stone."

"Donna worry. It's here."

She watched him reach into the hole in the stone and withdraw a dusty length of leather. He drew a sword from the scabbard, an iron blade, black as night and etched with strange symbols. The blade enchanted her, and although she couldn't actually hear anything, she could have sworn the sword was singing. Its voice seemed to vibrate against her skin.

"Whit're ye doin'?" Xavier asked when her hand landed above his on the hilt.

"I want to hold it."

"It's heavy. I have it."

"Just once. I... I need to."

Xavier gave her a strange look. She never had a chance to hold the blade.

The door swung open and Ned MacEachern stormed in, his own sword in hand. "Ye cost me ma wife!"

He lunged at Xavier, who thrust her out of the way and blocked the attack with Fairy Killer. The metal sparked where it connected.

"Run, Avery," Xavier ordered. "I'm right behind you."

She ran for the door and toward the place where Tàirn waited. Xavier burst out after her, dueling with Ned, who was clearly a master swordsman. Ned advanced and Xavier retreated toward the shore of the loch.

Everything stopped when a voice, hollow and mournful, rang out from the water. Avery saw the head of a seal bobbing on the waves, and behind her, the wild red hair of a woman with a crown of seashells. The woman embraced the selkie, then opened her mouth and sang. The melody reverberated around her, its sad and mournful tune causing Avery's heart to ache. She didn't understand the words, but the power that wrapped around her told its own story. The song, she sensed, was a tale about how her friend had been stolen from her and now returned, and the emotion behind every note brought Avery to tears.

The song's effect on Ned was far more dramatic. The man abruptly stopped dueling Xavier and dropped his sword. Face blank, he turned on his heel and strode directly toward the water's edge.

He didn't stop there. He walked right into the water, knee deep, then waist, then chest.

"Ned!" Avery called. She took a step forward, meaning to stop him.

Suddenly Xavier's arms were around her, holding her in place.

"He's going under!" Avery yelled in alarm. "We can't let him drown."

Xavier looked confused as she turned in his arms. "You're not drawn toward her voice?"

She narrowed her eyes on him and scoffed. "No. Why would I be?"

"She's a siren! Ye canna hear her song?"

"Of course I can hear it. It's lovely and sad."

He shook his head.

"Never mind. You've got to help Ned. We can't let him

drown!" She pointed her hand at the man whose head bobbed offshore as he tried to swim toward his wife and the siren. "He has a child!"

The boy named Fergus watched in horror from beside the barn, his wide brown eyes reminding her of his mother's.

"He's half selkie. Her song willna affect him."

"He needs his father, Xavier."

"Hold this." Xavier handed her Fairy Killer.

Finally! The sensation that traveled up Avery's arm was one she could only describe as a connection. It was like she'd just been plugged in. She didn't pay attention as Xavier presumably rushed into the water to rescue Ned. Instead, she circled the sword around her body in a wide figure eight. She'd never held a sword in her life, yet this one seemed to know her, to whisper to her like a lover.

I am yours.

A spluttering noise broke her from the trance she was in. She turned in time to see Mr. MacEachern spew a fountain of dark water from his lungs. After Ned's fit of coughing, Xavier helped him to his feet.

Avery looked out over the loch to find the seal and the siren gone. Ned's gaze darted from the boy to the loch to Xavier and finally settled on Avery. He rubbed his chest as if the feeling of waterlogged lungs was fresh on his mind. There was plenty of anger apparent on his face, but Avery could also see how grateful the man was that Xavier had saved him from the siren's song.

"Keep the sword," Ned rasped after a long moment. He hobbled off toward the boy.

CHAPTER NINETEEN

Everything about the sword was magical. Avery inspected the hilt as Xavier removed the leather scabbard from around his neck and held out his hand, beckoning it from her. She'd never seen such fine craftsmanship. A Celtic design decorated the grip, and ancient symbols paraded up and down the blade. She wasn't sure a modern factory could even produce such a fine design. She was blown away by the incredible idea that a blacksmith had made it by hand hundreds of years ago.

"I can carry that for you, lass." Xavier made a gimme gesture with his fingers. "We should put it away before ye get hurt."

"I'm fine. I'm looking at it. Give me the scabbard." She sighed, holding out her hand.

"But it must be heavy," he drawled. "Allow me ta carry it for ye. It will be too hard for ye on Tàirn."

"It's not heavy. Remarkably light actually. Do you think that's a clue to its authenticity? It's hard to believe a human made this." She snatched the scabbard from his hands and slipped the blade inside its sheath, then slung it over her shoulder so it hung down her back. "See? Not heavy at all."

Xavier raised a finger but seemed at a loss for words. She strode toward Tàirn, mounting the horse before Xavier could protest. He frowned up at her, frustration brewing. "I won't be able to hold ye in the saddle with it between us. Just give it to me, lass."

She rearranged the blade so that it crossed her chest in front of her instead. "There. Out of the way."

A muscle in his jaw twitched, but he climbed on behind her and kicked the horse on. After ensuring a distance between them and the cottage, Xavier shed his illusion and changed back into himself. Avery noticed because the hand around her waist grew larger and his widening chest pressed more firmly against her back.

"Odd, ye ken, that ye were immune to the siren's call." His lips were very near her ear, and his breath warmed her blood.

She shrugged. "Maybe it only works on men."

"Nay. I've been alive a long time, Avery. Have never seen a human man or woman resist the call of a grown siren. Ye've got some kind of magic about ye. Are ye sure ye're no witch?"

"You know I'm not. I couldn't have come through the wards if I were," she said defensively.

"Hmm."

"Men."

"Whit about men?"

"You would rather believe I was supernatural than admit I simply have a strong human mind."

He scoffed. "It takes more than a strong will to resist a siren."

She shrugged. What did it matter? So she wasn't

susceptible to sirens. She was sure many people here weren't. "Do you think the selkie was responsible for the siren's song?"

"Aye. Ned was about to run me through. The man is an exceptional swordsman. I believe she did us a favor by distracting him."

"Maybe that's why I wasn't affected. The siren didn't want me to be."

"Maybe."

"By the way, you can thank me now for finding the sword. If I'd left you to your devices, you'd have fisted Ned's face before the selkie told us anything."

His chest rumbled with his laugh behind her. "How do ye know a few punches were not what he needed to turn the blade over?"

She laughed. "You think if you pounded his face, he would have handed over the sword without resistance?"

"At that point I woulda taken it."

"You had no idea where it was or what it looked like. You would have been SOL, my friend."

"SOL?"

"Shit out of luck. I guess you don't use that expression here."

He laughed. "Nay. But I like it. I suppose it was a tense situation for a lass."

She scoffed. "No. I have tons of experience with tense situations."

"Whit now?"

"I've spent the past five years bartending and serving in New Orleans. We get all sorts of people in my family's pub. Doing what I do, you get good at resolving conflict really quickly. There's always some guy itching for a fight or trying his best to cop a feel. And women aren't much better, although they tend to be less aggressive. I have to protect women from themselves more often than not."

He made a low, Scottish sound deep in his throat. "You shouldna do this work."

His voice was edged in anger. Avery raised an eyebrow. That was interesting. By the tone of his voice, he almost sounded... jealous.

"No. I think I'm done bartending. But I'm very good at defusing tension."

"Good. I donna like thinking about men grabbin' you."

"No?"

"No. Ye should be treated with proper respect. Ye shouldna need these skills ye say ye learned. What type of world is it out there that would allow ye to be treated such?"

His mounting anger made a warm feeling spread in the general vicinity of her heart. He truly wanted to protect her. It was sweet. Avery wasn't used to being the one protected.

"I bet if you'd been there with me, no one would dare touch me," she said in a quiet voice.

"Not if they wanted to keep their fingers."

Avery quieted, suddenly more aware than ever of his nearness. He loomed warm and large behind her, and she closed her eyes and inhaled his smoky, fresh-grass scent. The feel of his powerful, corded arms around her as they rode together was almost too much to bear.

She placed a hand on his thigh beside her, leaned more fully against him, and said, "I would have liked that, to have you with me. Not that I couldn't defend myself, but it would be nice to have someone in my corner looking out for me."

The side of his face brushed against her hair. "I'm in yer corner now."

The man was temptation dipped in caramel and swirled

in chocolate. If she turned her head two inches, her lips would meet his, and she was sure she could find a way to enjoy a pulse-pounding make-out session right here on the back of this horse.

She forced herself to stare straight ahead. For all intents and purposes, Xavier was a man who lived by the rules of 1745. He probably wanted a woman who wore skirts and spent her time in the kitchen. Avery was not that woman. Besides, he wasn't a man, he was a dragon, one whose future was uncertain. There were too many ways a romantic attachment to Xavier could go wrong. She was here for one reason and one reason only—to help him kill Lachlan and then bring him with her to the outside world to help protect her family from Eleanor. A romantic entanglement would only complicate things.

Adjusting the sword on her shoulder, she used it as an excuse to put a hair of space between them. "I'm in your corner too."

CHAPTER TWENTY

Xavier struggled to keep his dragon from taking hold. It had been a long time since his beast had wanted its way, but his inner dragon chuffed and squirmed in a desperate desire to claim Avery. His skin prickled with need for her. He wanted to hear her cry out his name as he buried himself in her and her fingers clawed at his hair.

It had been too long since he'd been with a woman. His want of her was an ache he felt to his bones. *Turn your head.* If she did, he'd kiss her like she'd never been kissed before, and then he'd ask her to be his mate.

She sat up straighter, putting room between them, and stared straight ahead. He frowned. Had he misread her signals? Mountain help him—after everything, it might be Avery and not Lachlan who was the death of him.

As twilight stretched across the fairy hill, Tàirn's feet splashed down in the stream and they arrived at the brownie's cottage.

Xavier dismounted and helped Avery down. "I need to tend to the cow. The brownie will want his bowl of cream, and we donna want a hungry brownie on our hands."

She nodded once and avoided his eyes as she slipped into the cottage.

AVERY WAITED BY THE FIRE FOR XAVIER TO RETURN from the barn, but it was well past dark before he finally entered the cottage, and she didn't think milking the cow or feeding the brownie could account for his delay. Still, she was too much of a coward to ask what he'd been doing. More than likely he'd been avoiding her since things had become awkward. She couldn't deny her attraction to him, but acting on those feelings would be a disaster. The mixed signals she was putting off must have made him uncomfortable.

She sipped her tea, which she'd laced with a fair amount of whisky, and watched the flames dance across the logs on the grate.

"I thought ye'd be asleep by now. I hope ye did not wait up for me."

She glanced in his direction. "Actually, I did. I thought I would take the floor tonight. You can have the bed."

He grunted and gave his head a firm shake. "No."

"It's only fair. We can alternate."

"I'd rather not."

"Why?"

"Because I couldna rest knowing ye're out here."

She gave him a heated stare. "Why? Because I'm a woman?"

He jerked back as if surprised by her ire. "Nay. Because I'm a dragon. I don't get cold. The floor is as soft as a bed to my flesh, and if the fire sparks it will not burn me."

"Oh." She couldn't argue with that logic, but she

frowned and poured more whisky into her cup from the bottle beside her. She drank it down.

"Whit's wrong, Avery? Does it anger ye that I sleep on the floor?"

She turned to him, her head swimming with the effects of the whisky. "No. But I think you like being the hero. You probably want a woman who is helpless. Someone you have to save every other day. Someone who cooks and cleans and lets you do all the dirty work... Pops out babies like a salad shooter."

"Whit's a salad shooter?"

"Never mind." She waved a hand and drank more whisky.

"I donna want a helpless woman."

She scoffed, swaying where she sat. "Oh sure, a Highlander whose life has been suspended in 1745 Scotland for a few hundred years must be a feminist." She belched toward the fire.

He flashed her his famous crooked smile and rounded the bench to sit beside her. "I had a helpless wife once, but I dinna love her. She'd ha' these fits where she thought insects were swarmin' her skin or the wee folk were tryin' to kill her. I cared for her and did ma best to keep her well, but it was not a good feelin' when I found her dead. I wasna able to save Jane, and I would ne'er volunteer to be responsible for someone like her again."

"I'm sorry, Xavier." Avery shook her head. What a stupid comment to make considering his past.

"No, if I ever married again, I'd prefer a warrior. I reckon it's exhausting saving someone all the time. I'd much rather take turns. It seems I've needed my own saving now and again."

She turned her head and was surprised to find him

staring at her through a fringe of deliciously long lashes. His eyes moved to her lips, and he leaned in. Would he kiss her? God, she wanted him to. Her entire body tingled with the desire to feel his full lips on her own.

The warmth of his breath brushed her lips and sent a rush of heat pulsing through her veins that dwarfed the effects of the whisky. She inched forward and pressed her mouth fully to his, reveling in the soft, wet heat. From the day they'd arrived and he'd started the fire with nothing but his internal flame, she'd wondered at the temperature of his mouth. She wasn't disappointed. Her heart thudded ferociously at the feeling, racing as if she were drinking lightning. Her stomach clenched.

His fingers threaded in the hair at the nape of her neck, and she tilted her head to allow the kiss to go deeper, preparing herself for pure bliss. If she allowed this to continue, she would dive into him, straight to the bottom, and she wasn't at all sure she'd ever break the surface again.

Her eyelids fluttered, and she spotted Fairy Killer on the table. They had the sword. Xavier would soon use it to slay Lachlan, which meant her time here would soon be over. Everything would change. He'd come back to Mistwood with her, and then...

With all the strength she had left, she pulled away. Her head was spinning. "Wait, there's something I need to know."

"Anything," he said in a voice lined with cinders.

"After you kill Lachlan and take back Castle Dunchridhe, what happens then?"

"I'll need to set things right, ye ken. Fix what Lachlan has broken."

How long would that take? "And then?"

"I promised ye that I would return to Mistwood to

speak with my siblings and discuss their issues with Paragon. I plan to keep that promise. I won't leave ye to make excuses for me to Nathaniel."

"*Their* issues? Don't you mean your issues? It's your mother on the throne."

"'Tis not my war, Avery."

She backed up a step. "You don't plan to help them at all, do you? You'll meet with them because you owe them that much for sending me, but you have no intention of helping them oust Eleanor."

He stared at the fire. "My people are here."

"But what about... your family?" She'd almost said, *what about me*? But that would be silly. None of this was about her.

"I wish them the best of luck if they think Paragon is worth saving," he said coolly.

Avery suddenly felt a little nauseated. She nodded slowly, then set her cup down. "I think I've had too much whisky." She stood and moved toward her room. "Good night, Xavier."

CHAPTER TWENTY-ONE

Xavier slept fitfully that night. It was clear Avery did not approve of his ambivalence about Paragon. It was possible he'd misled her, although that hadn't been his intention. Had she assumed he'd run headfirst into a war for Gabriel's benefit? Of course she had; her sister was his brother's mate. Which gave Xavier another reason to deny his dragon's desire to bond with Avery. He had to stay strong while she was here. She'd be back in her world soon enough, and the temptation would be gone.

He was relieved when the sun rose. Unfortunately, any plans he had to advance his cause against Lachlan ended with a clap of thunder and the sound of rain against the roof.

Avery wandered from her room, rubbing her eyes. "Why didn't anyone tell me Scottish whisky was the devil?"

He grinned. "Weel, they say the devil was once an angel. Ye've had yerself a slice of heaven."

She laughed, then winced as if the sound hurt her head. Lowering herself into a chair at the table, she poured herself a cup of tea. Thanks to the brownie's magic, breakfast was already there on a tray beside the sword.

When her eyes refused to meet his, he wondered if he'd have to address the kiss and their conversation the night before. There was so much unsaid between them. So much at risk if they gave in to the attraction that even now prompted him to move closer to her.

"I thought you'd be scoping out the castle today, planning your attack." Avery's comment sliced through the thick silence, and relief washed over him.

"Canna in the rain. 'Tis a shortcoming of invisibility."

"Oh?"

He blinked out of sight, then opened the door and stepped out into the drizzle. She watched as the water made his form glisten.

"Weird. You're like a reflective ghost."

"Aye."

He stepped up on the porch and shook the rain from his shoulders. She smiled at him from the door, and the temptation to kiss her again was almost more than he could bear.

He lowered his gaze and took a step back. "I should tend to the cow. The brownie will want his breakfast."

He was halfway to the barn when he realized she was behind him.

"Aren't ye hungry?" he asked her. "Ye can stay if ye like. Out of the rain." He eyed the stormy sky warily.

"I want to help you milk the cow." She hastened and ducked into the barn, which was when he noticed she'd taken Fairy Killer from the table and was wearing it on her back.

"Am I ever goin' ta pry that sword out of yer hands?"

"No. I'm going to start sleeping with it."

"Lucky sword." He gave her a roguish grin and was

rewarded with a slight blush of her cheek. He wasn't sure why Avery was drawn to the sword as she was, but until he needed it, he'd let her have her way. It seemed to make her happy. "I'll eventually need it to slay Lachlan, ye ken."

She shook her head. "I like it too much. You'll just have to swing me at him while I hold the sword." Her eyes twinkled in the dark stable.

"Now ye sound even more like a *curaidh*."

"I'm not sure I'd call myself a warrior. I just don't think it's a good idea to let the one weapon that can kill Lachlan out of our sight."

Now that she put it that way, he agreed with the wisdom of it. He told her so as he passed her to get to Tàirn's stall and scoop a heap of oats into his trough.

"Why do you call him Tàirn? Doesn't that mean nail in Gaelic? Odd name for a horse."

"Aye, but he is a nail. He's the color of one, as black as wrought iron, but he also performs like one. Cuts right through the hardest wind and the steepest terrain. Drives fast like he's been pounded in with a hammer."

"I stand corrected." Avery tilted her head, a faraway look in her eyes. "We should have given the brownie a name. Calling him 'the brownie' seems rude. It would be like me calling you 'the dragon' or you calling me 'the human.'"

"But he doesna speak. We canna simply name him like a dog. How would ye like it if I started calling you Mary simply because I couldna speak your language?"

"Right. That is true." She shrugged.

He finished with the horse and then led her to the next stall, where he kept the cow. He pulled up a stool and a bucket.

"Ye donna have to stay and help," he said. "Don't ye have female things ta do?"

She laughed. "Like what?"

He shrugged. "Things women do!"

"No, I want you to show me how to milk her."

He grunted and made a face. "Ye donna ken how ta milk a cow?"

"Not a clue. And who would feed the brownie if you suffered a sudden bout of hand cramps?" She crossed her arms.

Standing, he pointed at the stool. "Weel, have a go at it."

She sat down on the stool beside him, gently chewing her bottom lip. Xavier raised an eyebrow as she stared at the bloated udder in front of her. The cow looked at her, its mouth full of hay, as if to express sincere reservations about her abilities. It stomped its feet.

"Relax, old girl," she said. "We'll get through this together."

"Now, take hold of two teats and pinch."

She tugged the teats straight down. The cow mooed.

"Nay. Not that way." It was too hard to describe with words. He squatted behind her, wrapped his hand around hers, and showed her.

"Oh! Like squeezing out toothpaste."

He wasn't sure exactly what she meant, but he grunted approvingly anyway. Her fist rhythmically relaxed and tightened, and milk squirted into the bucket. She squealed with pride and delight.

Her hand was warm and soft inside his. Clearly she no longer needed his help, but he was reluctant to move away. He inhaled the clean wisteria scent of her hair before forcing his inner dragon down within him. He slowly pulled away from her, his breathing heavy.

"You have it. As good as any milkmaid," he murmured.

She glanced at him over her shoulder as she worked. "Now that we have the sword, what's your plan for using it?"

"Hadna got as far as a plan. I think though, the key is the element of surprise. I'll take the sword, make myself invisible, creep up on Lachlan, and behead him."

"What if he recognizes your scent?"

"There is that chance. Fairies have a keen sense of smell and can penetrate the minds of the humans around them. It will be difficult."

"You'll need a distraction. I'll go with you. I'll cover myself in something, fish or..." She eyed the cow. "...dung if I have to. Anything to mask your smell. I'll say I was captured and tortured by you and have information about your whereabouts. They'll take me to Lachlan where you, invisible behind me, will strike."

"No."

"Why? It's a good plan. We should do it."

"Too dangerous. He might kill ye on the spot. He knows ye helped me. I reckon Lachlan is as confused as I am about how ye made it happen. He'll likely kill ye out of fear of ye if not for any other reason."

"I'm willing to risk it."

"I'm not."

The barn grew quiet aside from the sound of the milk spraying the side of the pail. He watched her, bewitched. Avery Tanglewood had to be a witch; she had enchanted his soul. Mountain help him.

"Avery," he said softly, "ye told me before ye werena spoken for in yer world."

"Spoken for... You mean married or have a boyfriend?"

He nodded. "Aye."

She flashed him an impish grin over her shoulder. "No, I'm not spoken for. Why? You interested in the job?" She bobbed her eyebrows.

He stared at her, wondering what the outside world must be like to create a woman with fire in her soul like her. The mischievous spark in her eyes reminded him of lightning in a summer sky. "Aye. I am."

The sound of milk hitting the side of the bucket stopped, and her smile slowly faded. Her gaze drifted to his lips. His dragon rose to the surface, just under his skin. He was all need and desire as he crouched to take her face in his hands, feathered his thumb across her jaw, and kissed her.

ALTHOUGH XAVIER MOVED TOWARD HER SLOWLY AND gently, crouching to reach her lips as she sat on the stool, she met him halfway. Their lips collided with an intensity she wasn't expecting, and he absorbed the momentum. His arms wrapped around her waist, lifting her.

Last night's kiss had been good, but this one rocked her world. There was something raw and feral about it, as if he couldn't help himself. Neither could she. She knew now that whatever this was between them was short-lived. This kiss was a flirt with heartache and she didn't care. She just wanted more.

A crack of thunder rattled the walls, and Avery heard the rain fall against the roof. Petrichor and the scent of green grass filled her nose. It was impossible to separate what was the storm and what was him. A shiver of intense feminine desire tingled through her veins. She wanted him, and it had been a long time since she'd wanted any man.

More importantly, she *wanted.* After years of everything feeling gray, he was like a roaring storm of color and light. He was just so good—loyal, strong, honorable, worthy. She'd come here to find herself, and this kiss felt like waking up.

She pressed against him and tangled her fingers in his hair. His lips were soft but demanding. His tongue dipped inside her mouth, and she opened for him, welcoming the invasion. The stroking rhythm ignited a long-dormant passion. He swept her off her feet, turned her around, and pressed her back against the stable wall. A husky moan escaped her and she kissed him harder. Oh God, with his body pressed against her, she could feel him, long and hard against her lower belly.

She reached down and stroked him through his kilt. Stars above, he was massive, but then wasn't that fitting given his general size? Even with her being above average height, she'd have to strain her neck to kiss him if he weren't holding her up. She drove the kiss deeper. Aggressive on her part, but she was enjoying this too much to not equally participate.

The sound he made seemed to rumble through the walls. It was like a purr but richer, much bigger than his physical body. That was new. He hadn't purred like that last night. It reminded her that she was holding a dragon in her arms, as did the fact that the temperature in the barn had risen several degrees. If they continued, would it set the hay on fire?

His hand worked at her thigh, gathering her skirt up around her hips. She helped him and moaned when his fingers connected with her bare thigh. She hooked one leg over his hip. That steel length pressed against her most sensitive flesh, throbbing with need through his kilt. She was almost certain it was only the tails of his shirt beneath the tartan and if she tugged both up, there would be nothing between them.

How long had it been since she'd had a lover? There weren't many in her past, and none of the boys or men she'd dated years ago in New Orleans had been serious. None had been as worthy or as magnificent as this dragon with his brave and loyal heart. She slowly worked the tartan higher in her hand.

"Mmm, I like that sound you make when you're excited," she murmured into his mouth.

He pulled back a fraction of an inch. Was that a blush staining his cheek? "'Tis my mating trill. 'Tis instinct."

"I like it," she said, surprised her own words came out throaty and seductive. She lowered her lids, tugged the tartan higher. "Wait... Mating trill? Do you want to mate with me?"

His eyes widened and searched hers. "Aye. I confess ma dragon has wanted ye from the beginning. Will ye be mine, Avery Tanglewood?"

Her mouth found his neck, and she worked her way from collarbone to jawline. She wanted to say yes—whatever it took to have him buried in her as soon as possible—or at least after a moment to shed their clothes now that it was at least ninety degrees in the small barn.

She brought her lips to his ear to whisper the word, but it caught in her throat. Wasn't there something about dragons and mating? What had her sisters told her about their bonds with their mates? She stiffened in his arms.

"Are we talking about sex here or something more?"

He gently set her down on her own two feet and straightened her skirts before caressing the side of her face. "More, Avery. I want ye to be mine in the way of ma kind.

Accept the mating bond, and I will have you as my own for all eternity."

It struck her then that his Scottish accent had given way to one that sounded more like Nathaniel's and Gabriel's when they spoke of their homeland. *Paragonian.* She was speaking to his inner self, his dragon. Xavier's blue eyes flickered with inner fire.

She pressed her back against the wall, shock and anxiety worming their way through her torso. Hand at the center of his chest, she gave him a firm push and was surprised when he stumbled back. "Hold up, big boy. I need a second to process this. Are you trying to bond with me? As in offering me a dragon mating bond?"

"Aye." His Scottish accent was back. He flashed that damned lopsided grin of his that was so sexy it made her knees weak. No man should hold that kind of power in his smile. He reached for her again.

"Wait..." Despite desperately wanting to give in to the pleasure he made sing in her veins, she held up a finger between them. She blinked rapidly up at him. "We've only known each other a few days. You live here, inside this... bubble in time and space. I don't. And you told me last night you have no plans to leave, not even temporarily to fight alongside your siblings."

"Once we kill Lachlan, this place will be ours again. Ye can stay here, with me. Live in the castle as Lady Campbell." His expression held nothing but joy and surety that she would jump at the chance.

As much as her instincts prodded her to say yes, she couldn't do it. She did not want to live in this place where time had stopped. She'd had enough trouble breaking from her own past and her history of putting her own needs aside for the sake of others. Here, she'd only lose herself more.

She wanted Xavier, but she could not commit to living in the *builgean.*

"When I came here, it was under the assumption that I would bring you back to the outside world, Xavier. Gabriel, Nathaniel, and the others are counting on your help. Your evil mother will destroy your homeworld if given the chance."

"Aye. I said I would come back with ye and deal with Gabriel. Once Lachlan's dead, I can come and go as I please. I can see it bothers ye that I donna want to fight for Paragon. If it matters to ye so much, I'll consider it."

"But you'll still live here."

"Aye."

"I won't," she said honestly, although it hurt her to say it. "I'll be there, in my world, the real world. I have a life there."

He took a step back. "I thought you said ye wanted to escape from that life. You told me ye had no idea who ye wanted to be or what ye wanted to do next. Here's yer answer. After we've helped in whatever way we can, ye'll come back here and live with me."

He said it as if it were a foregone conclusion and reached for her again. She sidestepped out of the way.

"No." As Avery said the word, a branching sensation tingled through her limbs as if that one tiny negative were a seed she'd planted deep within her. She could almost feel it growing, sprouting roots and branches. Spreading. Her spine straightened. She didn't have to think as the truth came barreling out of her throat. "I will not live here. It's not the future I want for myself. I want to wear pants and own my own home. I want to work. I'm not sure what I want to do quite yet, but I feel like it's right on the tip of my tongue and I just have to keep living to figure it out. I want to be in control of my own life, and I can't do that here, entombed in the past as you are. I just can't."

Xavier's face fell. He turned and paced the length of the barn like a wild animal. The cow, who'd been grazing lazily until then, seemed to suddenly realize there was a predator in the room and shuffled in her stall.

"Is that what ye think?" He snapped out the question. "That I'm entombed in the past?"

"What else would you call it? Hey, I get it—you built this place to keep you and your people safe. You saved hundreds of lives with your magic. But now it's as much a prison as anything else."

"A prison? Ye think this is a prison?" he gritted out.

"What else would you call it?" She raised her voice, willing him to understand. "Are the people here free to leave? Do they know enough about the outside world to even decide for themselves to stay or to go?"

He growled, and the cow tugged against the rope holding her.

"Careful, Xavier. You're scaring her. She'll kick over the milk."

"I donna care about the milk," he said in a low, gritty hiss. "You were goin' to accept. I felt the connection. You want me. Donna deny it."

Avery placed her hands on her hips and leveled a stare at the surly dragon. "Yes. I want you. I have never felt as strong a connection with anyone. Honestly, it seems to grow stronger by the day. But I can't... *mate* with you. It wouldn't be fair to either of us. I'd never ask you to give up your life here, and if you would ask me to give up mine, we shouldn't be talking about mating at all."

He dragged his hands through his hair, his face reddening. "Ye would have given yerself to me."

"Yep." She crossed her arms over her chest. "If you hadn't mentioned the bond, I'd be leaving footprints on the ceiling right now and have a back covered in hay. I won't deny it was painful to stop."

He was angry now, seething. "Are ye a tease? A harlot?"

She narrowed her eyes on him. Immediately she sensed he hadn't meant it, but it hurt anyway. "No. I'm a woman. That's all. But the fact that you'd say such a thing tells me I've made the right decision."

She turned and ran from the barn toward the cabin, the pounding rain mixing with her tears.

CHAPTER TWENTY-TWO

Everfield

Aborella accepted the hooded cape that Dianthe offered her. It was dark purple velvet, a color that reminded her of her natural skin tone. She answered to the name of Zinnia, carefully hiding who she really was under a strong illusion of rose-colored skin and oversized green eyes. Deep inside, in a place within herself she didn't want to admit existed, she wished the illusion was reality. Zinnia had friends and a purpose. Aborella had neither.

"Can you carry this, Zin?" Dianthe held out the tray of cookies they'd prepared together for the waning ceremony.

"Of course."

"Are you sure? They're heavy."

"I am well, Dianthe. Aside from a minor limp, I am restored."

Dianthe shook her head. "I've never seen anyone heal as fast as you. You must be blessed by the goddess."

Or cursed by the devil. Aborella understood that her speedy healing was thanks to the dragon's tooth that rooted in her belly. There was no other explanation for why she wasn't dead. Eleanor had fed her that tooth to keep her from dying so Aborella could endure the punishment of being buried alive. There had been no compassion in it, although she suspected there was strategy.

Eleanor needed her. Aborella now realized that the tug she'd felt deep within her torso was not guilt or apprehension as she'd assumed, but the empress calling for her down the bond of that tooth. More than once over the past several days, she'd felt the pull, almost painful inside her bottom ribs, felt that strong desire to return to the palace. She realized now that Eleanor was searching for her.

Only, Aborella wasn't ready to return to Paragon.

She told herself it was because she was collecting information on the rebellion to bring back to the empress. But there was more to it than that. There were feelings Aborella didn't want to examine too closely—belonging and happiness. Maybe even friendship.

Arms laden with cookies, she pushed thoughts of the Obsidian Palace aside and followed Dianthe out of the small cottage and down the trail toward the festivities happening in the heart of Everfield. Twilight in the fairy kingdom was nothing short of magical. Fireflies soared across purple skies where two orange suns descended behind a turquoise sea. She'd almost forgotten the beauty of this place, had taken it for granted as a child. Now it was like walking through a dream.

Cottages in Everfield were constructed completely of natural materials. The best of them had parts that were still growing. While homes in other kingdoms were concerned with straight lines and square angles, the architects of Everfield wove residences around and out of the natural life of the forest. They were organic additions to the landscape.

Living trees held up the walls. Branches were woven together to create a roof.

Everywhere, the buzz of wings met her ears as fairies flew overhead. She'd join them if it weren't for the cookies in her hands. She watched the others flying toward the gathering place and marveled at the way their gossamer wings caught the silver light of the rising moons.

"Do you miss flying?" Dianthe asked. "I can probably take that tray if you want to spread your wings."

Aborella blinked rapidly at the unexpected kindness. "No. I'll help you. It's been a while since I tried. I'd rather experiment later, when and where there aren't so many eyes."

Dianthe nodded then resumed her way toward the gathering. "I've received word Sylas is coming back tonight."

Aborella felt a chill run through her blood. She hadn't seen Sylas since the night he and Dianthe had rescued her, but Dianthe had never actually confirmed what he'd been doing. He was a potential source of valuable information on the activities of the Defenders of the Goddess.

"I hope he accomplished what he set out to do," Aborella said. *And shares it with me.*

"Tonight, after the festivities. I'll tell him about your interest in joining the rebellion. If all goes well, we'll have more to talk about tomorrow."

Aborella nodded. This was what she'd wanted. So why was she relieved when Dianthe turned her soulful eyes from her and continued toward the festivities?

They arrived at the gathering, and she helped Dianthe arrange the cookies on the dessert table, then chose a log close to the fire. Someone offered her a roasted narwit on a stick. Happily, she accepted and bit through the crispy skin to the juicy meat underneath. Across the gathering place, a fairy band played a song with an upbeat rhythm while a storyteller relayed the tale of the witch queen of Darnuith.

As she listened though, she was confused. She'd never heard this version of the story, not even as a child when she lived in Everfield.

"They tell it differently in Paragon," a deep voice said from beside her.

She raised her face to find Sylas standing over her, his chestnut hair neatly trimmed since the last she'd seen him. He'd also regained some of the bulk he'd lost during his stay in the Obsidian dungeon.

"You must be Sylas," she said. "I'm Zinnia. Your wife has been caring for me, thank the Goddess. I don't know what I'd have done without her."

Sylas's lips bent into a barely perceptible smile. "I know who you are." He sat down beside her. He gestured toward the storyteller. "Are you familiar with the Paragonian version?"

She nodded her head. "The story goes that during the fourth century, in the time when Eleanor and Brynhoff first rose to power over Paragon and Dracor and Villania stepped down to serve on what was then the Council of Elders, an evil witch cast a spell over a Paragonian dragon. The witch used the dragon in her thrall to attack the kingdom. She murdered Dracor and Villania and the rest of the Council of Elders in cold blood before Brynhoff and the Obsidian Guard could subdue her. Brynhoff bravely battled the witch and dragon and won, protecting Paragon from their evil clutches and clearing the way for the future of the kingdom. Afterward, a law was passed forbidding relationships between dragons and witches and establishing the Highborn Court to replace the Council of Elders out of a desire to maintain a permanent peace in the five kingdoms."

Sylas shook his head. "Sad, isn't it? How far that story is from fact. They used to tell it here that way not so long ago, until they learned the truth."

She narrowed her eyes on him. "What is the truth? I was trying to listen to the story, but now I've missed it."

"Brynhoff was not the eldest of his siblings."

Confusion wrinkled her brow. "Brynhoff had no siblings other than Eleanor."

Sylas laughed. "What makes you think so? He actually had two brothers, one older and one younger. His elder brother was supposed to inherit the throne, but he couldn't stomach spending time with Eleanor, whom he found cruel. Ruling by her side was a future he found distasteful. So he left Ouros centuries before his father's time to step down."

"Paragon," she said. Ouros was no longer an acceptable name for their world.

"At the time that happened, our world was called Ouros." Sylas rubbed the bridge of his nose. "It was only after the war that it was renamed after the kingdom of Paragon."

She nodded. She knew that much, but so what? Lands were often renamed once they were conquered.

"Brynhoff's elder brother, Tavyss, was gone for centuries. No one knows where he went, but while he was away, he met the woman who would rise to be queen of Darnuith."

Aborella suddenly felt queasy. How could that be true? She had never heard of this Tavyss. "What are you saying, Sylas?"

"In the fourth century, Tavyss returned to Paragon and challenged Brynhoff for the throne. As the eldest, he had every right to, and the Council of Elders supported him in his challenge. He'd already chosen a consort, the witch queen of Darnuith, and rumor was she was pregnant."

"No." Aborella shook her head. "That can't be true."

"Eleanor was terrified of Tavyss usurping Brynhoff. She'd been controlling Brynhoff from the start, using their unnaturally close and incestuous relationship to bend him to her will. She knew that if Tavyss became king, she'd be sidelined politically and lose all her power, especially considering the eldest heir to the throne would be the witch's child. But the Council of Elders would not hear her pleas to dismiss Tavyss's claim. They believed Tavyss and his bride were perfect for the kingdom and that the union would be pleasing to the Mountain because, as legend has it, Circe, the first witch, and Aitna, the Goddess of the Mountain, are both children of Titans and are close cousins.

"Backed into a corner, Eleanor and Brynhoff murdered the Council of Elders in cold blood before any of this could be made public. They framed Tavyss and his mate for the murders and then started the false rumor that Tavyss was held in the witch queen's thrall. Once they'd convinced the Obsidian Guard and everyone in the kingdom that Tavyss and the witch queen were murderers, they attacked. The Paragonians had just lost their entire Council of Elders. Dozens of ancient and wise dragons had been slaughtered. The citizens of Paragon took up arms and joined the Obsidian Guard in a surprise attack on Darnuith. By all known accounts, they killed Tavyss and his bride."

The stick with what was left of the narwit fell from Aborella's hands as a vision hit her squarely in her third eye. She was a seer, able to have visions of the future but sometimes also flashes of the past. This time it was the past. She saw Tavyss and his mate unconscious, covered in blood, saw

Brynhoff and Eleanor seething above them. It was true. It was all true.

"Brynhoff and Eleanor killed their parents and ancestors to keep the throne then, and now Eleanor is trying to kill her children to do the same," Aborella whispered. It was suddenly all so clear.

"Yes," Sylas said in disgust.

She blinked and looked around at the children laughing, dancing around the fire. The people were thin, most dressed in rags. She'd been so caught up in the beauty of Everfield, she hadn't noticed the poverty. The Highborn Court and Eleanor's unquenchable thirst for power and riches were draining the other kingdoms dry. And now the empress had even eliminated Brynhoff. She'd never stop, Aborella realized. Her cruelty would be as unending as her immortal life.

"I know who you are," Sylas said again.

She frowned and stiffened, her heart beginning to pound uncomfortably in her chest. "I am Zinnia."

"I saw you lying in that grave, Aborella."

He whispered her name, and she skittered back on the log, wondering if she should run.

"I wanted to leave you there to rot, but Dianthe insisted on healing you. She said she saw light in you. She said she'd never felt right about what happened to you as a child and thought bringing you here could be healing."

"What are you talking about?" Aborella's throat constricted on the words. "You couldn't have known who I was."

He threaded his fingers. "Dianthe suspected, but she didn't confirm it to me until later. I refused to stay in the same house as you, which is why she's kept you in that cabin this entire time. My mate says your mother abused you and that many fairy children made it worse for you. She thinks that's why you left Everfield."

Aborella's blood froze in her veins. How had Dianthe known? "Your mate is very perceptive."

"Dianthe is a seer like you."

At first Aborella was surprised, but then she recalled the signs. The deep hue of her skin. The strange eyes. Fairies were born in a diverse array of colors and shapes, but the darker the complexion, the stronger the magic. Dianthe was powerful. Some part of Aborella had always known that.

"Then she knows how cruel the citizens of Everfield were toward me." Aborella scowled.

"Yes." Sylas frowned. "But she's also seen you fighting on our side in the future. So I am here now, asking you to choose the potential my mate saw in you. Aborella, we need you. Join forces with your own people. Help us free the five kingdoms."

The music was loud, and the other fairies paid no attention to their close conversation. But Aborella couldn't help but wonder what the others would think if they knew who she was. She glanced toward the fire. "And if I don't?"

He drew a line in the dirt with his toe. "If you want to go back to the person who put you in that hole, you can go. I promised Dianthe I wouldn't kill you, not if you didn't attack first. But I promise you, if you hurt anyone I love, I will tear you apart and burn the pieces. I will not allow my mate, whose heart is bigger than her head, to save you again. Do you understand me?"

She stared at him, overwhelmed by the revelations and confused about what to do next. Pain radiated from her bottom ribs, sharp and quick. She almost doubled over.

Eleanor. She was tugging insistently on the bond. *Fuck!* The empress would wait no longer.

A vision filled her skull of Everfield overtaken by Obsidian guards, homes burning, fairy blood flowing. If she did not go to Eleanor, Eleanor would come to her. She closed her eyes against the vision. She could not lead the empress to this place, could not put Sylas or Dianthe in danger. The tooth couldn't be removed. Even if she wanted to help them, she'd only be a risk to their cause.

"I have to go," Aborella said. "Tell Dianthe goodbye."

He sneered at her and shook his head. "I knew she was wrong about you."

Aborella swallowed. "A seer is never wrong, but a picture only shows part of the story."

His eyes widened.

Calling on her deepest magic, she twisted her shoulders, dissolved into smoke, and transported herself to Paragon.

CHAPTER TWENTY-THREE

Through pouring rain, Avery stormed from the stables toward the brownie's cottage, her heart aching. Why did the first guy she'd cared about in years have to be a Highlander involved in some major political shit? The worst part was that after his kiss, her entire body felt weird, like he'd awakened something inside her that didn't want to fall back asleep. It was an internal fire she knew only he could extinguish. Or time. Lots of time. Maybe a lifetime.

She flung open the door to the cottage and came up short when a winged woman appeared quite suddenly in front of her.

"Jesus Christ!" Avery leaped straight back, somehow slipping through the door, over the porch, and landing in a crouch in the rainy yard outside the cabin with her skirts flared out around her.

Glenna stepped out of the house toward her. "How be it that ye can see me?" the oread asked.

"How could I not see you, Glenna? You were right in front of me. What are you doing here?"

"I'm looking fur Laird Xavier. 'Tis of great importance that I speak with him immediately."

"I am here." Xavier stood in the rain behind her, looking sexier than any man should be allowed to look. He hadn't rebuttoned his shirt, and her eyes sank to the sliver of exposed flesh between its folds. Just like that, she was horny again.

Xavier spread his arms, and Glenna ran into them. As he hugged her, the oread's skin glowed brighter, even in the rain. Avery realized the dragon was transferring his energy to the nymph. Her sister had told her about the symbiotic relationships between oreads and dragons, but the theory did not hold a candle to the reality. The transfer of light was both beautiful and intimate, and Avery understood suddenly that it was something she wasn't supposed to be able to see.

"Come inside," Xavier said to Glenna. "We can speak out of the rain."

Glenna was wild-eyed and frantic. "It's been horrible at the castle without ye. I did as ye asked me to. I spied on Lachlan. Now I've to warn ye of his plan!"

"What has Lachlan done now?"

Avery led the way inside and held the door for them. She wiped rain from her face and tried not to panic. The oread was shaking noticeably, her wings drooping as if the news she had to share was horrific.

"After he figured out ye came here to the fairy hills, he was enraged. He wanted to come after ye, but he couldn't get any humans to come here. Even his magic couldn't overcome their deep fear of this place."

"Aye."

"But he hates ye, Xavier. Hates ye wi' the fury of a thousand suns. He's never been loved the way ye were loved by yer people. He has to force them, and it takes a lot of magic to keep them under his mind control."

"What's he done, Glenna?"

"He called on every blacksmith in the *builgean* to take apart yer cage, melt down the metal, and fashion it into nets, chains, and weapons. He ordered four teams of hunters, the strongest men among the clans, to the castle and worked his magic on their minds. Lachlan has offered his weight in gold to the team that brings ye in. They plan ta set out for the fairy hills tomorrow ta search for ye."

"Let them come. They'll never find us here. If they somehow do, I'll be ready."

"There's more." Her otherwise smooth, pearlescent face crinkled with her frown. "He has decried that he will kill one of your clan every hour ye aren't found. He's going to start with Mistress Abernathy."

"No!" Avery yelled, unable to stay silent. "Mistress Abernathy was always kind to me. She gave me a job when I had nowhere else to go. We can't let him hurt her!"

Xavier gave her a reassuring nod. "Agreed, lass."

She pulled the sword and scabbard over her head and held it out toward him. "We have Fairy Killer. Let's go now."

"I agree we need to do *something*, but we have to be smart about it. Lachlan is trying to lure us in. He has weapons charged with my own magic. It's a trap."

"There's something else," Glenna said.

"I'm almost afraid to ask." Avery set the sword on the table but kept her fingers resting on it. Its presence gave her comfort.

The oread lowered her chin and focused her intense butterscotch-colored eyes on her. "You should be. He's put a price on yer head—one thousand pounds to anyone who ends yer life."

Avery's terror was interrupted by a resounding crack. Xavier's grip had broken the back of the chair he'd been holding in two. His expression twisted into a murderous visage.

"That bastard," he said through his teeth.

"Ye stood out ta him, Avery. He said ye seemed invulnerable to his magic." She glanced away. "Behind closed doors, he mentioned he might have killed ye then if ye weren't so bonny. He hopes to capture Xavier, but you he plans to kill."

The growl that rumbled up Xavier's throat was nothing short of threatening. Glenna took a step back.

"So, in summary, Lachlan wants my pretty head on a stick, has dragon-capturing tools, and is trying his best to lure us back to the castle." Avery drew a shaky breath.

An eerie calm came over Xavier. "What time has Lachlan scheduled the public execution of Mistress Abernathy?"

"High noon. Lachlan wants to give the hunters a chance to flush you out."

"We should go tonight, under cover of darkness," Avery said.

Xavier shook his head. "*We* won't go at all."

"What the hell are you talking about?"

"Lachlan will be ready tonight, and he'll have all the weapons he's made at his disposal, ye ken? But tomorrow, when the hunters leave to search for us, they will take some of those weapons with them. If I go then, there will be less men and less risk."

"If *you* go then? Where will I be?" Avery scoffed.

"On Tàirn, heading for the door to the *builgean*."

"And I suppose I'm to wait for you there while you fight Lachlan on your own?"

He nodded. "If there's trouble, I'll send Glenna to carry you through. I'm confident with all the modern magical devices ye've described to me ye can find yer way back to my brother. Tell him that if I survive, I will join his cause."

Avery ground her teeth. "You've got to be kidding me! Take your eighteenth-century, patriarchal, chauvinist attitude and shove it up your ass!"

Glenna gaped at her, then looked at Xavier as if she expected him to leap across the table and tear her to pieces. He did look decidedly livid. His eyes had narrowed, and she didn't miss the way the temperature in the room rose.

"You will go, fur yer own safety."

"Or?"

"Or I'll be forced to fly ye there and toss ye into Glenna's arms maself."

She snorted and met his stare with her own. Slowly, she drew the sword from its sheath and held it out between them. "Just. Try. It."

Xavier's growl shook the walls, but she stood her ground.

"Damn it, woman. I canna fight Lachlan and protect ye too!"

"I snuck into the castle and freed you from under his nose. I don't need your protection."

Xavier strode slowly around the table, his blue eyes never leaving hers. He didn't stop until the tip of the sword pressed against the skin of his chest. "There's a price on yer head. Ye don't have invisibility. Every clan member will be searching for ye."

Somewhere, deep inside, she knew he was right, but she

refused to admit it. She absolutely would not leave him to do this alone. "He'll smell you coming, Xavier."

He tipped his head. "I can take care of maself, lass."

"So can I." Her narrowed gaze lowered to the tip of the sword resting on his chest.

Glenna hissed, her wings jutting out from her back defensively.

Xavier held up his hand to her and shook his head. "Leave us. I'll call for ye if I need ye."

The oread scowled at Avery before dissolving into thin air.

Xavier turned back to her and curled his lip at the sword. "Will you run me through, Avery? Kill me before Lachlan has the chance?"

She glared up at him. "No. But I won't let you force me to go."

For three long breaths, they stared at each other in silence until he finally softened. "All right. If I promise not to force ye ta do anything, would ye lower the sword then?"

She withdrew the tip from his skin and slid it back into its sheath. "Yes."

He moved toward her slowly as if she were a skittish animal. "Only a few moments ago, I offered ye my mating bond, my very heart exposed." He gestured to his chest where the sword had just been.

"Yeah... I'm sorry about that—"

"I'm not looking for an apology, Avery. Did my brother teach ye nothing about a dragon's instincts?"

She shook her head.

His lids sank low and heavy over his eyes. "We only offer the bond to someone our dragon chooses, and a potential mate doesna come along often. You, in fact, were ma first. You can deny me, deny the bond, but ma dragon wants ye in the most feral way. My deepest instinct is to protect ye. If ye come wi' me tomorrow, I won't be able ta concentrate. I won't be able to do what I need to do to kill Lachlan, because ma every thought will be of protecting ye. Dragons are immortal, but we can be killed. I'm confident I can defeat Lachlan in a one-on-one battle, but if it came down to ye, I'd let him have ma head."

A lump formed in Avery's throat. It wasn't only his words. Xavier's expression was nothing short of genuine. He wanted her. Wanted her permanently. "Do you love me Xavier?"

"The human word for love doesn't fully encompass a dragon's need to bond, but I suppose it is as good a human word as any."

He took another step closer. Everything he'd said rang true. She'd seen the dragon mating bond in action with Raven and Gabriel and with Nathaniel and Clarissa. And the truth was, although she couldn't accept Xavier's bond for all the reasons she'd mentioned before, she too felt an inexplicable link between them. She would never want to do anything to put him in danger. And he was right—she would be a distraction.

"Okay." She glanced at her feet. And then she closed the space between them and took him into her arms.

CHAPTER TWENTY-FOUR

Xavier took Avery into his arms and buried his face in her hair. Wrapped around her like this, he was reminded how fragile she was, how incredibly human. He drew her scent into his lungs, sweet and clean. It would be so easy to give in to his urge to take her. The way she leaned into him indicated her willingness certain enough. What was it she'd said in the barn? If he hadn't mentioned the mating bond, she'd be leaving footprints on the ceiling.

All his instincts told him she'd be as accommodating now. But could he make love to her without the bond? Not without hurting himself. He was already in too deep. And she'd be leaving soon.

"We should eat and rest. We'll part ways in the morning."

She gave him a small nod, her eyes watery. He reckoned she felt it too, this immediate, consuming connection.

Stepping outside, away from her, he rejoiced in the feel of the rain, the cool breeze against his hot skin. Avery Tanglewood was an enigma, both a balm and a poison to his soul. There was no doubt in his mind that she'd been sent by the Mountain in answer to his prayer when he was Lachlan's prisoner, but given the circumstances, he wondered if the goddess had a sense of humor.

"I canna believe ye let her speak to ye that way." Glenna formed in front him, her wings sparkling in the rain.

He grunted. "How? Like ye talk ta me?"

She gasped. "That isn't the same. She's a *mortal.*"

"A mortal who holds ma heart," he murmured.

Glenna's face drooped with her wings. There was a long pause. "She's a witch. Has to be. She's ensnared ye with her feminine wiles."

He grunted. "A happy prisoner I may be."

"She is a witch, ye ken? She saw me when she shouldn't 'ave been able ta."

He furrowed his brow. "She saw ye like I see ye?"

"Aye."

Xavier's head began to ache as he thought about Avery. He rubbed it now as he considered Glenna. "Would ye do me a kindness?"

"Anything, ma laird."

"Make us supper."

"Ma pleasure. Anything particular ye might like, considering it may be yer last?"

He sighed. "Do your best with whatever you can gather. The brownie who lives here stocked the cupboards, but he can't cook like ye. I want it ta be special before..." He looked down at a puddle forming near his feet.

"Before ye have ta say goodbye."

"Aye." He lifted his head to meet her eyes.

Glenna's expression softened. "I'll make ye something ta remember."

She drifted toward the cabin, and Xavier returned to the stable and chores he'd left behind. An hour later with the cow milked and the brownie fed, Xavier returned to find the table set with a dinner only an oread was capable of. There was roast rabbit that she must have hunted herself, herbed root vegetables, boiled greens, and fresh bread.

Glenna was gone, but Avery was there, standing by the fire and dressed only in her shift. He had to force his mouth not to drop open.

Her deep blue eyes seemed to darken as she looked at him, as if he'd dived into the loch and was sinking into its depths.

"My dress was wet." She ran her fingers through her curly hair, the drying coils falling loose around her shoulders.

"You are... truly lovely." His throat turned hot and dry, as if he'd recently breathed fire. Oh, there was a blaze inside him, but it wasn't in his throat. He tore his eyes away from the bewitching way the fire's glow shone through her thin shift. "Are ye hungry?"

"Starving. I was just waiting for you." She strode to the table, and he held out a chair before taking a seat across from her. "How is it you're dry? You just came from outside."

He grinned. "Body heat. I dry quickly."

The light that came from her answering smile cut straight to his heart.

"I guess there are benefits to being a dragon."

He watched her fill her plate and start to eat. The meal was delectable, but he picked at his food.

"I think ye're wrong, Avery."

"About what?"

"About not being a witch."

She snorted. "We've talked about this before. There isn't anything special about me."

He shook his head slowly. How could a woman so beautiful and strong have absolutely no self-awareness of her many stunning attributes?

"I find ye utterly enchanting. Spellbinding, beyond explanation. You have bewitched me."

She lowered the piece of bread she was holding to her plate and stared at him. "You're the first one to think so." Her voice held a breathless quality, and she tucked her hair behind her ear. He wished he had done it for her. He longed to stroke one of her curls between his fingers. "And," she continued, "that doesn't mean I'm a witch. It just means your dragon has a crush on me."

He scratched his chin, studying her. "Nay. I think I may be seein' ye clearly fur the very first time."

She flashed him a demure smile. "Oh?"

"You told me our first day here that ye were the only one who could touch yer sister's egg aside from her."

"True." She tilted her head.

"And ye walked away from the brownie the first time he tried ta lead ye here."

"I was in a hurry. I needed to find you."

"Aye. Only, most humans can't resist such an invitation, or even see a brownie in order to feed him as ye did."

Her expression became thoughtful as she eased back in her chair. "I think I'd know if I had any supernatural powers. Believe me, I'd have used them many times over."

"Aye, but ye did. Ye lied to Lachlan's face while holding his hand."

"It wasn't hard. The man made my skin crawl." She shivered. "I'd rather eat dirt than give him anything he wanted."

"He's a fairy, Avery. Detecting a lie is one of his most notable powers. You were immune to it."

Her expression turned wary.

"And ye opened ma cell, although it was sealed shut with ma own enchantment."

Her fingers pressed into her lips. "Okay, that was odd."

"And ye resisted the siren's call at the MacEacherns."

A deep furrow appeared in her forehead and her eyes started to mist. "Xavier? What does it mean?"

"You did all these things, Avery, because ye have a very powerful and sophisticated magic, and I only now recognize it fur what it is." He laughed. "I felt it when I kissed you in the barn. Ye practically buzz with power, ye ken."

"Please, I don't understand."

He was upsetting her, but she had to know the truth.

"The egg canna hurt you because ye are immune to its defenses. Lachlan's mind control won't ever work on ye. Even my magic fizzles in yer hands, which is why ye could open ma cell door. You, Avery, are immune to magic."

She blinked at him, then laughed deeply. "That can't be true. I've had magic used on me before. I was part of a very strong spell to rebind me to my sisters."

"Rebind you. You were separated. No power. Isn't that what you told me?"

"Exactly, and still I could hold little Charlie... the egg."

He nodded slowly as his own understanding dawned. "Because yer ability to soothe is inherent in you, in your human body. I bet ye've always been good at calming people."

"Well, yes."

"Because ye were born with the innate ability to neutralize negative energy. You told me ye were exceptionally gifted at calming rowdy patrons at the Three Sisters."

"Anyone who works in the service industry develops that talent." She shook her head.

So defiant. He traced the firm set of her lips with his gaze. "I *was* wrong. You weren't immune to the egg's magic. Your very human self soothed it into trusting ye. And then ye came here, and yer magic woke and grew stronger still when ye encountered the brownie, and Lachlan, and opened ma cell."

She was shaking her head, denying it.

"Why can't ye believe that ye're special? There has never been anyone like ye, Avery. I have lived over five hundred years, two hundred in Paragon and another three hundred in this realm. I've met thousands of supernatural creatures and even more humans. I've communed with witches and fairies alike. But you, ye are a treasure."

He watched her carefully for her reaction and was disappointed when none came. She held perfectly still, not even a flutter of her eyelid giving away what she thought of his ode of devotion.

Finally her blue gaze met his. "I don't think I can leave you."

CHAPTER TWENTY-FIVE

Nothing could have prepared Avery for this moment. Nathaniel had tried to warn her the night he'd read her tarot cards when she'd flipped over the moon card, but she hadn't really understood what he'd meant. At the time, he'd told her it represented her transformation and a possible romance. She'd just never allowed herself to believe either of those things could actually happen.

But now here she was, changed. Her first instinct was to deny the magic Xavier had pointed out to her, to protest that she was as normal and human as she'd ever been. Only, what he said made too much sense for her to deny it. She'd never been able to explain to herself how Xavier's cell door had opened for her or why she'd been immune to the siren's call when Mr. MacEachern had practically drowned himself. Something else, she'd felt it, a strange unraveling inside her since she'd come here, since she'd been with him.

He wanted her to go. Wanted to keep her safe. But the thought of leaving him now, it made her feel nauseous.

"Say something." His expression grew demanding. "Tell me ye believe what ye are."

"I-I believe you." The sweet warmth of his breath grazed her cheek when he exhaled. "It makes sense. I know this sounds crazy, but I could feel it, earlier, when you were kissing me. It felt like a seed was growing in me. Spreading. I feel different. Stronger somehow."

Across the table, Xavier sat back and rubbed his fingers against his thumb in quiet contemplation. "Dragons give off magic. 'Tis what draws the oreads to us, what feeds them." The intensity building in his gaze was mesmerizing. "If ye have magic in ye, bein' near a dragon will strengthen it."

"But I've spent the past two months before coming here with most of your siblings and I didn't feel like this."

He gave a slow, decidedly masculine smile. "Maybe ye were wi' the wrong dragon."

Despite herself, she giggled and felt her cheeks heat. He was just so damn alluring. She recalled their passion inside the barn again, the feel of him in her hand. Her skin grew hotter and she covered her face with her hands.

"Donna hide from me, lassie. You're a work of art when ye blush." His voice was gritty and deep—the voice of his dragon. "I love it."

"It's embarrassing. I'm a grown woman." She sucked her bottom lip between her teeth. "It's just... what you do to me. I've never felt this kind of attraction to anyone."

She heard his chair slide back from the table, but his movement was faster than her eye could track. He was in front of her in a blink, extending his bear paw of a hand toward her.

"Xavier..." It would only make things harder if they acted on their feelings.

"Dance with me, lass." His voice dropped. "Ye needna do more than let me hold ye."

"There isn't any music."

"You can sing us a tune."

She snorted a small laugh. "No, I can't. I couldn't carry a tune in a bucket."

"All right, then mine will have ta do." He flexed his fingers in an inviting gesture.

Slipping her hand into his, she gasped as he tugged her out of her chair and against him easily, as if she weighed nothing. His chest was broad and hard, a veritable wall of flesh that made her feel tiny in comparison. She hadn't noticed in the barn, so distracted was she by other parts of his anatomy.

"Do ye know this one?" He started humming a tune with a familiar cadence and turning her about the room.

She wasn't familiar with the tune itself, but there was no mistaking the dance. "Where did you learn how to waltz?"

"Is that what it's called? I saw it done once when I was travelin', before I settled here."

She laughed. "Well, it became quite popular for hundreds of years throughout Europe."

He paused his humming and gave her a dashing smile. "Really? 'Twas considered scandalous when I witnessed it." His hand pressed into the small of her back as they circled past the fire in the small space.

Feigning outrage, she fluttered her lashes. "Mr. Campbell, are you saying you deliberately chose to lead me through a dance you thought was scandalous? Are you trying to ruin my reputation?"

"Considering I am the only one around to witness any scandalous activity, I reckon I'm attempting to learn what reputation ye deserve."

The laugh that tore through her caused her to miss a

step, but he lifted her easily by the waist until his guidance had her back on track. "Where I come from, it's not so bad a thing to admit when you want someone. It takes more than a waltz to scandalize the modern world."

"What does it take?" he whispered, his breath caressing the shell of her ear.

That voice was like warm honey, the voice of a man who had no business teasing her so mercilessly. It was an invitation to sin, and she was too weak to deny the temptation. He was taller than her, the top of her head level with his nose, and she raised her chin in small increments until they were face-to-face, only a matter of inches between their lips.

The rain poured harder now, battering the walls of the cottage. Wind howled in the darkening sky. The noise of the burgeoning storm was nothing compared to the low purr that started in his chest again, vibrating against her. What had he called it in the stables? His mating trill.

His lips were parted and near, but he didn't close the distance between his mouth and hers. What was he waiting for? The answer came to her in her next heartbeat. *He offered. He wants you to say yes.*

"I can't bond with you. It would be a promise I couldn't keep," she murmured, their breath mingling between them.

"I heard ye the first time." He didn't move. He didn't pull away. "We have only this moment, Avery. Nothing else is guaranteed. If ye knew this would be the last time ye saw me, how would ye like to say goodbye?"

The fire flickered. Somewhere a tree branch slapped the wall, scraping like claws against the stone. "Don't talk like that. You promised me you'd come to Mistwood to meet with Nathaniel and the others."

His arms tightened marginally. "I'll do ma best."

His best. He had no idea if he'd be successful. Lachlan was terrifying. Who knew what tricks he'd have up his sleeve tomorrow, and the entire village—people Xavier had known and loved—would be turned against him.

"Then, in answer to your question, I'd like to say goodbye in a way that will motivate you to succeed tomorrow. A way that shows you I fully expect you to keep your promise."

"Oh?"

She rose up on her toes and brushed her lips, featherlight, against his. His arms tightened around her, and his mouth became one with hers. He was so big she felt like he'd wrapped completely around her. She reveled in his embrace. The warm cocoon of his body felt like a shelter from the storm. The kiss grew in intensity, his mouth claiming hers. His fingers explored the contours of her face in a way that belied the size and strength of his hands.

"This will only make things harder for both of us." A storm was brewing in her, one far more tumultuous than the one beating the roof outside.

"I know."

She reached for his belt and started unlatching it. It rattled to the floor and his kilt dropped, leaving him in nothing but his long white shirt. She, on the other hand, was already stripped down to her shift. He traced her nipples with his thumbs through the thin fabric, and they swelled beneath his touch.

"Avery."

Her name on his lips filled her with pleasure. She ran her hands along his neck and over the outside of his arms.

"Take this off," she demanded, tugging on his shirt.

He did as she asked, and the effect was glorious. His arms, corded with thick muscle, bunched and stretched as he grabbed the back of the collar and pulled it over his head. Her gaze raked down his sculpted body, every part of him hard and toned, powerful.

"Do I please you?" Laser focused on her reaction, his knowing smile deepened.

She forced her eyes back into her head and gave him a nonchalant shrug. "It'll do."

Under her palms, his chest rumbled with laughter. He reached for her shift.

"What are you doing?" She backed up a step.

"Evening the score."

"Ah, but you took your own shirt off. To be fair, I should do the unveiling." Slowly, she allowed her fingers to drift toward her hem and lifted it in quarter-inch increments. It was half a minute before he could see her upper thigh.

Xavier growled and murmured, "I'm immortal, but the room may fall down around us."

At last, she put him out of his misery and pulled it over her head, casting it aside.

He swallowed hard and his trill grew louder. He cleared thickness from his throat before saying, "By the Mountain, ye're a bonny lass. Come here and prove ye're real and not a fairy trick."

Legs trembling with nerves, she moved to meet him. It had been a long time since she'd made love. Years. Could a woman ever prepare herself for sex with a dragon?

As their mouths met again in a passionate kiss, his hands skimmed along her spine and then her waist, her breasts. He mounded one in his palm and leaned down to draw her nipple between his teeth. There was an edge to this pleasure, the sharp nip livening the gentle pressure of suction and tongue. Avery moaned and dug her fingers into his auburn hair.

"The sounds you make," he rumbled. "Let's see if I can play a tune."

He swept her off her feet and whirled her around until she felt weightless and disoriented, then settled her gently on the furs and blankets that had served as his bed in front of the fire.

"What sound will ye make if I kiss ye here?" He pressed his lips to the inside of her elbow, his tongue tracing the vein there.

She moaned at the heavenly feeling and basked in the glow of his self-satisfied smile. Dragging her nails down his chest and the hard planes of his stomach, she wrapped her hand around his shaft. "Let's make it a duet."

He didn't disappoint. His trill rumbled and his wings unfurled above her, filling the small room. She stared at the webbed wonders, awed she could inspect them up close. She trailed her fingers along the edge that extended beyond his shoulder. The scales were coppery with a blue undertone that came from fine, almost invisible feathers between the scales. They blended down into a fleshy web similar to a bat's wings. At the apex of the arc, at the front of each wing, a talon as large as a bear claw extended toward her.

She hooked her hand in one. "These are intimidating."

He stretched and flapped the wing gently against her hold. "They should be. We use them to fight."

"Each other?" The thought of Xavier using the massive claws to fight another dragon made her stomach clench.

"Aye."

"DONNA BE AFRAID. I WON'T HURT YE." XAVIER HAD seen darkness in Avery's expression when he'd mentioned using his talons to fight. He hadn't meant to frighten her, merely to answer her question. Stretched out on the floor, he rolled off her and propped himself on his elbow beside her.

"I'm not afraid," she said quickly.

"These talons"—he flexed his wings—"have a purpose. You hook them into yer opponent's to hold him fast so he canna get away, and then ye pummel him bloody with yer fists."

"Sounds unpleasant." She stroked a finger along the shell of his ear. "Especially considering what you told me before."

Memories of the pit filled his brain and distracted him from their intimate moment. The earthy stench of spilled dragon's blood filled his nose, and the pain of his father, Killian, resetting his bones so that he'd heal faster filled his memory.

"We did it because we had to, not because we wanted to."

"What I don't understand is the why of it?" She frowned. "Was it to make a soldier out of you? To protect Paragon in case of war?"

"That's what they told us, but our kingdom hadn't seen war in over a thousand years. I believe it was for sport. Entertainment for the Highborn Court and those who wanted to be seen with them. They would often bet on our matches." He sighed heavily.

"Brutal."

"Aye."

She examined his face, and understanding sparked in her eyes. "Was that why you created this place? To avoid unnecessary violence?"

It had been a long time since he'd thought about why

he'd created the *builgean.* "As a dragon, I could have annihilated the Jacobites or changed the destiny of their cause."

"You chose door number three."

"Aye. I'm not above fighting, ye ken, but it wasna ma war."

"It wasn't your war, and you refused to be used as a weapon."

"Aye."

"Last night... you said what was happening in Paragon wasn't your war either. Is that why? Do you feel like if you join your siblings to battle Eleanor, you're just being used again? Only Gabriel can sit on the throne, and you've already spilled enough blood in the pits?"

He gazed at her, his heart swelling with affection. "It's as if ye know ma very soul, Avery."

She blinked. "I... I think I get it. You and I are so much alike." She shook her head. "I came here because I was sick of living my life for someone else. And you built this place for the same reason."

He rubbed a lock of her silky hair between his fingers. "Aye."

"Only, if I hadn't made myself vulnerable and stayed here to help you, I would never have understood my own power or fallen in love with you."

His heart skipped in his chest as his eyes bored into hers, seeking the truth. "You love me?"

"Yes, I do."

Xavier's heart pounded anew when she raised a hand to tease the talon of his right wing, then scraped her nails along the inside webbing. He shivered and closed his eyes. "Ye canna imagine how good that feels or how much I love ye in return."

"It must be incredible to be able to fly."

He opened his eyes and smiled wide. "I can take ye for a ride if ye wish."

She seemed to roll the offer over in her mind. "Okay. *After*."

Her fingers dug into his hair, and she drew him on top of her. He was more than happy to lose himself again in her sweet lips. It was the most natural thing in the world to lower his weight between her thighs. Propped on his elbows above her, he'd never experienced anything like her. She was a goddess, a formidable fortress, a fellow warrior. She wrapped her legs easily around his hips. All he had to do was reposition himself and he'd be inside her. His dragon surged beneath his skin, desperate to have her.

This was folly. This was madness. What would it do to him, to his dragon, to do this and then watch her leave tomorrow? They were from two different worlds. He might as well sentence his heart to hell.

Yet, if he didn't, he'd always regret it. To feel like this, even for a moment, was worth an eternity of pain. This was bliss. It was heaven. Who would refuse their only chance inside the pearly gates even if they couldn't stay?

"Please." She squirmed beneath him, positioning her hips. "Xavier, please."

Her expression was his undoing. She was begging, almost in tears for want of him. He lowered his hips and slid into her.

He thought he might come apart for the feel of her, warm and soft beneath him. The sigh of pleasure she released made his dragon rise to the surface. The instinct to claim her as his own was overwhelming, and he would. Even without a mating bond, he'd make her remember this.

"My God, Xavier. This is beyond anything... ever..."

She touched her forehead to his chin, braced herself on his shoulders, and thrust her hips into his.

He growled. He'd meant to go slow, to make love to her tenderly, but Avery had other ideas.

"Harder." She moaned, digging her nails into his back beneath his wings.

He gave her what she wanted, unleashing his inner beast hard and fast until he feared he might hurt her. Thrust for thrust, she matched his pace, and then in a feat of strength he wasn't expecting, she rolled him over. His wing slapped the bench, sending it skidding across the wood floor.

She rose above him, one hand braced on his chest the other grabbing and tugging the talon of his left wing. Her hips ground against his. Arching, she tipped her head back and cried out. The sight of her rising and falling above him drove him into a frenzy, and her rough play ignited his passion to a level between making love and a physical attack.

He sat up, driving deeper into her. A crack of thunder rattled the walls, and lightning lit up the windows. The storm outside was nothing like the one raging between them. She bit him lightly on the jaw and scratched along his ribs, scoring his skin. The pain was pure ecstasy.

Fisting her hair, he bent her head back and nipped her throat, soothing the bite with tender kisses. She only ground harder against him. Her breasts mounded against his chest, between their bodies.

"You're mine, Avery." His dragon hissed, wild and feral, from his soul. "You'll always be mine."

He thrust harder inside her, and her pleasure seized her in a violent quake that tipped his own over the edge. With a long, low growl, he emptied himself into her. Surely he'd died and gone back to the Mountain. Everything was fire and heat and his love for this woman.

He flopped onto his back, and she stretched like a lazy cat over his chest. "I donna know whit's changed in the outside world, but I'd no idea people did it like that."

"Like what?" She laughed.

"Rough. Almost violent. I hope I didn't hurt ye."

She blushed fire red. "Oh... They don't. I... I just couldn't help myself. You didn't hurt me. Did I hurt you?"

They both laughed. "Nay," he said softly, then added, "Not yet."

She slid off him and tucked into his side. He could have sworn he saw a tear roll from her eye. He wiped it away with his thumb.

"Are ye all right, lass?"

Her kiss landed on his jaw. "Just a bit of ash in my eye from the fire."

He grunted and pulled her closer, drawing the blankets up over her shoulders. He swiped a thumb under his own eye. It seemed the ash had gotten to him as well.

CHAPTER TWENTY-SIX

Avery woke in slow increments, recalling exactly where she was. Tucked into Xavier's side, she experienced a swell of affection for the Highland dragon. But she was also very, very sore. She suppressed a groan as she stretched and inspected herself. Her inner thighs were bruised, and more sensitive spots on her anatomy were equally tender.

She'd done this to herself, to be sure. She'd made love to Xavier last night as if she could permanently join the two of them if she just fucked him hard enough. The act was raw and primal. She hadn't noticed then how violently she'd participated, but she felt it now. Felt as if she could barely move.

None of her bruises held a candle to what was going on in her heart.

Xavier stirred beside her. His soulful and serious blue eyes gazed at her in silence.

"'Tis still vera early. Before dawn," he said. "But I think we should both be on our way. The hunters will be scouring the hills, and I want them nowhere near ye."

She nodded but didn't break eye contact. Couldn't look away. Didn't want to blink. And then a stupid thought led to a stupid action, and before she could stop herself, she said, "I don't want you to go."

"Aye. No one wants to go inta battle, but the war must be fought."

"No, it doesn't. Come with me... to the outside."

He shook his head. "You know I can't. I can't leave ma people to be murdered by that maniac."

"But..." She squirmed next him and blinked back tears. "I love you, Xavier. I do. I love you. You're the first thing..." She chewed her lip. "You are the first thing I ever really wanted for myself."

"Aye. I love ye too. Enough to offer ye an eternal bond. And I suppose what happened last night sealed that deal for me, although ye are still free of it."

She inhaled sharply. "Are you suggesting you bonded with me even though I wouldn't bond back?"

He nodded. "Sometimes we canna help it. Ma dragon wants ye. There will be no other for me—not ever."

She shuddered in his arms. "Ugh. This is stupid." She couldn't go. Not now. "I'm coming with you."

He leaned over her, not a hint of levity in his expression. "No. You're going home. You're going to live a long, happy life in yer world. If all goes well, I'll see ye at Mistwood in a day or two."

She searched his face, then said firmly, "I'm going."

He shook his head. "After last night, I canna risk it. Yer presence would put us both in danger. The second someone saw ye, Lachlan would use ye against me."

He was right. She knew he was right. And it was the hardest thing she'd ever had to do when she pushed him off her to stand up. "Fine. Then let's not prolong the inevitable."

"Avery!"

He called after her, and she made the mistake of glancing back at him. His fully nude form stood from a crouch, every muscle as etched and pronounced as she remembered. No wonder she was sore. The man was a marble statue whose sculptor hadn't skimped anywhere.

She closed her eyes, turned away, and marched into the bedroom, closing the door behind her. Her heart pounded. The memory of him filling her flooded her mind, and her hands trembled as she dressed. Never would another man live up to last night. She might as well become a damned nun when she returned home.

She laid the outfit the brownie had obtained for her on the bed and dressed in the one she'd come in, the leggings and the hiking boots. She repacked her bag, slipping it onto her back. By the time she exited, Xavier had dressed as well. He looked positively regal in his kilt, his hair braided and Fairy Killer hanging at his hip. She narrowed her eyes at the fierce sight of him. If Lachlan wasn't shaking in his boots about what was coming for him today, then he'd never truly known Xavier. This man was a warrior.

"I'm ready."

"That makes one of us," he grumbled.

Choking back her useless tears, she strode past him, out the door and toward the barn where Tàirn waited. Xavier's reasons were sound. She agreed they were both doing the right thing. So why did it feel so damned wrong?

Because you didn't say yes. She'd reached Tàirn but balked, the searing pain in her chest almost bringing her to her knees. Clarity exploded between her temples. Xavier was the first thing in her life she had truly wanted, and she'd rejected him because of geography. Talk about being so focused on the trees she couldn't see the forest! In her desire to keep nothing from thwarting her quest to find her future, she'd almost cast the most important part of it aside. Love.

Snorting her derision, she took Tàirn's reins and led the horse out of the stall to where Xavier waited in front of the cottage. "Ye ken where ye're goin', aye? Head due west, same direction ye arrived from. Ye'll find the place ye dropped in. I'd thought before that either Glenna or I would have to let ye out, but now that we know ye're immune to magic, I reckon ye'll be able to pass through the ward at the foot of the mountain on yer own."

She nodded, avoiding his eyes. Without being asked, he lifted her easily into the saddle, and she settled her skirts around herself, gathering the reins in her hands.

"By the Mountain, woman. After everything we've been through, are ye not even goin' to say yer farewells?"

Swallowing hard, she took a fortifying breath and looked him dead in the eye. "Yes," she said firmly.

He nodded, confused by her curt reply.

"Yes, I accept the bond."

His eyes widened until she could see white all around the blue of his irises. He reached up to touch her, but she pressed her calf to the horse and maneuvered away from his hands, shaking her head.

"If you want your bonded mate, Xavier, then kill Lachlan and come for me. I'll be waiting for you at the gate. I'll only pass through if I'm in danger. I *expect* you to succeed and come for me. Do you understand me?"

She wondered if it was a low blow, accepting the bond now, but she wanted his inner dragon to stop at nothing to get back to her. She needn't have worried. He straightened and gave her a wolfish smile that rocked her deep in her core.

"Vera well, ma *mate*. I will win back ma lands and then find ye, and when I do, ye best be prepared to have ma hands on ye."

The impish smile she returned held nothing but promise. "I look forward to it."

Before she could change her mind, she turned Tàirn and kicked him into a run.

SHE'D ACCEPTED THE BOND! FIRE RAGED IN XAVIER'S chest. His instinct was to go after her and never leave her side, but now not only did his loyalty to his people drive his steps but also her mandate that he succeed. Avery was a cunning woman, and she knew exactly what she was doing. He'd never been so motivated in his long life.

He fed the brownie one last time, just as the sun's rays broke the horizon. "Thank ye, ma friend, for yer help."

The fairy wrinkled its cream-covered nose and smiled at him. Xavier turned himself invisible, spread his wings, and flew for Castle Dunchridhe. The sooner he killed Lachlan, the faster he'd be back in Avery's arms.

He was thinking of her still as he arrived within view of the castle. His heart sank. Lachlan was expecting him.

The entire clan stood in the road leading to the castle, and every person was armed. Their arrows, swords, crossbows and bolts gleamed metallic in the sun. But the worst part was their eyes. Empty, dead eyes, as if they were in a trance. Completely within Lachlan's control.

His stomach twisted as he recognized each of them—his friends, his fellow clansmen. He soared over them toward the castle, and that's when he saw Lachlan and the cruel trick he'd played. He'd placed Mistress Abernathy on the castle's hoard, a noose around her neck. Lachlan stood beside her, so close that one of his feet rested precariously between her legs, a gleaming rapier in his right hand.

It was clear now that she was meant to be the bait. If Xavier showed himself, the clan would shoot him. If he flew straight for Lachlan, he risked the fairy tripping Mistress Abernathy and sending her tumbling over the wall, which would break her neck. If he soared into Mistress Abernathy and carried her back from the edge of the hoard, Lachlan would use the distraction to stab him with his sword, which was undoubtedly made from the metal enchanted to weaken him. If he got too close or tried to snap the rope encircling Mistress Abernathy's neck, Lachlan would smell him and either cause the old woman to fall as a distraction or simply stab him.

Lachlan was an excellent swordsman and faster than any human. Xavier couldn't take any of those scenarios lightly. Which left him only one choice.

He drifted high over Lachlan's head, careful to distance himself so that his scent wouldn't give him away. He circled around the castle and landed silently on the castle wall behind Lachlan. In that position, the villagers would not be able to shoot at him without hitting Lachlan first. He raised Fairy Killer and dropped his invisibility.

"Let her go, Lachlan, and let's settle this as men."

Lachlan turned his platinum-blond head slowly and stared at him with cold black eyes. "I'm no man, and neither are ye."

He swept Mistress Abernathy's legs out from under her.

Xavier moved as fast as he was able, swooping over the edge of the castle and catching Mistress Abernathy before the noose could close. He loosened the rope and pulled it over her head while twisting his body in flight to avoid the stab of Lachlan's rapier. Arrows flew from below, and Xavier dived and then climbed to avoid them, moving for the cover of the east stone turret. He landed with Mistress Abernathy inside the window and kicked in the leaded glass as a storm of arrows bounced harmlessly off the stone.

"Are you well?" he asked her, but her face was blank, her hands down by her sides. She might as well have been staring absentmindedly across the loch rather than recovering from a close call with death. Her lips twitched. He shook her by the shoulders gently. "Can ye not speak?"

She blinked rapidly at him; then her right hand tore from her pocket and thrust a dagger into his gut. The pain was instant and unbearable. He pushed her away and stumbled backward toward the window.

"Must slay the dragon," she mumbled. She screamed then, screamed for the guards as if he were ripping her heart out.

Betrayal shivered down his spine as Xavier tugged the dagger from his flesh and dropped it. Enchanted steel. Blood gurgled from the wound.

Mistress Abernathy bared her teeth and lunged for the weapon. One day she'd be free from Lachlan's control and regret this, but today was not that day. Xavier leaped backward out the window and allowed himself to fall fast. He landed in a crouch in front of the castle, facing a legion of his own clan, every one dead set on killing him.

A hand grabbed him by the shirt and pulled him behind the castle wall inside the raised portcullis before another barrage of arrows fell where he'd been standing. Glenna pressed her hands to his wound, which wasn't healing. It would eventually now that he'd pulled the dagger out, but the healing would be slow and painful thanks to the enchanted metal.

"Oh, she got you good. They're all under his control, my laird. All but me. And he's ordered them to fire at ye on sight."

"Then we take away their sight." He made himself invisible. Stripping, he dropped the sword on the heap of his clothes. "If I shift, I'll heal, and my scales will repel the arrows."

Glenna nodded her understanding.

"Bring these to me as soon as you are safely able. Guard the sword with yer life. 'Tis our only sure method of killing Lachlan."

"Aye, ma laird."

He bent and stretched, transforming into his true dragon form. He targeted Lachlan on the hoard. The fairy's eyes scanned the yard for him as he sniffed the air, no doubt catching his scent on the wind. As he slithered from behind the castle wall, his thoughts became simple as they always were when he was in his beast's skin. He must end Lachlan even if he had to bite the fairy's head off with his own teeth.

He beat his wings, lifting into the air and sending a downdraft over the people below, strong enough to make them raise their arms in front of their faces. They lifted their weapons and aimed at the source. Invisible or not, Xavier didn't have much time. He didn't need it. All he had to do was break Lachlan's hold over the clan and he'd be home free.

He snapped at the fairy's head, but Lachlan stumbled back from the edge. Xavier missed. Lachlan pointed his sword straight at him.

"I donna need to see ye to run ye through," Lachlan

said. "Come, dragon. 'Tis time for the fairy to slay ye for real."

Xavier couldn't speak in his dragon form but inhaled a great stream of air into his lungs and, with that breath, sent a blast of dragon fire to consume the wicked fairy. The flames completely engulfed Lachlan, sword and all. Xavier didn't stop until every flicker of flame had left his lungs. He wasn't sure if dragon's fire could kill a fairy, but if he was going to try, he was going to give it his best shot. But when his fire finally dwindled, Lachlan was gone. Not ash. Not scorched. Gone.

The clatter of chain links preceded a heavy weight landing on Xavier's back. His invisibility flickered out and his wings stopped working. He tipped over the edge of the hoard and crashed onto the grass in front of the castle, his body wrapped in enchanted chain mesh.

Lachlan strode toward him. Xavier tried to raise his head and failed. His horns caught in the mesh, but no matter what he tried, he couldn't shake it. The fairy placed his hands on his hips and his boot firmly on Xavier's neck. The net drained his magic, left him helpless.

"Ye've always underestimated ma abilities, Xavier," Lachlan said to him. "Fairies are masters of illusion. Look at me! I've slain the dragon again. What songs they will sing while ye rot in the dungeon where ye belong."

A wave of nausea overcame him as the enchantment in the metal forced him to shift back into his human form. He lay in the grass naked and helpless.

"The problem is ye never understood why I need this place more than you. A fairy changeling, Xavier, is left when the fairies steal a human child. The fairies want the baby, but they also want to get rid of the changeling. My kind were cruel to me in the land of light. They left me behind in the *builgean* to rot in the shadow of yer human clan. But I am far more powerful than those bastards ever knew. This is my world now, and all will serve me." Lachlan grabbed the back of Xavier's head and dragged his face up from the grass to see his evil grin.

With Xavier's last ounce of magic, he attempted to reach out to Glenna via the oread's bond.

Tell Avery to run. Tell her to go to Mistwood. If the oread responded, he didn't hear it. Lachlan let Xavier's face crash into the grass again, and then his boot came down on his temple and the lights went out.

CHAPTER TWENTY-SEVEN

Avery could barely see and was thankful that Tàirn seemed to know where he was going. Her eyes were practically swollen shut from the endless crying she'd experienced after leaving Xavier. Even now she sobbed as if she'd ripped out her own heart and left it in that cottage.

"Stop! Avery, stop!"

Avery tugged on the reins and brought Tàirn to a halt at the sound of Glenna's voice. She knew it was serious when the oread flew at her, fully visible, and hovered at her side.

"Glenna, what's happened?"

The oread looked positively distraught.

"Lachlan captured Xavier." Glenna's voice cracked. "He told me to tell ye to go on to Mistwood." Tears glittered like diamonds on the oread's cheeks.

Avery's heart clenched. She turned Tàirn around.

"Didn't ye hear me, mistress? He wants ye to go!"

"I heard you, and I will do as I please."

To her surprise, Glenna gave her a barely perceptible smile.

"Do you have the sword? Do have Fairy Killer?" Avery asked.

A bundle of clothing and a scabbard appeared in Glenna's arms, and the oread handed it all to her. Avery snatched up Fairy Killer and slung it over her head and shoulder, the blade verily singing to her from its scabbard. She wiped under her eyes and shoved Xavier's clothes into her saddlebag.

"What do ye plan ta do?"

Avery smiled in a way that must have been chilling based on the expression on the oread's face.

"I'm going to go save my mate."

TÀIRN SEEMED TO UNDERSTAND THE GRAVITY OF Avery's situation because the stallion all but flew for the castle. She'd never ridden this hard or fast, and she clung to the horse's mane, giving the magnificent beast full rein. By the time they reached the castle, she was sure her joints were going to come undone.

She slowed Tàirn and surveyed the road leading to the castle. People were drinking and singing, dancing in the street.

Without dismounting, she reached down and grabbed the collar of the closest man to her. "What's going on?"

"Lachlan killed the dragon!" he said excitedly. His eyes locked on her face. "You're that girl." He drew his dirk and swung it in a wide, drunken arc toward her.

Avery's blood ran cold. She caught his wrist and stopped the blade from reaching her. In her higher position on Tàirn, it would have landed in her gut or thigh. He opened his mouth as if to scream her identity to everyone around them, but she grabbed his bottom jaw with her opposite hand and squeezed. Tàirn stomped his feet at the shift of her weight in the saddle, but she used her legs to keep him in place.

All at once, Avery became aware of a tingle in her fingers, that same electric current she'd noticed when she'd opened Xavier's cell. The man blinked rapidly up at her as if he were waking from a deep sleep.

"Where's Lachlan?" she asked.

"Who are ye? What do ye want wi' Lachlan?"

Avery's eyes narrowed. The man's pupils had gone from rheumy to clear, and he seemed to no longer recognize her. "Can you help me? I need to find Xavier."

"Xavier?" He shrugged. "In residence at Castle Dunchridhe, I ken?"

"You know Xavier?" A flicker of hope ignited in her chest.

"Of course. He's laird and chief of our clan. Ye have a strange way of speakin', lass. Who are ye?"

At once she realized Xavier was right about her abilities. She was immune to magic and could use her power to break the spells over these men and women. And the best part was, once she did, they *remembered.*

She released him, then urged Tàirn forward. People in the crowd had started to recognize her. They pointed and seethed, reaching for their weapons. Avery grabbed the face of the biggest man she could find. To her pleasant surprise, it was Aeden, the bouncer from the Lion and the Hare. She breathed a sigh of relief as he shivered at her touch, then stared at her quizzically with clear brown eyes.

"Avery? What's happened?" He looked toward the castle. "Lachlan... That fairy bastard!"

"You remember?"

"Aye."

"Aeden, Xavier's in danger. I need your help."

Avery dismounted and, with Aeden's help, hurried from man to woman—anyone she could touch—until she had a small army of supporters and had neutralized all those who recognized and wanted to kill her.

"Lachlan has captured Xavier, and I need your help getting him back," she said to the group.

Aeden acted as translator, explaining her plan in a way they could understand. If you could call it a plan. Her best idea was for them to distract Lachlan while she snuck into the castle to save Xavier.

A redheaded woman at the front of the crowd shook her head. "How do ye expect us to defend ourselves against him, lass? I want to help Xavier as much as anyone, but the fairy's had us all in his thrall for years. He's too strong!"

The crowd murmured their agreement. Avery glanced at Aeden, but the big man's gaze shifted to his toes. They were afraid. They should be. These people had only known peace thanks to Xavier. They weren't soldiers, and their fear of fairies was well-founded.

Avery sighed. "This is dangerous, I know that, but we will win against Lachlan because... because..."

The crowd waited.

Closing her eyes, Avery inhaled a deep, cleansing breath and drew Fairy Killer from her scabbard. "I am Avery Tanglewood, and I am a powerful witch immune to fairy magic. It was my sorcery that freed you from Lachlan's hold. I will protect you, but I need your help."

A murmur crept through the crowd. She had broken Lachlan's spell, and although they feared her magic, they also trusted in it. For several tense moments, Avery prayed their gratitude would outweigh their instinct to fear the unknown. Stories of witches burning at the stake filled her mind. But finally there was a collective nodding of heads.

"Aye. We'll help ye," the redhead said.

Avery's plan was rushed at best. The idea was that the villagers would cause a commotion in the castle yard and yell for Lachlan, distracting the guards, thereby allowing her to sneak inside and rescue Xavier. But as they closed in on the castle, any hope of that scheme becoming a reality collapsed. A battalion of soldiers guarded the gate and Lachlan watched, waiting from the castle hoard. Beside him, a narrow-shouldered man stared absently over their heads.

"My dear friend Angus tells me a witch has come to Castle Dunchridhe to challenge my rule. Show yerself, witch!" Lachlan yelled down from above. A chill ran the length of her spine, and she exchanged glances with the men and women around her.

Aeden shook his head. "Angus MacKenzie. He must have seen what ye were doin' and run to warn the bastard."

Avery swore. She'd known the number of people she'd been able to touch and free from Lachlan's hold was less than the number she'd initially seen in the street, but she'd thought the others had gone back to their homes or wandered off drunk. Now she knew the truth. Lachlan, the clever fairy, had a fail-safe.

She walked to the front of the crowd and drew Fairy Killer.

"I'm here, Lachlan," she yelled. "I've come for Xavier."

He sneered. "Well, if it isn't the kitchen wench. I always knew there was something odd about you. You're too late, lassie. Xavier is back where he belongs, and he's going to stay there." Lachlan focused on the others around her and said in a voice laden with magic, "Go back to your work. This has nothing to do with you."

The power in Lachlan's words was palpable as they washed over her and the people behind her. She closed her eyes, and the tingle of it made her skin itch. Beside her, Aeden groaned.

She reached out and touched his wrist. "Fight it," she murmured.

He shook his head, as did the others around her.

Avery smiled. Whether Lachlan was too far away or her magic had helped ward off his fairy powers, the villagers were still hers. She felt his influence blow away like dust on the next wind.

"Give us Xavier!" Aeden yelled, thrusting his sword in the air.

The others cheered him on, offering a collective chant for Xavier's freedom.

Avery lifted Fairy Killer. "Free Xavier or die!" she bellowed.

The small crowd roared behind her. For a moment, Avery thought Lachlan might cave. His eyes widened and his mouth bent into a scowl as if he were legitimately shaken by his failure to subdue the crowd.

He answered her only with an intense, condescending stare. An evil smile spread across his face, too broad, showing too many teeth. She wondered what wicked thoughts had spawned such a grin, then learned the answer straightaway as Lachlan shoved Angus off the wall.

CHAPTER TWENTY-EIGHT

Deep in the dungeons of Castle Dunchridhe, Xavier lay naked on the stone floor of a dungeon cell. A blanket of chain mail fastened to the floor held him in place and painfully drained his energy. Eyes closed, all his thoughts turned to Avery. He hoped she'd made it to Mistwood safely.

He would be tortured with thoughts of Avery as he rotted in this stone tomb for the rest of eternity. Of lost opportunities. Of lost intimacies. He'd loved her like he'd never loved anyone or anything. In that instant, it occurred to him that he'd never properly thanked the goddess for bringing her into his life. Although his time with her had been too short, he would do it all again.

"Goddess of the Mountain," he whispered hoarsely. He wished he could kneel, but he was too weak to raise his head from the floor. "Thank you for sendin' Avery to free me from the dungeon and for every minute ye gave me with her. Also, if ye can see fit to send me help to get out of this mess, I'd be yer humble servant."

He felt the air shift in his cell and forced his eyes to

open. He could have sworn he saw a flash of gold, but there was nothing there.

And then a woman whispered in his ear. "I want Paragon. It *is* your war, Xavier."

He tried to turn his head to see who it was but couldn't move. "Who's there?" he cried.

"By the Mountain, laird, quiet down. Ye'll catch the attention of the guards if yer not careful." Glenna appeared in front of him with a long metal bar in her hands.

"Glenna, careful. If ye touch the mesh, it'll drain you," he murmured.

She scoffed and dug the metal tool under one of the spikes holding the netting to the floor. "I have lived in this castle for two years without Lachlan being any the wiser to my presence. It helps, ye ken, bein' a mountain nymph and able to merge into the stone. He doesn't know I exist."

"Thank the Mountain ye're safe," Xavier murmured weakly.

"Oh, shut yer fat head."

The stake came loose, and she used the metal rod to toss it across the cell.

"Lachlan I can see underestimating me, considering he doesna know I exist. You have no such excuse, Xavier."

"Huh?"

"Do ye ken this thing in my hands is from the kitchen? They use it to scrape the burned crud from the sides of the oven. I'm wishin' I could use it on yer skull 'bout now."

The second stake came free of the stone and clattered across the floor.

"It's occurred to me ye might be miffed about somethin', Glenna. Why not come right out and say it?"

"Ye have a bad habit of actin' like ye've no one in the

world to trust but yourself." She hooked the rod on the corner of the chain links and peeled them back.

He took a deep breath, the relief from the removal of the netting feeling like pure heaven.

"Ye underestimate every woman in yer life. Me and that mate of yers, who is out there right now, facing Lachlan."

"What?" Xavier's stomach dropped and his gaze snapped to Glenna's as he staggered to his feet.

She reached down and swept his clothes from the floor and tossed them at him. "Ye'd better hurry if ye want to kill him. She might get there first."

CHAPTER TWENTY-NINE

"Angus!" Avery rushed forward, but the man lay in an oddly angled heap near the base of the castle wall. Blood oozed from his nose under empty, unseeing eyes. He was dead.

She lifted her gaze to glare at Lachlan. "Are you such a coward that you'll kill a man in your thrall but won't cross swords with a simple kitchen wench?"

His laugh was cold and cruel as he drew his blade. "If ye choose to die by the sword, who am I to deny ye?" He leaped down from the hoard and landed on the grass in front of the castle, some twenty yards from her. "Well, come take yer due, *witch*."

Behind her, the castle guards rushed the villagers and the raucous howls and clangs of war raged around her. Once again, Lachlan had caused infighting amongst the clan. To stop it before someone else died, she had to kill Lachlan. She attacked.

Avery had always been stronger than most of her friends. At the bar, the staff would bet her on how many cases of beer she could carry up from storage, and she always won. She was also fast. For someone who only ran for fitness, she'd always been told she had a professional's pace. Still, something had changed. She moved on Lachlan in a flash, Fairy Killer colliding with a clang that reverberated in the bones of her arm. She kicked him in the gut, leaped back, and thrust again.

How on earth did she know how to even use a sword? Avery hadn't held a weapon like this in her life, but the connection she felt to this blade was undeniable. Fairy Killer became an extension of her arm. A part of her. As did the knowledge of how to use it.

The iron sword seemed to sing in her hand as she attacked. Her blade connected with his at the base. She swept the blade around, trying to disarm him. He retreated and parried, then thrust. She sidestepped, parried, and lunged for his neck. The razor-sharp tip nicked his throat.

Lachlan retreated, bringing his hand to the wound. Dark, mud-colored blood smudged his fingers. Avery watched fear slither into his eyes like a snake entering tall grass. That's right—the kitchen wench could use a sword. At least *this* sword. She advanced. He stabbed and she dodged.

"Your hands are shaking, Lachlan," she said. "Give me Xavier, and I'll let you live."

"Nay, witch, 'tis you who should be afraid. Time to sleep." He leaped backward and thrust his hand into the dirt. Instantly, plants sprouted all around them, thicker between Lachlan and her. Avery had never seen anything grow so fast.

Clouds of crimson pollen exploded from the flowering sprouts. The sounds of battle behind her stopped abruptly. Out of the corner of her eye, she saw a few villagers attempt to outrace the explosion of red, running for the village.

They didn't make it. Neither did the guards. They all toppled like plastic soldiers. Aeden called her name before a fit of coughing consumed him and he succumbed as well.

"Aeden!" She ran into the crimson fog and crouched beside him, but a cursory inspection showed he wasn't dead, merely asleep, as Lachlan had threatened. The dust was all around her now, painting her red, but unlike the others who dropped like flies and snored in a heap around her, the dust had no effect on Avery except to make her cough.

She covered her mouth and nose with one hand as the red dust coated her, turning her arms and skirts blood red. Through a crimson haze, she watched Lachlan, who was confidently smug with his hands in the dirt in front of the castle. Gripping Fairy Killer's hilt tighter, Avery rose from a crouch. Pieces of her hair drifted in front of her face, bright red from the flower's pollen. She must have been a sight. Even to her own eyes, the parts of her she could see looked doused in blood. Images of Carrie danced through her head, and just like the scorned prom queen, she intended to have her revenge.

Fueled by sheer determination, she faced Lachlan and raised Fairy Killer. She took a step toward him, then another. Her legs felt heavy. The damn skirts—they were caked in pollen and mud, weighing her down. Suddenly it occurred to her she didn't need them anymore. She untied the waist and pushed them off. When she stepped out of the cloud of pollen toward Lachlan, she wore nothing but her leggings and top and the knowledge she could not fail.

"What are ye?" Lachlan asked through his teeth, visibly shaken. He pulled his hands from the dirt and scrambled for his sword.

Avery could see he'd hit her with his best shot and missed. She wasn't snoring like everyone else in a visible radius, and the weapon in her hand was still stained with his blood. She spread her lips into a wide, avenging grin. "I'm Xavier's mate."

She launched herself forward, thrust, parried, kicked, and ducked. Metal met metal, her arms flashing red in front of her. *Clang, clang, clang.* The sound rang out across the grounds with every strike, her arm aching from the force of each blow.

Mustering her strength, Avery backed Lachlan against the wall of the castle. He tried to dodge left, and she circled his blade with her own, twisting it from his hand. It fell from his grip.

Truly frightened now, Lachlan flapped his gossamer wings and flew straight up. The one thing Avery couldn't do was fly. She swore as he rose out of her reach. Even if she could now rescue Xavier, they'd never rest as long as Lachlan was free.

A long, dark shadow blocked out the setting sun. Avery squinted against the light as the silhouette of a dragon rose over the castle.

Xavier!

Seeing him like this, Avery was overcome with awe. Her breath left her in a whoosh. His shimmering amber-and-blue scales glinted in the light of the sunset, and the roar that broke from his throat vibrated along her skin.

Lachlan turned his head slowly, his eyes growing wide at the sight of Xavier. His wings flapped furiously as he tried to flee, but there was no escape. Not now. Not in the face of one very pissed-off dragon.

A flash of claws and teeth later, Lachlan dropped from the sky in front of her. Her body moved of its own volition—all instinct or all magic, she didn't know which. Her boot landed on the fairy's stomach, and she pressed the tip of Fairy Killer over the evil son of a bitch's heart.

Lachlan held a palm toward her. "No. Please. I surrender. I beg of you."

Xavier landed beside her, his blue dragon eyes burning with fire. He bared his teeth and chuffed.

She glared down at Lachlan. "Should I show you the same mercy you showed Xavier? Give you his cell? I wonder if a fairy will do as well as a dragon in perpetual darkness."

His expression turned into a sneer. "Death!"

At first Avery didn't understand what he was saying. Was he begging for death? But then a mushroom exploded from the ground beside his hand and flung black spores into the air around her. Xavier roared.

But Avery just shook her head and grinned. "You should have learned from your first mistake."

She thrust the sword between his ribs until it met dirt on the other side. Lachlan's mouth opened to cry out, but his breath gurgled in his throat. The light flickered and faded from his cruel dark eyes.

"Avery, his head." Xavier had shifted back to his human form and was standing beside her naked. "Never trust a dead fairy with its head still attached to its shoulders."

She could have beheaded Lachlan herself, but after everything, she thought Xavier needed the closure. Shoving the hilt into his hand, she nodded her support. With a crooked smile, Xavier lifted Fairy Killer over his head before bringing the edge down on Lachlan's neck. The fairy's head rolled from his body, tangling in his white hair as mud-colored blood seeped into the earth.

Xavier's gaze locked with her own. "What happened to

yer skirt?" he asked, eyeing her leggings. Even stained red, they left nothing to the imagination.

"What happened to your kilt?" Her eyes darted to his obvious lack of clothing.

"I told ye to go to Mistwood. Instead, ye came back for me."

"Glenna found me and told me what happened."

"Ye shoulda followed my orders. Ye're lucky ye weren't killed!"

Avery didn't care for the accusatory tone even if it came from his fear. She planted her hands on her hips. "I hate to break it to you, Xavier, but you mated a defiant, willful, and disobedient woman who will never do what you say unless she wants to."

At first he stared at her openmouthed, but then a deep, rumbling laugh shook his chest. "Aye, I suppose I did. And I wouldn't have it any other way."

CHAPTER THIRTY

Paragon

Aborella arrived at the gates of the Obsidian Palace, feeling stronger than ever before. Her skin once again glowed with her natural deep purple luster, and her wounds had completely healed. She'd even managed to replace a few of the tattooed magical symbols she'd lost when she was injured.

But despite her efforts to neutralize it, the tug at the bond between her and Eleanor had become a persistent and painful one. No longer could she avoid heeding the dragon's call. Which meant everything she'd learned about dragon bonds was true. She could not die of anything short of beheading as long as Eleanor lived. Eleanor could command her presence and track her by following the bond. And although the empress couldn't force Aborella to do her will, she could make it highly uncomfortable if she didn't, an unfortunate reality that had driven her back here.

"I've come to see Eleanor, empress of Paragon," Aborella told the young man at the gate. A mere boy, it seemed. She did not know his name. One of the newer recruits.

"Of course." He bowed awkwardly. "You're Aborella. She's been expecting you. I'm to escort you directly to the throne room."

"That won't be necessary. I can find her myself."

"I-I'm sorry, but I have to," he squeaked, fidgeting with the weapon at his hip as if he couldn't decide if he feared her or the potential retribution he might endure more.

She tolerated him beside her all the way up the mountain to the veranda where she crossed the jeweled mosaic of a dragon curled around a fruit tree. For the first time, she contemplated the ancient art under her feet. It had been there long before her time. Who was it? What did it mean? She'd never asked, and none of the dragons she'd encountered had ever mentioned it.

The young guard opened the door to the throne room and cleared his throat. Looking up from the mosaic, Aborella raised her chin and entered. Eleanor was waiting, standing impatiently with Ransom on the dais. She looked livid.

"I was beginning to think I'd have to hunt you down myself." Eleanor's sharp tone reverberated in the open space. "When Ransom couldn't find you in your hole, I was worried you'd deserted us."

"You told me to lie in the hole, not to stay there. I've been recovering in Hobble Glen in the back of my shoppe. It's been closed for some time, but it gave me the respite I needed to truly recover."

She scoffed. "Was that before or after you visited Everfield?"

Aborella's blood ran cold, but she raised her chin. "Before. I returned to Everfield only recently to follow up on a rumor I heard in the village during my time recovering. I overheard a man claim Everfield was the seat of the rebellion. I was on a reconnaissance mission for the kingdom but came as soon as I felt your call."

Eleanor ordered Ransom away and took a seat on her throne. The way she crossed her legs and bobbed her foot, it was clear she was annoyed. Aborella could almost hear her trying to puzzle out how Aborella had managed crawling out of that hole alone in the condition she'd been left in. But then, Eleanor had likely forgotten about her those first few weeks. The empress had no proof, just a suspicion of Aborella's dishonesty.

"What type of intelligence did you gather?" she asked, lines forming around her tight lips.

"I found nothing in Everfield itself. Only rumors substantiated by more rumors. The people seem to be bored and entertaining themselves with stories of insurrection. A mason said he'd heard the movement was gathering support but he himself supported the monarchy. You're very popular there." The secret to a great lie was to believe the words when you said them, and Aborella did in the moment. She had practiced the speech all the way from Everfield and ensured there wasn't a bit of tightness to her expression as she recited it.

She couldn't fully explain to herself why she lied to the empress. For years she'd considered the woman a friend. Yes, Eleanor had betrayed her, tortured her by burying her alive in that hole, but Aborella would be a fool to think the rebels held any more love for her than this woman on her throne. Truly, she had no friends in the five kingdoms. No one she could trust. Whether it was the promise of revenge on Eleanor or some fragment of loyalty toward Dianthe, she wasn't sure, but she was no longer willing to do the empress's will.

"Hmm." Eleanor's eyes raked over her. "You will use your gifts to try to find these rebels?"

"Of course. As soon as I return to my rooms, I will consult my crystals." She spread her hands. "There are limits, you understand. If I had a name, things would be easier, but..."

Eleanor sneered. "Yes, I am fully aware of your limitations."

Aborella bowed and started for her chambers.

"Wait." Eleanor held up her hand. "There is one thing I want you to do first, a priority over all others."

"Yes?" Aborella swallowed nervously and waited to hear the empress's will.

"The egg. I want to know when and where Raven and Gabriel's spawn will hatch. We must strike the moment the whelp emerges from the shell. All three will be at their weakest. We must kill the youngling immediately, before its power can be used against me."

Aborella bowed low. "As you wish. I'll devote all my resources to it."

With a flick of Eleanor's hand, Aborella was dismissed. She hurried to her chambers, thankful to put a locked door between them. Directly, she strode into her ritual room, but she didn't bother with her crystals. Instead, she crossed to the window and threw it open wide, whistling for her familiar. After a few long moments, Abacus landed in front of her in a flurry of silver feathers. She scratched the back of the bird's head and received a warning nip on the finger.

"I'm sorry, sweet friend. I know I've left you to your own devices far too long." Although the bird could take care of herself and had the past several months, as her familiar, the animal would not feel complete away from her magic. Abacus buried her head against her hand, her large hooked beak clacking. "Yes, I know. But I need you now. Will you help me?"

The bird bobbed her head, and Aborella stroked her feathers.

The truth was, Aborella knew exactly when Raven's whelp would be born. She'd known for over a week. It wouldn't be long now. All that was left to do was to decide what and when to tell Eleanor. She scribbled a note on a piece of parchment and bound it to Abacus's leg. "Take this to Dianthe of Everfield."

The bird flapped her silver wings and flew toward the forest beyond. Steeling her resolve, Aborella reached into the pocket of her cloak and retrieved the one item she'd stolen from Sylas and Dianthe's cottage during her stay in Everfield. If she played her cards right, she'd both punish the empress and ensure a place in her court again. All she had to do was stay one step ahead of Eleanor.

CHAPTER THIRTY-ONE

For a dragon, nothing held greater power to heal than treasure. It had been far too long since Xavier enjoyed its pleasures. The vibrations from the gold and jewels that surrounded his scales revived his strength and healed the damage the enchanted weapons had caused him.

As good as it felt though, he did not linger in his treasure room. Once he regained his strength, he shifted into his human form.

"Thank you, Glenna," he said, finding clean clothing spread out on the bench near the door. He dressed quickly, needing to find Avery. They had unfinished business.

He burst from his treasure room and headed for the stairs that led up into the east wing. He stopped short when Mistress Abernathy saw him and broke into sobs that shook the woman and echoed in the hall.

"I suppose you'll be havin' me head for what I done, but I swear to you, my laird, I didna ken I was doin' it till it was done."

With nothing but gentleness, he approached her and gripped her shoulder. "Nay. Lachlan was an evil changeling, ye ken? Had ye under his spell. I'll not blame ye for it."

"Oh, my laird. Ye're good and kind. Ye deserve better than the likes of me." She wept violently until Xavier had no choice but to pull her into his arms.

"Ah weel. Let it all out then." He patted her back. "When ye can see fit to dry your tears, I need yer help though."

"Help? What with?" She wiped under her eyes.

"Avery. Have you seen her?"

"Avery from the kitchen?" Mistress Abernathy gave him a curious look.

"Aye. She is my betrothed. I need to find her."

The woman's round shoulders shook with renewed sobs. "Your be—?"

"Why are ye cryin'?"

"I fear I've made another error. I put her in one of the servants' chambers. I didna know she was yer betrothed, or I'd have put her in a proper room."

He wiped the woman's tears. "All will be forgiven if ye just tell me whit room?"

"The one next to mine! Down the hall from the kitchen."

"Aye." He strode away from her.

"Wait! Is it true what they say then, that it was she who killed Lachlan? I didna believe, but..."

He considered that for a moment. Avery *had* delivered the fatal blow to Lachlan's heart. The beheading by Xavier was to avoid any magical healing or resurrection. Besides, if he gave Avery the full credit for the kill, Mistress Abernathy's skill as a gossip would carry the news to every corner of the *builgean*. Xavier's deepest wish was that his clan love her, love her as much as he did.

"Aye. It was she who did it."

Mistress Abernathy's hands pressed into her lips. "And I gave her a servant's room! I deserve to be flogged." Her tears began to flow anew.

He returned to her and spent more precious minutes soothing the woman before assuring her he'd sort things out with Avery.

At last he freed himself from the woman's clutches and passed through the main hall where a group of men and women were celebrating at one of the long tables.

They raised their glasses when they saw him and cheered. "The fairy is dead. The laird and chief returns. Let us drink to his health! *Slainte.*"

"*Slainte,*" the others yelled.

Everyone drank.

"Aye." Xavier clapped the men on the back but refused the whisky they offered.

"Celebrate with a whisky?" the one called Aeden asked.

Xavier shook his head. "Perhaps another time."

"I ken the woman was a sorceress the day I seen her turn whisky into water and water into whisky at the Lion and the Hare." He lowered his voice. "That's why she was immune to Lachlan's fairy magic."

"Are you sure she's a sorceress?" Xavier asked. "That sounds like a miracle. Perhaps she's truly an angel."

Murmurs and speculation continued as Xavier excused himself and hurried from the hall toward the kitchen and then around the bend toward the room Mistress Abernathy had mentioned. He raised his hand and knocked on the plain wooden door.

"Just a second," Avery yelled.

There was a clatter inside and then she opened the door quite forcefully.

"Xavier!" She seemed surprised.

"What are ye wearing?" He grimaced at her garb. Her skirts and stays were too large, and they hung off her like an ill-wrapped drape. Coupled with their dull brown color, the ensemble made him long for the fairy-made blue dress the brownie had given her.

"One of Mistress Abernathy's castoffs. I only had the one outfit Nathaniel's oreads sent with me, and it was stained and torn beyond repair in the battle. I didn't take any of the clothing the brownie made for me. I didn't think I'd need it."

He made a guttural sound and backed into the hall, grabbing the first maid he could get his hands on. "Go find the tailor, Mr. MacGowan. Tell him he is needed immediately."

"It can wait, really," Avery protested.

He hoisted the fabric up on her shoulders. "Nay, it canna wait. I'll have Glenna get started on a few pieces as well. She's faster, ye ken, but Mr. MacGowan will be insulted if he's not asked."

Avery tucked her freshly washed hair behind her ears. "Xavier, we need to talk about when we're going ba—"

He grabbed her and kissed her firmly on the lips until she sagged against him like a sack of flour. He stood her back on her feet and slipped his hand into hers.

"First, come with me."

He led her from the room, through the castle, and up the stairs to the highest point of the highest tower. The view from here was his favorite in the castle. One could see the entire village from its window, all the way to the kirk. He stared at the cross on the steeple and tried to find the words he wanted to say to her.

"I ken these are not ideal circumstances, and ye need to

go back from whence ye came." She opened her mouth to speak, but he silenced her with a gentle press of his finger to her lips. "Ye're my mate. I can't bear to be away from ye long. So I 'ave no choice but to go with ye."

"Oh, Xavier..."

There was something else he didn't mention—that strange voice he'd heard in the dungeon. It wasn't Glenna who'd told him that taking back Paragon was *his* war. Had it been the goddess? A vivid hallucination? He supposed he'd never know for sure, but it was clear to him that helping his siblings was the right thing to do. He didn't mention that to Avery now because being with her was the only thing that mattered anyway. Mysterious voice or no, he'd go with her because he had to be near her. Everything else was just geography.

"I have one condition," he added, "one thing I want ye to do for me before I make arrangements to leave with ye."

She raised her eyebrows. "Anything. What?"

He took her face in his hands. "I want ye to marry me."

Avery blinked slowly. Had he just asked her to marry him? She couldn't have heard him correctly. "Huh?"

"Marry me. Tomorrow. In that kirk." He pointed to the chapel on the hill, barely visible in the light of the full moon.

"We've known each other... less than a week." She reworked the math in her head but came to the same conclusion. It seemed far longer since she'd rescued him from the dungeon, but truly it had only been a matter of days.

"Ye mated me. A mated bond is far more permanent than a human marriage."

"True."

He stepped in closer. Darkness clouded his narrowed eyes like a gathering storm. "Ye did mean it when ye accepted the bond?" It was a statement, but there was clearly a question in it as well.

Avery scraped her teeth along her bottom lip. "I did mean it, Xavier. It was possibly the first thing I've ever been sure of in my entire life. I still mean it. I will always mean it."

He beamed, his lopsided grin holding a modicum of smug satisfaction. "Then marry me."

Avery sighed. She'd always pictured her marriage as a grand affair as her sister Raven's had been, with a dozen bridesmaids and her parents and sister looking on. She'd fantasized about a designer dress and sprays of white lilies to line the aisle. Marrying him here didn't fit the future she'd painted for herself, but then, loving a Highlander didn't either. She was officially blazing a new trail here. All of her old dreams didn't hold a candle to her new ones.

Xavier was offering to give up his life and come with her into the outside world, and all he was asking was that she marry him in the place that was home to him first. These were his people. This was his church. Which reminded her, there was something more she needed to sort out before she could rest tonight.

"Xavier, you told me Lachlan couldn't kill you because it was your magic supporting this place. That must be true, because he imprisoned you twice even though he had the chance to do more."

"Aye."

"These people aren't ready for the modern world. If you leave, what happens to them?"

He leaned a shoulder against the side of the window and stared out over the village. "Leaving and being dead are two very different things. My magic has seeped into this place for centuries. As long as I'm alive, the magic I've put in place here will survive. If Lachlan had killed me, yes, the wards would have fallen, and even if he used his own magic to replace them, the variety of crops we grow here, the animals we raise, they wouldna thrive the way they do under ma care."

"But you can't leave forever."

"Nay. I'll need to come back regularly. Maybe a month or two every year. Do ye think ye could stand bein' Lady Dunchridhe part-time?"

Avery looked out over the village toward the people who had helped her save Xavier. Some, like Aeden, had become friends. All of them needed Xavier in order to maintain the life they'd made here. And the truth was, they'd all needed her. While she had a choice—Xavier could and would come here alone if he had to—she realized she didn't want that. She cared about this place too.

"I would be honored."

"Then ye'll marry me, here, tomorrow?"

A long pause stretched between them as she contemplated his question. "Would you consider getting married twice?"

He gave her a quizzical look. She gave him a wide, sheepish smile. He didn't even ask her for an explanation.

"Aye. I'll marry ye as many times as ye like."

"It's just, my family is there."

"Aye." He raised his eyebrows. "I promise ye we'll have it in the way of yer people as well."

She stepped into his arms and raised a hand to his cheek. "Then yes, I will marry you."

Xavier beamed as if she'd given him the greatest gift he'd ever desired. He cradled her face and kissed her solidly on the mouth. Avery gave herself over to him with reckless abandon, trying her best to wrap a leg around him in her oversized clothes.

He pulled away much too quickly. "Now, let's find ye a proper room."

"What? Don't you want to stay together? In the same bed, I mean?" She frowned up at him.

He raised a scandalized eyebrow. "What type of man do ye take me for, lass? Not before we're married!"

CHAPTER THIRTY-TWO

The next morning, Avery was jarred from her slumber by Mistress Abernathy and a gaggle of her friends. It was barely dawn, but the women propped her in front of a mirror, poking and prodding her as they arranged her hair in various styles. After some insisting on her part, they allowed her to use the chamber pot and have a little breakfast, which she ate wearing only her shift as Mistress Abernathy styled her hair in a series of intricate braids.

"I really don't think this is necessary," she said. "Something simple—"

"Hush. I won't hear of it."

"What is that noise in the hall? It sounds like someone's chopping wood?"

"Oh, but that's exactly what it is," Abernathy said, her round cheeks mounding with her grin. "Xavier ordered all the furniture to be removed from his chambers and all new brought in. He didna want anything in there Lachlan had touched. Anyway, a few of the men decided it would be easier to remove if they chopped the bed into firewood. I don't blame 'em. It would be right unlucky for anyone to use it. Might hold a fairy curse."

Avery's first instinct was to laugh at the idea of anyone being afraid of cursed furniture, but then the memory of those bright green plants shooting out of the ground and spraying her with poison pollen filled her head. Thank the stars above Xavier was replacing it all. Even the thought of touching something Lachlan had been in contact with gave her the heebie-jeebies.

"Mistress Abernathy, can you help me find—"

She was cut off when a man with a narrow face and highly arched brows burst in, a bundle of wrappings in his arms.

"Ah, this is Mr. MacGowan, our tailor," Mistress Abernathy said. "He's brought your dress."

Avery's mood brightened.

"Come, lass." Mr. MacGowan beckoned. "This is my own creation. I hope ye will forgive that I did not make it specifically for ye. It was something of a labor of love actually. I keep it in my workshop to inspire me, but I believe it will fit ye with a bit of light tailoring."

She stood and peeled back the wrappings. "I'd love to try it."

"It would be my honor."

He and Mistress Abernathy helped her pull it over her shift and lace up the bodice. The dress was constructed of fine pale silk hand stitched with silver thread in an intricate pattern of falling feathers. Once laced, the bodice cinched in her waist, giving her naturally curvy shape more definition. Billowy fabric skimmed her arms to her elbows and then flared out in a wide, oblong cuff that draped to her wrist at the back of her arm but ended just past her elbow at the front. Over that, he helped her with a hooded, sleeveless coat that was the same color as Xavier's ring and constructed of fine velvet lined in pearls. It fastened at the waist with a pearl brooch. When Mr. MacGowan had finished helping her into a pannier to make the skirt appear full, the effect was breathtaking. Silver, gold, and positively regal.

"I love it."

The tailor smiled. "It suits you, and aside from letting the hem out to accommodate your height, I have few alterations to make. I'll have no problems having this ready in time."

Mistress Abernathy started to cry. "The amber brings out your eyes! Xavier is a lucky man."

Avery looked at herself in the mirror and smiled. Everything about this felt right. Better than she'd ever imagined.

After Mr. MacGowan measured her for some additional dresses—something she supposed she'd need if she came back here with Xavier on occasion—he left, and Mistress Abernathy kept her busy with choosing a menu for the feast to follow. The kitchen staff had already planned several things, and Avery made sure to keep her requests simple and easy to prepare. She told them all she expected them to attend as well.

As the afternoon sun began to descend, she changed into the now perfectly tailored dress and donned the pearl-encrusted slippers the cobbler gave her. She descended the stairs to the sound of cheers. It humbled her to see all the women who worked in the castle gathered below, dressed in their finest.

"Where are the men?" she asked Mistress Abernathy.

"Xavier wanted to be the first to see ye. They're all at the kirk."

A carriage, drawn by a handsome white horse, was

waiting for her outside the castle. One of the servants helped her inside. She looked back at Mistress Abernathy.

"Donna worry, lass. We're right behind you."

As she traveled through the village toward the kirk at the end of the road, Avery thought about her journey here. Every choice she'd made along the way had brought her closer to this, closer to Xavier. And it was with some surprise that she realized she was happy. She did not resent a single day she'd been here. She did not feel taken advantage of. She felt powerful and wanted and like her whole life, the best of times, was just ahead of her.

The carriage stopped. She peeked out the window and saw that the women from the castle had arrived in carriages behind her and now flooded into the kirk. A line of men with bagpipes formed outside the door, and Avery laughed when she saw they all had their eyes tightly scrunched shut. At the prompting of their leader, they began to play the sweetest tune she'd ever heard. Her door opened, and the driver, whom she now saw was a woman, helped her down.

The doors to the church opened and there was Xavier, standing at the altar. When he saw her, even at a distance, his body's physical response was apparent. His eyes flared, his grin broadened, and his chest seemed to puff with pride.

Placing a hand over his heart, he bowed.

She curtsied her reply.

And then he stomped his foot.

The men, who up to this point had either had their backs to her or their eyes closed, turned to look at her, and there was a collective gasp. Her cheeks warmed.

The music changed.

The world faded away. There was only Xavier and her.

Somewhere in the back of her mind, she registered an ancient-looking priest who began muttering in Gaelic. She wished she still had the mole Nathaniel had made for her. She had no idea what the priest was saying.

Thankfully, they exchanged vows in English. Their hands were bound. And then he was kissing her, and it was like someone had turned on the lights and the sound again. Her surroundings came back into sharp focus.

The cheers were deafening as he led her back to the carriage, smiling and waving. She breathed a sigh of contentment when they were finally alone.

"You are breathtaking, Mrs. Campbell."

Her cheeks heated at the name. "There's something I've forgotten to remind you of. I've mentioned it before, but I'm sure with everything you don't remember. This all happened so fast."

"Oh? What's that?"

"It's my family's tradition for women to keep our surname. I am a Tanglewood witch. My last name must remain Tanglewood."

A hint of dissatisfaction curled his lip. "Keep yer own name? You were serious about that."

She frowned. "It isn't that unusual where I'm from. It's the rule of my family."

His brows knit low on his forehead.

"If it helps, I can be Mrs. Campbell here. I don't think anyone on the outside will care what they address me as in the *builgean*."

For a moment they rode in silence, the gentle clip-clop of the horse's hooves counting down the moments as he seemed to consider her offer. Her stomach clenched. The Tanglewood name was not something she was willing to give up, not now that she understood who and what she was. Relief came in the form of his lopsided grin and a nod.

"Aye. In Paragon, we go only by first names, ye ken? The idea should not bother me."

"But it does." She saw the slight damping of his smile.

He hesitated a moment, then shook his head. "Nay. I have ye as ma mate. People can call ye whatever they want as long as they respect this and the bond it represents." He held up their joined hands, and the beautifully cut golden-topaz-and-diamond ring that looked so much like his own sparkled in the low light.

They arrived back at the castle, and he helped her down from the carriage, ushering her into the grand hall where a feast was set. Xavier introduced her to the guests, and she tried her best to remember everyone's names, but there were far too many to commit to memory. What she did remember was the thankfulness, the warm and heartfelt words of gratitude for her ending Lachlan's reign. And although she tried to explain that she couldn't have done it without Xavier, the clan seemed convinced that the glory should go to her.

"I'd do it again, you know," she told Xavier. "I'm not a killer, but I don't regret turning Tàirn around or ending Lachlan."

"Good," Xavier said. "Ye shouldna regret bein' a hero."

By the time they had the luxury of a seat at the head table, her feet hurt and her stomach was growling. The hall quieted and the bard, the same one she'd first seen at the Lion and the Hare, began to play. He played the same tune, but the words sounded different.

"What's he saying?" she asked, wishing again she'd not lost Nathaniel's magic.

"It's about ye," he said. "It's a song about how ye freed the village, killed Lachlan, and rescued the dragon."

"That's flattering." She squeezed Xavier's hand beneath the table.

"Aye. Already writin' songs about ye." He winked. "Ye'll make a fine lady."

She looked out across their guests, her clan, and decided that come what may, she would try to be.

Although Xavier had wanted to do right by Avery by having her sleep in a different room the night before, now that they were married, he struggled to maintain his patience. He wanted her, enough that his inner beast roiled uncomfortably beneath his skin. He hadn't been with her since she'd consented to be his mate, and his innermost instincts craved to mark her as his own.

No sooner had she finished eating than he started the process of saying their goodbyes and moving her in measured increments toward their chambers. Thankfully, she didn't fight him on that and soon the door was closed behind them.

Avery gave a sigh of relief. "I thought we'd never get out of—"

He cut her off with a kiss. Thank the Mountain, she didn't resist when he drew her to him and covered her mouth with his own. His mating trill rumbled against her chest. Laughing, she playfully thrust him away, hard enough he actually took a step back.

"Ye're stronger."

"Yes. Whatever brand of witch I am, I fight like a superhero."

"Whit's a superhero?"

"Never mind. Get me out of this dress. I can hardly breathe."

That he would happily help her with. A talon extended

from his right hand, and he sliced through her laces. She raised her eyebrows as the gown fell to the floor. "I only meant for you to untie me, but I suppose that will work."

"Come, wife." When he reached for her, she dodged his hungry fingers, seeming to revel in her newfound speed. He grunted. Xavier narrowed his eyes and grinned at the challenge. "I can think o' no better way ta test yer newfound abilities than with ye under me."

"You put a ring on my finger, and you think you can bed me anytime you wish?" she taunted playfully.

"Aye," Xavier growled. Once more, he tried for her and she sidestepped his reach. "That's the way of things. Now come to me."

She shook her head, a few tendrils of hair falling from her braids and framing her face. "You can have me when you can catch me."

"Do I have yer word on that?" He gave her a low warning growl. If that was the game she wished to play, he'd be happy to oblige. He lowered into a predatory crouch.

She responded by dropping her shift, leaving herself naked across the bed from him. His vision focused in the way of a dragon. He noticed every hair on her arms, every microscopic shift of her skin.

He dived across the bed, his wings knocking a tapestry off the wall as he pivoted midflight. She was faster now than any human, but she could not fly. He snagged her waist near the window, and she turned to him, wild-eyed and breathless.

Sweeping her into his arms, he tossed her facedown on the bed to the sound of her squeals, then hitched his fingers into her hips and drew her to the edge on her knees. She looked over her shoulder at him, the luscious mound of her arse in the air, begging for him to take her. Her chest rose and fell in pants. He could hear her heart pounding in her chest.

Drawing his hand back, he smacked her bottom hard enough to get her attention. "That's fur teasin' me."

She fisted the fur blanket on the bed and gave a sultry moan. "I think I should tease you more often."

"Say yer mine."

She gave him a defiant smile.

He spanked her again.

She spread her knees wider. "Xavier, please. I'm going to combust."

He trailed a finger between her legs, into her moist heat. She was wet and hot, and his feral need for her was almost uncontrollable. Almost.

He dropped his kilt and positioned himself at her opening. His dragon chuffed to bury himself in her. "Say you're mine, wife."

She gazed over her shoulder at him through her lashes, her heavy lids halfway closed. "I'm yours. Always."

He drove into her, burying himself inside her in one slick thrust. She moaned, clawed the bed, and pushed back against him. He skimmed his hand along her waist, cupped one of her breasts, and pinched her nipple.

She moaned again and ground against him. "Xavier."

"Say it again."

"I'm yours. Only yours."

He drew back slowly and thrust into her again. This time she cried out and her muscles gripped him in a way that was sweet torture. He circled her waist with his hands and started to move in a gentle rhythm. But she met his gentle strokes with hard, sharp bucks, driving his thrusts deeper. He stroked along her spine, her skin, soft as silk.

"More," she cried.

And that was all he could take with being gentle. He spread his wings and pounded into her. He worked one knee onto the bed, and she spread wider to accommodate him. He filled her completely, her body tight around him until his thrusts became almost frantic as she clawed the fur and begged him for more. Finally her body seized, and she cried out, her inner muscles gripping him in a delicious rhythm that sent him over the edge.

As he released inside her, the possessive growl that tore from his chest rattled the walls. He supported her through the aftershocks, then collapsed onto the bed beside her.

"By the Mountain, you'll be the death of me, woman."

She laughed. "I think I'm the one wandering into the dragon's den."

"I didna hurt ye, did I?"

"You didn't."

"Good. I was afraid I got a bit rough with ye. Every time I try to be gentle, ye drive me harder. Makin' love to ye is like doin' battle."

"I like it rough," she said, and he noticed her cheeks pinkened. "I never knew that about myself until I met you. You've unlocked so many secrets for me, Xavier."

He glanced down his body toward his cock. "If the key fits."

She laughed. "You know I mean more than that. Don't you think it's like a miracle that we were born worlds apart, in different times, from different species, and somehow we found each other, like... soul mates?"

Finding her hand, he threaded his fingers into hers until the metal bands of their rings clinked together. "Maybe not. I did pray to the goddess of the mountain to send you to me."

"You did?" She rose on one elbow and looked down at him inquisitively.

He gave a crooked smile. "I'd been in that dungeon for so long. I thought I might lose my mind, so I got down on my knees and prayed for a way to escape or for death. I thought I'd improve my chances with the goddess if I gave her a choice, ye ken? I was never a vera religious dragon, even when I lived in the mountain. It's a hard thing to have faith in something ye canna see when yer world is full of trickery, magic, and illusion. But when I prayed to her, I did so earnestly." He sucked in a breath and slowly let it out. "And then ye were standing there, just as if the goddess had opened heaven and sent ye herself. Ye were a sight. That beautiful ebony hair, yer eyes the color of the loch on a rare sunny day. Ye are beautiful, Avery. I thought ye were a goddess when ye opened the gate." He turned his head to look at her. "I was right. Ye are a goddess." He placed a firm kiss on her forehead.

"My sister told me we are descended from the goddess Circe."

"Truly? By the Mountain, I guess the goddess did send ye then."

She snorted. "I came of my own free will. I didn't believe Raven until now, but when I wielded Fairy Killer against Lachlan, I felt like a different person. I could feel energy inside that was never there before. I felt like a goddess."

He kissed her gently. "Aye. Ye are, and a blessing to me, Avery mine."

"Tell me you're mine as well."

He shifted on top of her, ready again and wanting her desperately. She wrapped her arms and legs around him.

"I am yours, Avery Tanglewood, until my dragon scales and jeweled heart turn to dust."

He took her again then, showing her with his body everything he couldn't say with his words.

CHAPTER THIRTY-THREE

After a short honeymoon, Avery agreed to give Xavier time to begin the process of healing his clan from Lachlan's rule. But eventually they could put off going back to the modern world no longer.

Xavier appointed an old friend named Bernard to lead the clan in his absence. Avery thought of Bernard as a kind old grizzly bear of a man, big and cuddly but capable of tearing his enemies apart if provoked. The Scot took the position seriously, and it was clear to Avery that Xavier trusted him completely.

They left for the ward on foot, considering they couldn't take Tàirn with them where they were going. When Avery grew tired, Xavier scooped her into his arms and flew her the rest of the way. They passed through the door out of the *builgean*, and Xavier flew her to safety at the base of the mountain.

Avery assumed they'd need to hike to the nearest cottage to call Nathaniel for a ride, but his vehicle was waiting on the side of the road, Emory in the driver's seat. When Nathaniel saw them, he sprang from the car and bolted across the distance where he embraced first Avery and then Xavier with unrestrained relief.

"Thank the Mountain!" Nathaniel said.

Avery shook her head. "How did you know we'd be here? It's been weeks."

"Five and a half." Nathaniel took her by the shoulders and shook gently. "We've all been worried sick. Nick offered to go in after you, but without any information about what happened to you, it was too dangerous. For all we knew, you were killed instantly by something inside the *builgean*. We couldn't allow him to risk his life too, although it took Rowan to stop him. Raven has been beside herself with worry." He tugged at the cuff of his shirt. "All we could do was wait. I'm only here because my tarot cards suggested you'd return soon. Of course, divination is an often-inaccurate discipline. We've been waiting here daily all week."

An icy wind sheared off the side of the mountain and Avery instinctively pressed herself into Xavier's side. Nathaniel's penetrating gaze scanned both of them before locking on the ring on her finger. One of his eyebrows arched, and he gave his brother a curious look.

"What exactly kept you so long, Avery?" he asked through a growing grin.

"I'll thank ye to get my wife out of the cold," Xavier demanded.

Nathaniel sputtered. "Wife?" When Xavier glared at him sternly, Nathaniel shook his head and pointed toward the car. "Please. There will be plenty of time to speak on the way to Mistwood."

Avery hurried to the vehicle, but Xavier seemed perplexed. He ran his hand along the shiny black exterior, frowning. She was halfway into the back seat when she noticed him scowling at the sedan.

"You've never ridden in a car?" Of course, she should have guessed he hadn't, but it was still hard to believe. She held out her hand. "I promise you, the ride is smoother than Tàirn's."

He hesitated for only a second, put his hand in hers, and crawled in beside her.

"You're married?" Raven took Avery's hand in her own and shifted the ring back and forth under the light. She widened her eyes at Clarissa, who looked just as flabbergasted at the revelation.

Avery had tried to explain everything to Nathaniel on the long ride to Mistwood, but there weren't words for what she'd experienced. She felt like an entirely new person. She'd changed so much over the past five weeks. How did she even begin to explain how different she was, how she'd experienced love and done things she never thought she could in order to save an entire clan from an evil supernatural being? It sounded so over the top, so unrealistic.

"Do you love him?" Raven had stopped inspecting the ring and was staring, expression quite serious, into her eyes.

Avery blinked. "Like I've never loved anyone aside from you and Mom. I love him like he's the thing that has kept my heart beating my whole life without my realizing it. I love him like I'd walk through fire to be with him."

"Wow." Clarissa rubbed the side of her jaw. "She's not just married; she's mated."

Avery stared down at her ring, feeling herself glow as bright as the stone. "Yes, I'm mated."

Raven pulled her into a hug, and Clarissa wrapped her arms around both of them and squeezed. But Avery hadn't even told them the best part. She pulled back and took her sisters' hands in her own. "I'm also a witch."

"What?" Clarissa shook her head.

"But you can't be. You passed through the ward," Raven said.

"As it turns out, I'm immune to magic. I can pass through any ward, Raven. The reason I could always hold Charlie is because I was entirely immune to his or her defenses in the beginning and then, by the time we all lost our powers, my little niece or nephew was used to me."

"No shit!" Clarissa blurted.

Raven simply shook her head.

"Go ahead. Attack me with your magic. Try it out," Avery offered, smiling.

"I'm not going to attack—" Raven began, but Clarissa's voice already filled the kitchen.

A fork flew from the table and raced toward Avery's eye. She lifted her skirt and kicked in a rounded swipe that knocked the fork harmlessly aside.

"Not that way," Avery said. "Although now you've seen another of my newfound abilities. I can fight like a freaking ninja!"

"That's badass." Clarissa spread her hands. "Okay. What kind of magic did you have in mind?"

"Try to poison me or put me to sleep."

Raven raised her hands. "This isn't a good idea."

But Clarissa was already singing. Avery quirked her eyebrow, waiting for something to happen. She remained unscathed.

She shrugged. "See?"

"I was trying to set you on fire," Clarissa said. "I've used that one before. I know it works."

Avery shrugged. "Nothing magical works on me."

Raven drew her into a hug and squealed. "My God, Avery, you really are a witch!"

"Really and truly." She pulled away, offering Raven an apologetic look. "Now, I've got to get out of these clothes. You have no idea how heavy these skirts are or how much I've missed makeup." She headed for the stairs and the room where she'd stayed before this all began.

Raven called after her. "Avery, I hope you know how happy I am for you. You're positively glowing."

She was about to say thank you when the word *glowing* sparked a thought. "How is Charlie?"

Raven glanced at Clarissa before answering. "Before you take that shower, let me show you."

She led the way toward Nathaniel's office. "We moved Charlie in here so that Gabriel could work at Nathaniel's desk and be nearby. We're afraid to leave him or her anymore, even for a second."

They entered the large room with its bookshelf-lined walls, and Raven pointed toward the fire. Avery's throat caught at what she saw there. The egg was huge. It had at least doubled in size since Avery had last seen it, and the shell had smoothed, its formerly pearl-like exterior now silky.

"Oh my God," Avery murmured.

"Gabriel thinks Charlie will be born any day now. He says this happens right before. I've never seen anything grow this fast, Avery. This past week... I was worried you'd miss it."

Avery found her hand and squeezed. "I'm so glad I made it in time. Oh my God, Raven, you're going to have a baby. An actual living and breathing baby. Any day now."

Raven smiled, but Avery could see the worry lines form around her mouth. Her worry was warranted. No one knew what would come out of that egg. It could look like a dragon or like a human child. No one in the history of dragons and witches, as far as any of the dragon siblings were aware, had ever birthed a dragon/witch hybrid. The folklore though was clear. The citizens of Paragon were taught this offspring would be a monster, a nightmare, a soulless killing machine with unlimited power that never tired in its thirst for destruction.

"Raven?" Her sister turned to her, and Clarissa rubbed her shoulder supportively. "Whatever comes out of that egg, I can handle it. I'll be immune to it. Do you understand? I'll help you."

Tears formed in Raven's eyes and she hugged Avery, hard enough to make it count. "Go. Change. You must be dying for a hot shower," Raven said. "I can't imagine what it's been like for you in that... bubble all this time."

Avery sighed. "Honestly, I had the time of my life."

CHAPTER THIRTY-FOUR

Xavier opened the refrigerator door, closed it again. Opened it. Closed it. A tiny light in a glass bulb illuminated all the food, a small cellar's worth stored on glass shelves. The inside stayed cold all the time without the benefit of ice or the outdoors.

He raised an eyebrow, opened the door again, and grabbed a container of chicken in a yellowish sauce. He sniffed it skeptically.

"I can get you a plate," Avery said.

He turned to find her standing behind him in the same style of clothing the other women wore here, a pair of form-fitting blue breeches and a navy-blue shirt that clung to her like a second skin. He quashed the urge to cover her with his own body as if she were naked. This was the way in this place, although how men functioned here without a permanent *stauner,* he had no idea.

"Are ye cold? Might ye be more comfortable in a sweater?" He stared at her breasts, the texture of lace visible through the stretchy fabric of her shirt.

She shook her head, her lips spreading into a lazy smile

as if she saw right through him. "No. It's a comfortable seventy-two degrees in here. Besides, how could you stare at my tits through a sweater?"

He grunted and jerked his gaze from her chest to her face. "Well, ye have them there for all to see, Avery, in all their glory. Whit do ye expect?"

She laughed. "The same thing you expected from me the first time I saw your bare knees." She glanced salaciously at the hem of his kilt and bobbed her eyebrows.

"That's not the same and ye know it."

She made a low, lecherous sound. "That's what you think. One flash of a well-muscled calf and I'm wet between the legs."

"Avery!"

"You'll get used to it," she promised, her eyes glinting with laughter. She took the container from him. "This is Laurel's famous curried chicken salad. I'll make you a sandwich. Have a seat."

With a jab of her chin, she indicated a stool next to the counter and he reluctantly sat. His kilt rode up and he was tempted to straighten it. Instead, he raised an eyebrow at her and left his knee bare.

She narrowed her eyes. "Playing with fire?"

"Come warm yer hands."

She rolled her eyes at him and smirked at the sandwich she was making. "How did things go with your siblings?"

He scratched the back of his head. "Gabriel is still an arse, but I suppose anyone would be in his position. He's the heir, ye ken. The rest of us are spares as far as the Mountain is concerned. Expendable. But it's Gabriel should be on the throne. What Mother is doing is liable to get people killed. The goddess won't tolerate it forever."

A plate clanked down in front of him with bread

slathered in a thick layer of the chicken. Avery wiped off the knife she was using on the top slice, and Xavier couldn't help but be reminded of a warrior wiping blood from his blade. She carried a sort of intensity now that she hadn't had before. It was right damn sexy. He picked up the sandwich and took a giant bite, never breaking eye contact.

She sat across from him and folded her arms on the table. "Don't take this the wrong way, but you seem more accepting than I would be if I found out my mother was a killer."

He swallowed before answering. "I was ne'er the favorite, ye ken? I'm not surprised Mother is a killer because I never cared much for the woman. To be honest, it was Killian who raised me—that was her consort, my biological father—and I mourned him centuries ago. This new revelation, it does not surprise me as much as ye might think it should." He shrugged as he placed his food on the plate. Thoughts of his mother's coldness and the evil done to Marius turned his stomach. "It's different for Nathaniel. He was always close to our mother. Never fought in the pits with the rest of us. And Gabriel, he's the one that's got to oust the madwoman without getting himself, his wife, or his whelp killed. It hasna as much to do with me, really. I'm here for you before them."

"Me?" She chuckled. "I've little to do with it aside from helping my sister."

He frowned. "Haven't they explained to you that you're one of the Three Sisters?"

She scoffed. "I know. Raven, Clarissa, and I are sister witches. Our magic binds us together. The Three Sisters. It's actually the name of my mom's bar. Apparently there's a history of magic in the Tanglewood family."

He shook his head. "Aye, all that, but more as well. The

Three Sister Witches was a story told to us when we were young. We thought it was folklore, ye ken, not anything real. Something to keep us up at night. Make us do our chores."

"There's a story from Paragon that makes us out to be boogeymen? Great."

"No exactly. As the story goes, centuries ago there was a dragon who fell in love with a witch, the queen of Darnuith—that's the witch kingdom of Paragon—and he came under her thrall. She used him to attack Paragon and try to overthrow the kingdom. My uncle Brynhoff was credited with thwarting the attack and killing both the dragon and the witch. It was the type of political story that all of us in the palace knew was probably load of dung, somethin' invented at the time to lead people to idolize the king. In truth, Brynhoff was ne'er much of a fighter. If he hadna used the element of surprise to kill Marius, he'd have ne'er gotten 'way with it. Marius was a damn good swordsman."

Avery circled her hand impatiently. "So what does this have to do with the three sisters?"

He lowered his voice, digging into the tale. "Right. Right. Legend has it that the witch queen of Darnuith was one of three sisters herself, and the other two were enraged when they heard their sister was murdered. They cursed the kingdom of Paragon and vowed that one day three sisters—their direct descendants—would enact their revenge and topple the kingdom of Paragon. 'Twas said that when they returned, lava would flow and the mountain would shake. One of these three will have enthralled a dragon, and their offspring will be a monster with the power to bring about the end of the kingdom as we know it." He leaned in. "It's why all dragons are forbidden from mating with witches. It seems my brothers and I have been naughty dragons, eh?" He grinned and took another bite of sandwich.

Avery drummed her fingers on the table. "So Charlie is presumably the aforementioned monster?"

"Aye."

"And we are the foretold sisters destined to destroy the kingdom?"

"Aye."

"Great."

"About that, it seems now, in context, the others believe the legend isna about destroying Paragon itself but the kingdom of Paragon. 'Tis about overthrowing our evil mother and reclaiming the throne for the goddess. That's what I want to help wi'. Ye and I, I ken once we succeed in gettin' Gabriel and Raven on the throne, can go on wi' our lives."

"Right." Her face fell.

"Are ye worried about doing it? Ye're a good fighter. And Gabriel says his wife and Clarissa are powerful witches. Ye're foretold to survive."

She blinked and looked up at him. "I was just thinking, what does going on with our lives look like to you? I mean, after this is all over?"

Lines formed around her lips again and Xavier noted the tension in her shoulders. "You're wondering if I'll want to stay in Paragon?"

"Yes."

"Nae."

"You don't miss home?"

He grinned at her and gave her a wink. "I thought ye understood. Home is where you are, *mo ghaol*. With the exception of taking care of my clan, I will go where you go."

Avery leaned across the table and kissed him solidly on

the mouth, only pulling apart when they heard her sister scream.

"AVERY! AVERY!" RAVEN SCREAMED HER NAME FROM the second floor.

Avery sprinted for the stairs, Xavier right behind her. They pulled up short outside the door to Nathaniel's office. Raven and Gabriel stood frozen in the center of the room, staring toward the fire where the egg, now almost as big as the opening to the fireplace, was rocking back and forth on the grill. A hairline crack ran the length of its shell.

"Oh my God," Avery whispered. "It's hatching. What do we do?"

No one answered her.

"Seriously, what do people in your world do?" She glanced between Gabriel and Xavier, but both had practically gone catatonic at the sight. "Should someone boil water? Should we take it out of the fire?"

Nathaniel arrived with Clarissa in tow, Maiara and Alexander behind them. Avery moved to stand next to Raven, and the four filed in behind her, mouths agape.

Nathaniel stared at the egg in wonder. "By the Mountain, it's happening."

Avery repeated herself to the new arrivals. "What are we supposed to do? Are we supposed to help it hatch or let it fend for itself?"

Maiara leaned toward the egg and sniffed, then frowned. Maiara's dark eyes found hers. "I do not know this type of birth, but I smell... I don't know the word." She pressed her narrow fingers to her chin. "I sense that we should help it."

"Dragon males never see this," Gabriel muttered, rubbing his neck. "It's not allowed."

Raven started at the statement, blinking from her reverie. "We need Rowan."

"I'm here!" Rowan entered the room with Nick, who stopped in the doorway rather than further crowd the room. She approached the fire. "I've never done this." She looked wide-eyed between Raven and Avery. "I've read... I mean, they taught us—myself and the other Highborn females—that sometimes the baby isn't strong enough to get out and the mother has to help pull the shell apart with her talons."

Raven rushed forward and reached for the egg, then yelped and tugged her hands back. "The shell is too hot. Why is the shell hot? It's never been hot to the touch before."

Rowan frowned. "Sorry, I forgot about that part. Right before birth, the shell starts taking on heat. We're supposed to pull it out of the fire. May I? Or would you rather, Gabriel—"

"Just do it," Raven cried, cradling her burnt fingers.

Without hesitation, Rowan reached in and gently lifted the egg from the fireplace grate. She carefully rested it on the Persian rug in front of the desk.

"At least it didn't zap you." Avery hovered nearby in case Rowan needed help.

"Right." Rowan frowned. "I... I'm not sure that's a good sign."

Raven's face turned ashen, and Avery hugged her shoulders to offer support.

"Can't you bust out some talons and get it done, Rowan?" Avery said.

Raven nodded.

"I would, but I'm afraid." Rowan pushed her dark curls

over her shoulder. "My talons will bounce right off dragon scales. But this baby is part witch. If Charlie's human side has manifested first and it's not a dragon in there, my talons could injure or kill him or her in the process of opening the shell. We need a way to see what's inside."

"We need Tobias," Avery said. "He's a doctor. He can help."

"He and Sabrina are still asleep. It's barely twilight," Raven said.

"Fuck that. Consider me his new alarm clock." Avery bolted from the room and careened around the corner and down the stairs, into the basement where Tobias was staying with his vampire mate.

"Help! Tobias, you need to come. Now."

She grabbed the dragon by the neck of his royal-blue pajamas and hauled him out of bed. He stumbled onto his feet, blinking.

"Whoa." The blond dragon rubbed his eyes. Behind him, Sabrina lifted her head. "What's going on?"

"It's Charlie... The egg is hatching. Slowly. Rowan thinks—"

Tobias grabbed his black doctor's bag from the end of the bed. "Lead the way."

"I'm right behind you," Sabrina said.

She led them back to Nathaniel's office where Rowan and Gabriel were hunched over the egg.

"There's something wrong," Gabriel said when he saw his brother. "I can feel it."

A deep wrinkle formed between Tobias's brows. Kneeling beside the egg, he opened his bag and removed his stethoscope. He listened, then shook his head. "I can hear a heartbeat, but it's too slow. We need to get Charlie out of there."

Raven gasped.

Tobias took her hands. "Raven, it's a good, strong heartbeat, just slow. I don't want to scare you, but I'm concerned that your baby isn't strong enough to crack the shell from the inside. We need to help free it."

Rowan's fists opened and closed as if she wanted to take action but feared the result. "But if it's not a dragon in there, won't our talons hurt it?"

"Possibly. That's a risk we face, but I have to trust that Mother Nature thought of that. Whatever this baby looks like on the outside, both Gabriel and Raven contributed to their genes. Let's trust that this hatchling is most similar to a dragon." Tobias looked between Rowan and Gabriel. "My advice is to try to pry the crack apart rather than stab directly into the shell."

Gabriel sprouted talons. "I'll do it."

"Gabriel..." Raven pressed a hand to her chest.

He gave her a steadying gaze. "Trust me."

She nodded. He inserted his claws on each side of the crack and pulled, his muscles straining against his shirt with the effort.

When it was clear he was struggling, Rowan came to his aid. "Maybe if we both..."

"Try," Gabriel said.

She sprouted her own smaller set of talons and went to work on the crack. But the egg wouldn't budge.

"Step aside." Xavier drew his dirk. "I'll try ma blade."

Avery placed a hand on his arm. "No, it could slip and hurt the baby. A dragon's talons are curved. That's too straight and sharp."

"I agree," Gabriel said. "Xavier, lend us your strength instead."

Xavier sheathed his weapon and wedged himself among

the others, trying to dig his fingers into the crack. Nothing worked. The egg might as well have been made of solid marble.

Nick scoffed. "You were worried about the knife. I'm not sure a jackhammer could get into that thing."

Alexander, who looked like he wanted to help but couldn't find a place around the egg, gave him a hard, desperate look. "If three dragons can't get into it, you're right about that."

Maiara stroked the healing amulet around her neck. "Perhaps the young isn't ready to be born yet."

Tobias shook his head. "I don't think so. The heart rate is slowing. The baby is in distress. We have to get it out of there."

Clarissa crossed her arms. "All I know is that if I were in there, I'd be afraid to come out with all those talons around me."

A thought popped into Avery's head. She grabbed Clarissa's shoulders and shook. "You're a genius."

"I am?"

Avery pushed the dragons aside to get to the egg. "Charlie is protecting himself!"

Everyone stopped to stare at her. "Think about it. Charlie isn't zapping you anymore with magic because it's found another way. This baby has woven a ward around itself within the shell. The problem is, in keeping itself safe from the outside world, it's also trapping itself inside. Charlie is half witch. We keep treating it like it's a dragon, but it has magic too."

Clarissa approached the egg. "Rowan, you said the dragon mother usually helps the eggs hatch, right?"

"Sometimes the babies are strong enough to do it on

their own but yes, it is common for the mother to help," Rowan answered in an exasperated tone.

"Well, this baby's mother isn't a dragon. She's a witch," Clarissa said.

Raven closed her eyes and nodded. "Of course. Avery, you're brilliant! We need to open it with magic, not brute force."

"Exactly," Clarissa said.

The dragons backed away from the egg as Avery, Clarissa, and Raven stepped forward. "I'll neutralize Charlie's magic," Avery said, kneeling beside one point of the egg.

"I'll sing to crack the shell." Clarissa positioned herself at the opposite end from Avery.

Raven glanced between the two of them and knelt at the middle of the egg. "I'll pull the shell apart. I think Charlie needs to see me first." They all exchanged glances and tentative nods.

Avery placed her hands on the egg and experienced the now familiar tingling she associated with magical energy. Scalding heat like pavement in summer burned her palms, but she forced herself to hold on. "It's okay, Charlie. We're here to help." The magic fizzled beneath her touch and the shell cooled. "I think the ward is down."

Clarissa began to sing a soft tune Avery recognized as a lullaby. The music itself was soothing, but the power it held caused cracks to branch across the shell like a growing spiderweb.

Avery met Raven's panicked gaze with calm confidence. "You can do this. Let's meet your baby."

Raven dug her fingers into the widest part of the opening and pulled. A chunk of shell broke off. Avery noticed it was bright gold on the inside and was surprised when the scent of honey reached her nostrils.

"Do you smell that?" Avery whispered.

Raven ignored her to tear away another chunk. It wasn't easy. Even with Clarissa helping, Avery could see Raven break a sweat from the effort. Finally the hole was big enough to see inside. Something downy and white shifted, and a human fist punched out from the shell, chubby and golden.

"Help me," Raven demanded.

Avery started tearing at the shell. Clarissa, still singing, helped too. For a moment, all Avery could see was her sister's hands and hair as they worked over the egg.

The crack of splitting stone echoed through the room, and the shell completely shattered. Clarissa stopped singing. Charlie came into view, steadied between Raven's hands.

"It's a girl," Clarissa whispered.

Avery couldn't speak. Charlie did not look like a dragon at all. She was the size of a six-month-old baby, golden-skinned, with silky blond curls as pale as spiderwebs.

"She has your eyes," Avery said breathlessly, marveling at the bright blue.

Gabriel knelt down beside Raven and brushed Charlie's curls aside to expose two crescent-shaped birthmarks beside her right temple. "She has at least one thing from me." He brushed the hair off the back of her neck, and Avery spotted the three vee-shaped ridges there, indicative of their species. She also noticed two ridges below her shoulder blades.

"Are those...?"

Gabriel stroked along the baby's spine. Everyone in the room gasped as two white wings unraveled, unlike any dragon wings Avery had ever seen. They had no talon at the arc, or scales, or fleshy webbing. Instead, they were covered in downy white feathers.

"How?" Raven asked. Her gaze sought out Rowan's. "Is this… normal?"

Rowan shook her head, eyes bulging.

"She is a gift from the Great Spirit. It is a sign," Maiara said.

Clarissa circled Charlie and Raven to get a better look. "She's not a dragon; she's an angel."

As if in response, Charlie chose that moment to belch, sending a ball of fire coursing from her mouth. It singed Raven's hair, and Gabriel had to pat out the fire with his bare hand.

"Oh, she's a dragon," he said, taking her into his arms and bounced her gently. His grin was filled with nothing but pride.

Avery rose, stepped over the golden shell fragments, and took refuge in Xavier's arms, suddenly overwhelmed by it all. The joy of having a new baby niece. The fear of the unexpected. The deep desire to protect the people in this room.

"Aye. It's a wee bit strange, but they're just a few feathers." He tipped her face up to look at him. He gave her wink. "Ye're not going weak in the knees on me now, are ye? There wasna even any blood."

As always, Xavier's crooked smile held nothing but lighthearted joviality. Nothing ever seemed to shake him. He was her rock.

On tiptoe, she kissed him. "Not a chance."

"She'll need fresh meat and blood." Nathaniel moved around the desk.

"Blood?" Raven's voice rose an octave.

"No worries. I'll call the butcher." Nathaniel reached

for the phone. His hand froze as the silver candle on his desk blazed to life.

Clarissa's brow furrowed deeply. "I thought you said you gave the other shadow-mail candle to Sylas?"

"I did. Someone hit the lights."

Avery slapped the switch, plunging the room into darkness. All of them stared as the shadow-mail candle's light flickered. Shadows danced along the desktop. Dark and light twisted together. Charlie mewled softly in the silent room.

The shadows bent into letters. Nathaniel's eyes widened. Avery leaned forward to read what was written across the light.

She's coming. Run.

CHAPTER THIRTY-FIVE

One of the keys to a successful existence, Aborella mused, was understanding control—when you had it, when you didn't, and when you could change the locus to your advantage. She'd hesitated to tell Eleanor about her vision, but in the end there was only so long an egg could take to hatch. She'd described her vision in detail, and the empress had used her magic to bring them here.

Now she stood beside Eleanor at a crossroads in the English countryside in a place called Oxfordshire. Although they hadn't even entered Nathaniel's fortress, the empress smiled as if she'd already killed the babe within. She definitely looked the part of the Angel of Death. Dressed in head-to-toe black leather, her eyes were winged with dark kohl, her lips painted blood red. Two jewel-encrusted daggers hung from scabbards strapped to each of her thighs. Why she'd come armed, Aborella couldn't fathom. The empress's magic was far deadlier than any physical weapon, and she'd brought Aborella and Ransom along to do any dirty work she couldn't accomplish herself.

"All but two of your offspring are guarding the whelp,

Eleanor. Killing it will not be easy," Aborella warned. "And, of course, there's Raven herself."

"As you've mentioned twice before." Eleanor rolled her eyes. "Honestly, Aborella, since your accident, you've become such a wet blanket."

"My accident?" Fury bloomed in the pit of Aborella's chest. She checked it and forced her jaw to loosen before saying, "Are you referring to the day Nathaniel almost killed me and you buried me alive?"

She shrugged. "I fed you my tooth, didn't I? You are standing here thanks to dragon magic."

Ransom cleared his throat. "Empress, are we in the right place? I thought Nathaniel's manor—"

"Oh, shut up. Of course we are in the right place. Can't you feel the magic?" Eleanor waved her hand toward the bucolic moor in front of them, Earth's single sun low but rising over its rolling green beauty.

Ransom shook his head slowly, his chiseled features turning pink with embarrassment. Goddess, the male was dumb. Aborella chuckled internally at the guard's blank look.

"Would you like me to attempt to blast through the wards?" Aborella brushed some dust from the cuff of the gold vilt jacket she wore. She loved the color. It brought out the blue in her amethyst skin.

"No need. I learned something from Nathaniel the last time we were together. It didn't take me long to deconstruct the spell. One is never too old to learn a new trick." Eleanor reached into a small box concealed in her belt and removed a long, thin cigarette like the ones Aborella had seen humans smoke in years gone by. Dragons had no reason to smoke. Only the Elves of Rogos made it a habit and then only from long, hand-carved pipes.

Eleanor blew a bit of fire across the end to light the tobacco and then took a long steady drag. She exhaled the smoke in a ring that formed a pentagram-shaped dial with glowing arcane symbols in each of its sectors. Eleanor dug her fingers in and turned the dial as if she were cracking a safe.

A chill ran through Aborella's bones when she felt the ward give way. Nathaniel's defenses were the most powerful work of magic Aborella had detected in some time. The idea that even this could be so easily deconstructed at the empress's whims was truly terrifying.

Ransom's eyes grew large as they stepped across the threshold onto a cobblestone path that led to the grand manor beyond. The place had sprung into existence in front of them only seconds before, and Aborella didn't miss how the magic made Ransom's hands shake. A carriage arrived, pulled by a giant black horse. There was no driver.

Ransom moved to get in, and Aborella had to stop herself from slapping the side of his head.

"It's a trap, you fool," Eleanor said, gripping Ransom's upper arm. "We fly."

She sprouted wings and soared toward the mansion. Aborella twisted into a column of smoke and manifested beside her. Ransom caught up, his hand on the rod at his hip, a Paragonian weapon meant to stun.

Once there, Eleanor raised her hands as if to blast open the door with her magic, but Aborella reached forward and tried the knob. It was unlocked. The heavy door swung open, and the three stepped inside.

"Where—" Ransom tried to speak, but Eleanor pressed a finger over his lips. Her black-painted nail was filed to a point and speared the skin under his nose. He shut up and held perfectly still. Maybe he was smarter than he looked.

Aborella pointed to the stairs. They climbed to the second level. Eleanor lifted her nose and inhaled sharply, then gestured down the hall. A light was on, and they entered an office that smelled faintly of smoke.

"What have we here?" Aborella knelt down and fished a three-inch shard of gold from under the sofa in front of the empty fireplace. She held it up between her thumb and forefinger.

"Dragon shell," Eleanor hissed. "Search the rooms. Search the entire house."

The empress left Aborella behind as she hastened from the room, seething. Ransom bumbled after her. Aborella stayed where she was. Scanning the room, her gaze caught on a splotch of silver wax on the desk, next to an empty candleholder. A breathy laugh bubbled up inside her, and she took care to suppress the sound.

That's right, Nathaniel, she thought. *Keep that with you. I can't help you without it.*

Eleanor's voice screeched from a room down the hall. "They're gone! They are all gone!"

Aborella narrowed her eyes in the direction of her empress and dropped her chin. *Oh yes, Eleanor, they are long gone. And unfortunately for you, this is only the first in a humbling string of frustrations to come.* Well, if Aborella had anything to do with it.

CHAPTER THIRTY-SIX

"No, Mom, I'm not coming home." Avery stood on the bow of the cruise ship with her cell phone to her ear, Xavier behind her. She felt his supportive kiss land on the top of her head.

"I don't understand. When will you be back?" Her mother's voice sounded desperate and Avery's stomach clenched. As usual, she was tempted to appease her. Old habits died hard. It would be so easy to just give in and say two weeks, a month. But the truth was, she wasn't sure if she'd ever set foot in New Orleans again.

"I need to be very clear about this, Mom, because I think I've been too weak to tell you the full truth in the past. It's unfair to you how I've put you off, and I apologize for that. I do. But I've done some major soul searching, and it's time for me to tell you the truth. I'm quitting the Three Sisters."

Her mother's gasp filled her ear and then the line went absolutely silent for three long breaths. "You're quitting for good?"

"Yes. I don't want to run a bar. I don't want to serve, or cook, or bartend, or be the manager or even the owner. I don't want to live in New Orleans. It's been a good experience and I've learned so much from you about business and about people, but I want more. This is my chance to move on, and I'm taking it."

"So you can work in a bookstore instead?" Her mother's tone was incredulous.

"No. This isn't about what I'm going to do instead. This is about what I'm not going to do. I am not going to take over the Three Sisters from you. I'm not sure exactly what I want to do with my life. Maybe I'll go back to college. Maybe I'll try something new. What I do know is that I won't be coming home anytime soon. I want you to hire my replacement. You can't keep waiting for me. It's time for you to move on."

Silence. "I suppose this goes for Raven too?"

"Yes. We're together and we're safe."

"I should have known when she married Gabriel that things would change."

"This isn't about Gabriel." Avery sighed. "Raven spent so many years a prisoner to her illness, and you and I, we lived our lives around Raven. Now that she's free, I want to be free too. We're going to travel, and yes, Gabriel is funding it. This isn't goodbye forever. I just can't have you holding on, thinking we'll be back any day now. You need to look out for yourself and your business. Hire my replacement. Move on with your life."

"So this is what it feels like to have an empty nest." Her mother released a deep sigh.

"Don't you think it's time?" As hard as it had been for Avery to rip the Band-Aid off, now that it was over, a deep sense of relief came over her. "It might not seem like it now, but this will be good for you too, Mom."

Her mother's long silence on the other end of the line caused Avery to question if she'd lost the connection.

But then her mother said, "All right. I hear you. I love you, Avery, and if this is what you need to be happy, you have my full support. I do think you're right on some level, and someday I might feel better about it too. Until then, please promise me you'll stay safe."

"I promise."

"So will you be staying at Mistwood then, for now?"

"No. Actually, we've decided to take a cruise to Greece."

"Greece?" Her mother's breath caught in her throat. "How exciting!"

"I can't wait. But listen, the island we're going to has terrible cell service, so don't worry about us if you call and can't reach us, okay?"

"How will I know you're safe?"

"I'll call when I can. Maybe I'll send you an old-fashioned letter." Avery glanced over her shoulder where the rest of her family was waiting. "I've got to go. I love you, Mom."

"I love you too, Avery. You know, I never wanted this place to be a cage for you. Every mother dreams of giving her daughter wings and teaching her to fly. I thought this could be your launching pad. I'm happy you're doing what speaks to your heart, and I hope you find what you're looking for out there."

Avery's eyes filled with tears as she said her goodbyes, hung up the phone, and turned in to Xavier's embrace.

"I'd like to meet yer parents someday."

She kissed him gently on the jaw. "I'd like that too."

They joined the others on deck. Charlie was sleeping peacefully under a blanket in a bassinet that, for the moment, was doing a good job of hiding her wings. After the shadow-mail candle had ignited and the warning had come for them to run, each of them had packed their things in record speed while Sabrina booked this cruise at Nathaniel's request. They'd barely had time to feed Charlie before they were barreling away from Mistwood.

"Why Greece anyway?" Avery asked Nathaniel.

Nathaniel turned to the others. "When I freed Sylas from the dungeons of Paragon, he told me about a Greek island called Aeaea."

"Mythology," Tobias said. "It doesn't actually exist."

Nathaniel shook his head. "It does exist. Humans can't find it, but dragons can. Sylas did. South of Rome, in the Tyrrhenian Sea."

Raven's hand went to her throat. "Does Circe still live there?"

"Sylas told me he met her."

Breath caught in Avery's throat. Could it be possible? According to Raven, they were descended from the goddess, but she'd considered it only in abstract terms, no more seriously than she had considered tales of Zeus and Hera from her childhood. Could they really be headed to the goddess's actual home?

"There's more," Nathaniel said. "Sylas told me the island is a bridge between worlds. It connects Earth and Ouros, the realm of the five kingdoms." Nathaniel rubbed his forehead as if his head had begun to ache. "Sylas sent us that message, and I believe he will be there, waiting for us. It's the only place where we can hide and be safe while we decide our next move." His gaze fell on Charlie.

Xavier wrapped his arms tighter around Avery. "Well,

with a goddess on our side, I predict we'll have Gabriel back on the throne in no time."

No one said a word, but one by one, they looked out across the ocean and toward a future Avery thought even Nathaniel's tarot cards could not predict.

EPILOGUE

Far above this world, in the palace of the gods on top of Mount Olympus, Hera sneered into her looking glass. Eleanor should have wiped out her filthy progeny by now, but instead the Treasure of Paragon traveled for the safety of Aeaea. If they made it there, they would be out of Eleanor's reach. Out of *her* reach. Even Hera would be helpless to interfere. The Titans had gifted the island to Circe as both her jail and her sanctuary, and although she suspected the goddess occasionally used her magic to venture out of her wall-less prison, only one god of Olympus had successfully broached her shores.

"You tell that yellow-eyed witch that if she allows the dragon spawn onto Aeaea, she will have to answer to me." Hera turned to Hermes, pointing at the table where her looking glass showed her the six dragons and their mates barreling across the ocean.

The messenger of the gods inspected his nails. "It seems she already has you to deal with. Aren't you the one who secured the tonic from Hades that is even now being used to keep the goddess of the mountain sedated? You know Circe and Aitna are cousins and quite close. Circe is within her rights to retaliate."

Hermes passed his hand over the mirror, and a warrior woman dressed in flowing red magma appeared in the glass. Her eyes were closed and her chest rose and fell in a soft, slow rhythm.

"I had every right to act against the Mountain. She hides my book of magic within her boundaries." Hera bared her teeth and pointed at Hermes's face. The god was much too attractive for his own good. How she'd love to ruin that pretty face and teach him a lesson. "And Circe... Do not tell me about that sorceress's rights. She hid her children in my garden, and one of her brats seduced my dragon and stole my book of magic! They must pay. That book was given to me by Zeus himself."

Hermes crossed his arms and returned her explosive tantrum with a look of utter boredom. "There is no proof the book is even within the realm of Ouros. The three sisters might have hidden it anywhere."

"It's there. The witch queen of Darnuith admitted as much before she died."

Hermes shrugged, a barely perceptible grin turning the corner of his mouth. He was always sickeningly smug.

Hera perused his golden skin and ivory tunic with contempt. "You only resist me because you've taken Circe as your lover."

He rolled his blue eyes. "I have had many lovers, Hera. I cannot be expected to favor every one of them."

Hera rushed him, lightning crackling in the air around her. She fisted his tunic. "Take my warning to Circe, messenger, or I will inform Zeus of your dereliction of duty. Tell her I have ways of making her suffer that do not involve Aeaea."

Hermes jerked away from her and smoothed his tunic. He offered her an exaggerated bow. "As you wish, Goddess."

The wings on his shoes began to flap, and he moved for the edge of the palace balcony overlooking the worlds below.

"Oh, and Hermes"—Hera straightened, her pupils burning with her anger—"tell Circe her protection is only worthwhile if the dragons actually make it to Aeaea."

Thank you for reading HIGHLAND DRAGON. If you enjoyed Xavier and Avery's story, please leave a review.

When Dianthe's misinterpreted vision leads Everfield to ruin, Sylas feels he must take decisive action to protect the Defenders of the Goddess from exposure. Only cutting off his mate from her work for the rebellion drives a personal wedge between them, one that threatens to destroy Sylas from the inside out. It's all made more complicated when his siblings arrive and his plans to take back the kingdom must be accelerated.

Get your copy of HIDDEN DRAGON Now!

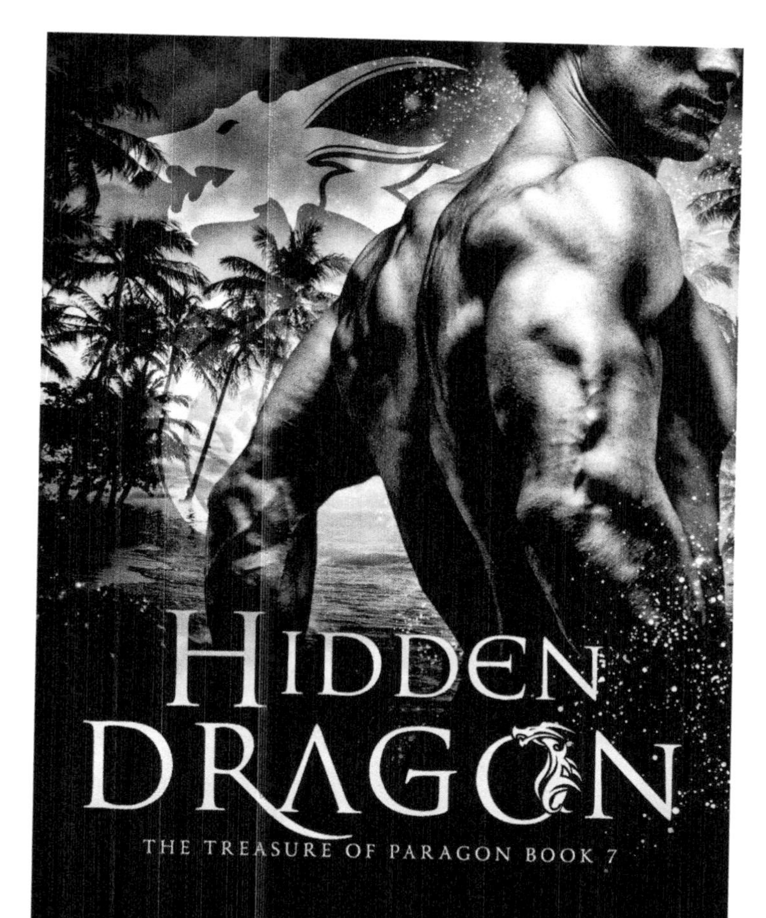
HIDDEN
DRAGON
THE TREASURE OF PARAGON BOOK 7
USA TODAY BESTSELLING AUTHOR
GENEVIEVE JACK

ABOUT HIDDEN DRAGON

Her gift was to see

Dianthe's second sight has always been both a blessing and a curse. She can't control her visions, yet they're unerringly accurate...until an erroneous prophecy results in the destruction of her homeland. The revelation crushes her spirit and endangers her role as an officer in the rebellion to take back the kingdom of Paragon.

Until their future was hidden

Sylas, dragon shifter and exiled prince, is the leader of the rebellion, but he can no longer rely on his mate Dianthe's psychic powers. His inner dragon is secretly pleased to relegate her to the sidelines. Even if his decision temporarily drives her away, he'd rather have her angry than dead or worse.

No one ever promised forever would be easy

When changing circumstances accelerate the rebellion's plans, Dianthe's fairy roots make her the only one who can perform a dangerous and necessary task. Her need to prove herself soon collides with Sylas's desire to protect her and strains their connection to the breaking point. Dragon mating bonds are eternal but if Dianthe and Sylas don't find a way to successfully work together again, not only will their marriage fail, their mission to take back Paragon will as well.

Get your copy of HIDDEN DRAGON, today!

CHAPTER ONE

Every time Sylas thought of his wife, Dianthe, he pictured her in the kitchen. When the light poured through their cottage window and caught the flecks of gold—color that had shed from her wings like glitter—on her mahogany skin, everything in his world felt right. Something about watching her bent over a bowl or inspecting a freshly baked tray of cookies proved to his soul that the world was good. How could tragedy befall anyone surrounded by the smell of warmed cinnamon?

Not that Dianthe's talents were limited to the domestic arts. On the contrary, her healing powers were legendary among her kind, and her second sight had proven invaluable to the resistance. Before he'd even known who the Defenders of the Goddess were, Dianthe had been a high-ranking officer and an integral part of the formation of the rebellion.

Their relationship had taken root on the island of Aeaea where he'd hidden after he and his siblings had been scattered to the four winds following the murder of his eldest brother, Marius. One of Dianthe's visions had led the

Defenders of the Goddess to the same island for the purpose of establishing a base camp. Once she'd discovered who he was, a Treasure of Paragon, one of eight remaining heirs to the kingdom, she had been the one to tell him the truth about his wicked mother. In Eleanor's bottomless thirst for power, she and his uncle Brynhoff had murdered Marius. Dianthe was the reason he had joined the rebellion and risen through the ranks, finding his purpose in the cause.

She was a warrior even if her only weapon was her mind.

Still, after so long away from home, picturing her in the kitchen had become his way to ground himself. Dianthe always seemed happy there. All the muscles of her face and shoulders relaxed, the tiny lines of tension loosening around her eyes and mouth. Her pupils grew large, the amber irises focused evenly on her task, completely empty of worry, completely content. In the kitchen, she was above it all. Nothing could touch her.

That's how he chose to think of her. There was too much blood, too much violence, to see her as she truly was, a fairy who'd chosen a life fighting by his side, fighting his evil mother's lust for power and risking her life to defend the five kingdoms. She'd chosen the fight before they met, but he'd always recognized it was his fucked-up family that had brought darkness into her life.

Now he joined her at the kitchen table and dipped his finger into the batter inside the powder-blue bowl she worked over. He stole a taste. "Mmmm. You're making crizzle rolls. My favorite."

"Sylas!" Dianthe smacked his shoulder. "That's for the party tonight. You don't want to show up at Elder Tree empty-handed, do you?"

"They won't miss a mouthful." He smacked his lips. "There's something different."

"I added a little lemon and fever fruit. Trader's spice."

He scooped up another dollop and popped it in his mouth. "Yes, the trader's spice makes it," he mumbled around his finger.

"Goddess have you, Sylas, I'm serious! Get your hands out of my bowl." She turned the full weight of her heavily annoyed stare on him.

He took it as a challenge. "Hmm. If I can't have the batter, what can I do to keep my mouth busy?" Reaching for her, he traced along the skin of her shoulder with the back of his nails.

She lowered her chin and stared up at him through impossibly thick lashes. "If I hadn't known what I was getting into mating a dragon, I'd tell you to go suck an egg." Wings fluttering, she allowed the spoon to clink against the side of the bowl. She wrapped her arms around his neck. "Lucky for you, I knew exactly what I was getting into mating a dragon, and I have far better uses for that naughty mouth."

A deep, vibrating purr rumbled in his chest when her mouth met his, her full lips tasting of crizzle batter and the remains of her smile. He hoisted her up his body, felt her legs wrap around his hips. The world melted away. All his responsibilities, the horrors he'd seen over his years leading the rebellion, all of it retreated to the back of his mind and pure joy filled his heart. Goddess, he wanted her. Wanted to bury himself in her for days. Wanted to taste every inch of her.

He pushed the bowl aside and lowered his mate to the table, reaching for the buttons of her dress.

"Sylas, stop. Wait." Dianthe's lashes fluttered.

Sylas froze. Her eyes rolled back in the way they did when she was seized by a vision; her stomach tensed rigidly. A tremble rattled her body. He supported her with his arms as the magic rolled through her.

"What is it? What do you see?"

Her eyes widened in terror, her entire body quaking under him.

He held her tighter. "I've got you. I've got you. Tell me what you've seen."

"Everfield... on fire. The Obsidian Guard is coming."

"When?" He stood up and lifted her from the table, placing her on her feet.

A tear cut along her cheek and her voice shook as she blurted, "Now."

Screams cut through the cottage from the forest outside and Sylas inhaled deeply, then cursed. He smelled smoke. "Mountain help us."

He ran to the door and peeked out. Fire. Chaos. Fairies screamed as they fled from dragons in black-and-red uniforms who were kicking in doors and dragging people from their homes before they set those homes on fire.

He closed the door. "They're burning Empyrean Wood."

"Oh goddess, Sylas. What can we do?" Dianthe began to weep in earnest.

Taking her by the shoulders, he denied his instinct to comfort her. They'd both known this was a possibility. Dianthe could fall apart. He couldn't. He had to follow the plan and get her out of there.

He grabbed the bags he'd packed for just such an emergency and handed one to her. He strapped the other onto his back. "We go together, out the back, hand in hand. I'll cloak you in invisibility. Don't look back."

Dianthe stared at the backpack in her hands. "When did you pack these?"

"You know when."

She frowned. "We can't just leave, Sylas! People will die. The Obsidian Guard is here. They're showing no mercy. You have to shift. We have to fight!" She clutched the strap of the bag until her fingers turned white.

He shook his head. "I'm not strong enough to face the Guard alone, and calling on the rebellion now would undermine everything we've worked for. They're not ready. We'd lose and all would be for nothing."

When she didn't move, he hoisted her bag onto one shoulder. If she wouldn't carry it, he would.

More screams filtered through the walls, closer now. A knock came on the door, followed by the voice of a young fairy. "The Guard is coming. Save yourself. Run!"

Sylas grabbed her hooded cloak off the rack and wrapped it around Dianthe, dressing her as if she were a child. He thanked the Mountain she was still wearing her boots. "Out the back." He tugged her toward the rear door.

She pulled up short of the exit and glanced woefully at the healing branches of the tree that grew at the center of their cottage. "Sylas, the zum zum! It's one of the last of its kind."

It was much too large to move, big enough to support the body of a full-grown male now and capable of curing fairies of most ills. Dianthe had healed many friends, neighbors, and community members in that tree, as well as the one fairy he'd begged her not to heal—Aborella.

Dianthe had claimed she'd seen a vision of Aborella fighting on the side of the rebellion, but her visions were open to interpretation. That one was exceptionally nebulous. But when they'd come across the fairy, gravely injured and buried alive outside the palace walls in Paragon, he'd allowed Dianthe to talk him into bringing her here. His mate had spent days painstakingly caring for and healing the fairy. But once she was healed, Aborella went straight back to the Obsidian Palace. He was almost certain she was behind this raid. Why else would the Guard be in Everfield now?

He gave Dianthe a mournful look. "We have to leave it. There's nothing we can do."

"Sylas—"

"Shhhh." He made them both invisible before throwing open the back door and ushering her out onto the path.

All fairy homes were built from living materials, and their cottage was no exception. The walls consisted of tightly woven branches, creating a large, leafy dome completely integrated into the forest. Outside, the scene of utter chaos that met them turned his stomach. The entire north side of the Empyrean Wood was on fire. Everyone was evacuating. Those not fast enough to flee found their faces plunged into the dirt by soldiers wearing the black-and-red uniforms of Paragon. Blood flowed. Everything was on fire.

He tried to cover Dianthe's eyes to save her from the sight.

"Don't bother. I saw it in my vision." She shoved his hand away. "I'll be seeing it in my nightmares for as long as I live."

He tugged her forward, breaking into a run when he saw a guard at the neighboring cottage, kicking down the door.

"By order of the empress of Paragon, I am here to exact punishment for aiding a fugitive of the crown." The guard's pronouncement came through a haughty grin before he charged into the abode.

Sylas heard the screams of their elderly neighbor, Willow.

"Oh my goddess, Sylas. What will they do to her?"

"I don't know. Keep moving."

"We have to help!"

He repositioned the bags, yanked her against him with his free arm, and spread his wings, taking to the air. The position of the bags and uneven weight set him off-balance, and it took his best effort to climb above the trees and soar beyond the limits of the village. It was a relief when Serenity Harbor came into view.

"Sylas, answer me!" Dianthe sobbed. "How could you just leave her there to deal with those... those cretins alone?"

He landed on the docks and swept her toward the sailboat he'd kept at the ready. He tossed in both bags, then turned to his mate. "Get in."

"Not until you talk to me."

He swept her under his arm and carried her onto the boat, then went about untying it from the dock. His oread, Indigo, appeared beside him, and together they pushed off the dock and rowed out to open water.

Indigo readied the sail. "To Aeaea as planned?"

Sylas nodded.

"Aeaea?" Dianthe asked. "We're going back to Circe's island now? What about Everfield?"

"There's nothing we can do, Dianthe. There're too many of them. Any attempt to help would reveal our identities. We'd both be in the dungeon by nightfall." Sylas's throat was thick and gritty. He'd held back his emotions from the first sniff of smoke. Just a few more minutes. He couldn't allow himself to break, not until he knew they were safe.

Dianthe looked back the way they'd come and broke into deep, wrenching sobs. Even though Sylas told himself not to, he looked back too. Flames engulfed Everfield, licking over the trees and turning the entire sky red and hazy. Fairies gathered on Serenity Beach, holding each other as their homes burned. He thanked the Mountain for every single one he saw. At least they were alive.

His mate grabbed his arm as if she were holding on for dear life.

"We'll be safe soon." The words sounded hollow, completely inadequate.

Her sobs abated. A far darker emotion moved in, clouding her eyes and causing her lips to peel back from her teeth. "Safe? You think I'm worried about being safe! How could you just leave them like that? We could have helped. We might have saved Willow from whatever fate befell her at the hands of *your* people!"

That was it. Sylas could abide no more. Heat flooded his face, and all the muscles in his back tensed. "Willow would be fine if you hadn't invited a viper into our home."

Dianthe pushed away from him, hugging herself against his words.

"Why do you think the Obsidian Guard was there? Didn't you hear them say this was retribution for taking in a fugitive? Who do you think told them there was a fugitive in Everfield? Who is the only other person who knows who I really am and that I've been living with you there?"

"No. It can't be. I saw... I saw her helping us." Dianthe shook her head vehemently.

"Your vision was wrong. Don't you get it?" He pointed a

hand at Everfield in flames. "You made a mistake, Dianthe, and Everfield paid the price!"

She gasped as if he'd slapped her.

"I'm sorry to put it so bluntly, but you knew there was the possibility. You told me yourself that visions are open to interpretation. People have free will. They can change their minds."

"Yes, but I befriended her. She's changed. She was kind."

"Give me a break." Sylas held his head. "She was kind when you were giving her what she wanted! When she needed you! I told you she was evil."

Dianthe's already red eyes began to tear again.

"You gave her information. I know you did. Not a lot, I'm sure. But you wanted to endear yourself to her. I know you, Dianthe. I know you had good intentions. But if you'd seen her face when I told her we knew who she was. If you'd seen how quickly she fled... Everfield is burning because of Aborella."

Dianthe's knees seemed to give out and she sat down hard, her hair blowing in the saltwater breeze. All light drained from her eyes and her mouth gaped. Beyond the stern, the ever-reddening sky over Everfield was thick with smoke from the active fires. How long would Empyrean Wood burn? Would there be anything left by the time they put it out?

"You think Everfield is burning because of Aborella, and Aborella was there because of... me." Dianthe grimaced as the truth set in.

Sylas wished he could tell her she was wrong, but he'd known this would happen. Aborella was as evil as they came. She couldn't be trusted. "It's not your fault. You've always been able to trust your visions in the past. It's just now..."

"Now what?"

Every part of Sylas felt heavy and bone weary. He didn't have the heart to tell her that Aborella might have infected her or polluted her gift with a dark curse. He didn't know for sure, but he suspected they could not trust Dianthe's visions any longer. Not right away. Even tonight's prophecy had been far too late to be of much help. She was off her game. They'd have to be cautious.

He couldn't tell her now though. Not like this. Not when her homeland was burning and she had no idea if the community she'd grown up in, the people she loved, were well and safe. He sat beside her and slid his hand into hers.

"Nothing. We're safe. I'm here. This is the best we can do for now."

He was relieved when she seemed to accept it. She laid her head on his shoulder and watched helplessly as the forest of her childhood and the home they'd built together blazed.

MEET GENEVIEVE JACK

Award winning and USA Today bestselling author Genevieve Jack writes wild, witty, and wicked-hot paranormal romance and fantasy. Coffee and wine are her biofuel. The love lives of witches, shifters, and vampires are her favorite topic of conversation. She harbors a passion for old cemeteries and ghost tours, thanks to her years attending a high school rumored to be haunted. Her perfect day involves a heavy dose of nature and one crazy dog. Learn more at GenevieveJack.com.

Do you know Jack? Keep in touch to stay in the know about new releases, sales, and giveaways.

Join my VIP reader group
Sign up for my newsletter

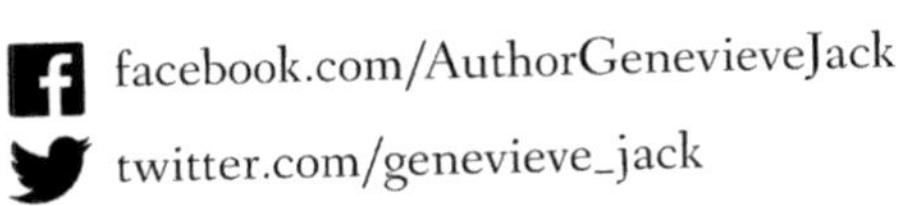
facebook.com/AuthorGenevieveJack
twitter.com/genevieve_jack
instagram.com/authorgenevievejack
bookbub.com/authors/genevieve-jack

MORE FROM GENEVIEVE JACK!

The Treasure of Paragon

The Dragon of New Orleans, Book 1

Windy City Dragon, Book 2,

Manhattan Dragon, Book 3

The Dragon of Sedona, Book 4

The Dragon of Cecil Court, Book 5

Highland Dragon, Book 6

Hidden Dragon, Book 7

The Dragons of Paragon, Book 8

The Last Dragon, Book 9

The Three Sisters

The Tanglewood Witches

Tanglewood Magic

Tanglewood Legacy

Knight Games Series

The Ghost and The Graveyard, Book 1

Kick the Candle, Book 2

Queen of the Hill, Book 3

Mother May I, Book 4

Logan, Book 5

Fireborn Wolves Series

(Knight World Novels)

Vice, Book 1

Virtue, Book 2

Vengeance, Book 3

ACKNOWLEDGMENTS

When I outlined *Highland Dragon* over a year ago, my plan was to visit the Scottish Highlands in June of 2020. In 2019, my husband and I booked a ten-day tour where I intended to sample the local dialect, get a lay of the land, and learn about Jacobite and Clan Campbell history firsthand.

Then the pandemic happened. I watched my plans to research this book go up in flames as we all were locked down and masked up. On top of losing the trip, I now had family home and wrestled with distractions galore. Then one of my children caught Covid and everything became more complicated. She recovered, but I had to start the book anew, having lost my momentum.

I'd originally planned to release *Highland Dragon* in October, but after turning to nonfiction books and videos for research and working my writing around the effects of the pandemic, I had to change those plans. I am so thankful that *Highland Dragon* is finally here.

To the fans of this series, thank you for coming along with me on this journey and being patient as *Highland*

Dragon came to fruition. Thanks to Victory Editing for helping me create a book I'm proud to share under less than ideal circumstances. Also, a big thank-you to the authors of the High Tea Society for your long-suffering support and encouragement.